THE
STONE
WORLD

THE
STONE
WORLD

A Novel

JOEL AGEE

MELVILLE HOUSE
BROOKLYN • LONDON

THE STONE WORLD

First published in 2022 by Melville House

Copyright © Joel Agee, 2020

All rights reserved

First Melville House Printing: December 2021

Melville House Publishing

46 John Street

Brooklyn, NY 11201

and

Melville House UK

Suite 2000

16/18 Woodford Road

London E7 0HA

mhpbooks.com

@melvillehouse

ISBN: 978-1-61219-954-2

ISBN: 978-1-61219-955-9 (eBook)

Library of Congress Control Number: 2021947660

Designed by Betty Lew

Printed in the United States of America

1 3 5 7 9 10 8 6 4 2

A catalog record for this book is available

from the Library of Congress

I wish to thank the American

Academy in Berlin for granting me a generous fellowship.

Work on *The Stone World* began there,

in good company and under ideal conditions for writing.

For Beckett and Johanna

Infancia mía en el jardin:

¡Reina de la jardinería!

—RAFAEL ALBERTI

1

The boy liked to lie with his ear pressed against the cool shaded stone of the patio. Zita, the maid, might be hanging clothes on a line. There was a stone tub in the garden where she did some of her washing. There was green slippery slime on the edge of the stone that the boy liked to touch. For a big wash, Zita would go to the nearby stream, where other women went also to wash their clothes. Sometimes the boy went there with her. He would lie in the grass reading books or just dreaming, listening to the women's talk and to the sound of the stream. Those two sounds flowed together so that sometimes it seemed that the water was talking and laughing and the women were part of the gurgling and sloshing of the stream. But he also liked to lie on the cool stone patio, feeling its coolness against his face and listening.

His mother asked him once what he was doing. He said he was listening. Listening to what, she asked. To the stone. Really, she said, what does it say? It doesn't say anything, he said, laughing: Stones don't speak! Then what do you hear? I don't know, he said. I just like to listen to it. She didn't ask any further.

His mother was a musician. She played the violin every day. She was practicing, she said. Why do you practice, the boy asked. So that I can play better, she said. But you play good already, he said. Play well, she said. Yes, I play well, but I still can play better, and that's why I practice. Later, when my playing is perfect, I'll play for other people to hear it. That's called a performance. I'm practicing so I can give a good performance.

A *perfect* performance, he said.

Maybe, she said, smiling.

Zita pronounced the boy's name like a Spanish word, "Pira." Other Mexicans and even some American children who spoke Spanish called him that too. Some called him Pedro. Otherwise, his name was Peter. He liked the sound of his name the way Mexicans pronounced it. That made him feel Mexican, more Mexican even than Pedro did.

Playing in the street with Mexican children, he didn't like it when his mother and father called him by his American name. Americans were gringos, so Peter was a gringo name.

It wasn't good being a gringo. Sometimes the other boys used that word. Always they were talking about someone who wasn't there, or even about all the gringos in the world, and always the word sounded mean. He knew that he could be called a gringo because he was American and his mother for sure was a gringa even in the way she spoke Spanish. His father was German, but that didn't make Pira less of a gringo.

And yet nobody ever called him that. Once a boy cheated at marbles and Pira called him a cabrón, which he knew was a bad word, and the boy, instead of calling him "gringo," said "chinga tu madre," which was one of the really bad expressions that he was told never ever to use. That proved how bad a word "gringo" really was.

Sometimes Pira prayed to be allowed to be Mexican.

*

Pira's last name was Vogelsang. That was a name he liked even though it wasn't Mexican at all. It was his German father's name, and it meant birdsong.

His father was a writer. When he went into his room to write, he said he had to work. The room where he worked was always full of smoke, and he always looked worried when he wrote. That room was his office. On one wall near his desk was a bright red picture of a man's arm making a fist above some German words. On another wall was a picture of the house of a famous writer from long ago, with pretty trees around it. There was a bookcase full of books, and on top of the bookcase stood ten or fifteen ídolos, green ones and brown ones, tall and little. Pira wasn't allowed to play with them.

Zita worked too. She swept and mopped the floors, she made the beds, she went shopping, she did the laundry. That was Zita's work. Sometimes his mother helped Zita make meals, but otherwise she didn't work. She practiced. Maybe that was work too. She said it was. But she was also playing.

Soon Pira would be in first grade and there would be homework. He looked forward to that. But now it was summer and all he did was play. He played with the children in the street, and also with two special friends: Chris, an American boy who had no mother and whose father was rich, and Arón, who had no father and whose mother was poor. Chris lived in a big white house that had a machine gun in the garden. A chauffeur drove him around in a car. Arón lived nearby in a dark apartment full of crucifixes. He had only one toy, a skeleton that waved its arms and legs when you pulled on a string. Once Pira gave Arón a toy car to take home. The same day, Arón brought the car back, crying. His mother had whipped him with a strap, he said, for taking something that wasn't his, even though it *was* his because Pira had given it to him. Pira's mother talked to Arón's mother. "Your son suffers a lot, Señora," she said. "Please don't beat him. We all love him."

"I will beat him as much as he deserves," Arón's mother said.

Chris was beaten too, but not as often. He once showed Pira a welt on his behind that his father had raised by spanking him with a hairbrush.

Every once in a while, the three boys played together.

But on many days Pira played alone, and he liked that. He liked to ride his scooter on the patio. He liked to race on the scooter with a floating silk cloth tied around his neck and pretend he was Superman. He liked to play with his metal soldiers and Indians. He liked to listen to Paco, the parrot, chattering in the banana tree behind the house. He liked to throw a stick for Tristan, the dog, which Tristan loved. And he had recently discovered how to read, and that was fun too. That discovery happened all by itself. His parents were always reading to him from books and he would watch their fingers moving along the line, and suddenly he realized he could read.

Often, he would climb the big zapote tree in the garden. He used to need his father to help him get up on a big branch, but now there was a ladder leaning against the tree so he could climb up by himself. Standing on the branch and holding on to another branch above it, he could imagine he was a sailor in the rigging of a sailing ship, especially when the wind was blowing. He could sit on the big branch too, hugging the tree's trunk for support. From there he could look across the valley all the way to the snow-topped volcanoes, Popocatepetl and Iztaccihuatl.

Zita had told him a story about them. Popocatepetl was a great Aztec warrior. Iztaccihuatl was a princess. Popocatepetl loved Iztaccihuatl and asked her father for permission to marry her. Her father said he would first have to fight against a bad king who lived far away. Popocatepetl set out for that faraway kingdom and fought against the bad king and killed him. But it took him a long time to come home. Another man who also loved Iztaccihuatl told everyone that Popocatepetl was dead. So her father said the other man could marry her. Iztaccihuatl didn't want to marry the other man, but her father said that she had to. Then Iztaccihuatl became so sad that she died. No sooner had she died than Popocatepetl returned. Everyone had to cry. It was the saddest day. Popocatepetl said he would take Iztaccihuatl away and never come back. He carried her body high up into the mountains and laid her down there and stood looking at her day and night and never moved. Then it snowed and snowed until Popocatepetl's head and Iztaccihuatl's head, chest, knees, and feet were covered with snow, and there they stayed forever.

Pira no longer asked Zita to tell him that story. It was there in his memory and in the mountains themselves, Popocatepetl standing tall with his head slightly bowed, Iztaccihuatl lying on her back before him. And instead of Zita's low, slow-talking voice, he heard the birds and the vendors' cries in the street.

*

One of his favorite books was the *Just So Stories*. Every once in a while, the person telling the stories said "Best Beloved" or "O Best Beloved," and at those moments Pira always felt a special pleasure, as if he personally was being addressed in the most kind and respectful way imaginable. The way the words were capitalized made them look even grander than they sounded. The "O," when it came, was like the bow you make before a king: "O best beloved!"

Another thing the person telling the story said from time to time was "Listen and attend." He said it in different ways:

"Now listen and attend!"

"Now attend and listen!"

"Hear and attend and listen!"

"Now attend all over again and listen!"

Sometimes when Pira lay on the patio doing nothing, those words came in his thoughts and reminded him that he could listen.

*

It was Zita who taught him how to pray. "You can pray to God, or to La Virgen de Guadalupe, or to el Señor Jesús," she said. "El Señor Jesús is the god of love. Fold your hands like this and ask him to help all the people and all the animals. Then you can pray for yourself and the people you love." When Zita spoke of God and el Señor Jesús, she used special words that weren't used in ordinary speech. Poderoso, for instance. It meant "powerful" but the Spanish word sounded that way: poderoso. Another word she used was gracia: that was something the Virgin gave you if you prayed to her—gracia y cariño. Pira knew that cariño meant kindness, but he didn't know what gracia meant, and when he asked Zita, she didn't know how to explain it. So he asked his mother:

"What does gracia mean?"

"It means thank you."

"No, not gracias—gracia."

"Who taught you that word?"

"Zita. She said she couldn't explain it."

"It's hard to explain. It means grace in English. Grace is similar to beauty, but it's not the same. Ballerinas are graceful—the way they move, the way they stand on tiptoe. A ballerina may be beautiful, but if she's not graceful . . ."—she made a dancer's movement with her hands—"like this . . . then she's not a really good dancer. Grace is a special kind of beauty."

He nodded.

"There's grace in music too," she said. "I'll show you."

She took her violin case from the drawer where she kept it, took out the violin and the bow, tucked the violin under her chin, and with the bow drew a single long, clear note.

"That's beauty," she said.

He understood.

"And now: here's the same beauty but with a grace note." And again she drew the long swelling sound, but with two fingers she produced a delicate, dancing quaver near the end.

"That's grace," Pira said, making little waves with his fingers to imitate grace.

His mother agreed. She put the violin and the bow back into the case and the case back into the drawer and closed the drawer.

"Actually," she said then, "Zita has grace. She's beautiful too, but she's graceful as well."

"Like a ballerina?"

"Kind of. The way she holds her head when she walks, the way she stands, the way she sits."

"How does she sit?"

"You know . . . very straight. Very dignified."

"What's dignified?"

"Graceful!" she said, and they both laughed.

"It comes from balancing things on her head," she said.

Pira pictured the way Zita walked beside or ahead of him on the way to the stream and back, carrying the laundry in a basket that was balanced on her head. Sometimes she supported the basket with one hand, and sometimes she walked with both arms by her sides and the basket never fell.

"Zita says she gets grace from La Virgen de Guadalupe," he said.

Now his mother looked surprised. "Oh," she said. "That's a different kind of grace. The same word, but it means something different."

She thought about it. Pira waited.

"It's a little bit like luck. When religious people are lucky, they believe it comes from God, or a goddess. So they pray for grace. And sometimes they get it, but it's not because there's a god."

Pira was no longer curious about grace. It seemed to be something for women, and he was going to be a man. If he prayed, he would pray to el Señor Jesús, the god of love, who was muy poderoso.

But after a while, when he thought about Jesus, it was hard to imagine him being poderoso, because he was nailed to a cross. How could he help anybody? He needed help himself. So when Pira prayed, which he did once in a while, he prayed to God. God was the father of el Señor Jesús. He knew everything and could do anything, so it made sense to pray to him.

*

On the other side of the stream where the women went to wash clothes, there was a meadow where cows grazed. At the far end of the meadow was a canyon. Pira's father took him there once when he was little. They dropped stones off the edge of the cliff and heard them hit the ground far below.

"Never go near this edge by yourself," his father said. "It's too dangerous. If you fell the way these stones are falling, you would be dead."

Pira never went back to the canyon. Often when he sat near Zita and the other women by the stream, he would look up from his book to watch the cows grazing on the other side of the stream. Some of them went near the cliff, and he wondered if they knew how dangerous it was.

*

Pira's mother's name was Martha. She called Zita by her first name and wanted Zita to call her Marta. A few times Zita tried to do that but couldn't. It sounded strange to her. She called her "Señora Marta." When they talked to each other they both said "usted" instead of "tú."

Pira asked his mother, "Is Zita your friend?"

"Of course she's my friend," Martha said. "I love Zita."

"Why does she say Señora Marta and not Marta?"

"Because she works for us and we pay her. She doesn't call Bruno 'Bruno' either." Bruno was Pira's father's name.

So Zita and Martha were friends, but not in the same way that Martha and her other friends or Zita and her friends were friends. He didn't understand, but there was an explanation.

Other children used different names for their parents too. But that didn't need explaining, it just was that way. Arón called his cruel mother Mamá. When Chris spoke to his father, he said "Dad," and when Chris's father asked Chris a question, Chris would say "yes, sir" or "no, sir." Pira called his parents Bruno and Martha. For a while he tried calling them mommy and daddy the way American children called their parents in books, but that sounded like make-believe parents, so he went back to calling them by their names, just as they called him Peter. But when speaking to Zita about them, he always said "mi madre" or "mi padre," never Martha or Bruno. It would have been strange to do otherwise.

*

Usually Paco, the parrot, just chattered and squawked and made clicking sounds, but once in a while he said things like "Sí, cómo no!" and "Caramba!" and sometimes he called his own name: "Paco?" "Paquito!" He sounded like a man, probably the man who had taught him how to speak. Once, sitting on Bruno's finger, he said "Cristo es vivo, cabrones!" which Bruno said was the funniest thing he had ever heard. Martha tried to teach him English words, but Paco wasn't interested.

Martha loved Paco almost as much as she loved Pira and Bruno, and Paco clearly loved her more than anyone. He would sit on her finger, cocking his head, while she spoke to him softly: "Paco, my sweetheart. You beautiful bird." He cocked his head when she played the violin too. Martha said he was musical.

*

Bruno was Pira's father, but Pira had another father named David who lived in New York. David was his first father, and Bruno was his stepfather. Martha said Bruno was just as real a father to Pira as David was, and in a way more real, because David was far away and hadn't seen Pira since he was a baby except for a few weeks when he was four. But just for that reason, Martha wanted Pira to know that David was his father. "One day you will meet again and you'll see that he loves you," she said, "even though he hasn't seen you since you were little." She told him a lot about David.

She told Pira that David was a musician, like herself. That he played the piano. That David and Martha used to give concerts together. To show Pira, Martha put on a record that she and David had made together. She said that she and David had separated because they didn't get along, and that now she loved him as much as ever, but not in the same way that she loved Bruno. Sometimes she sent photographs of Pira to David. Then David would write to Martha, and Martha would tell Pira that David had said that he loved Pira and was proud of him.

Once Martha suggested that Pira write David a letter, so he dictated the words to Martha, telling his first father about the zapote tree and Iztaccihuatl and Popocatepetl and Bruno and Zita and Tristan. Then David wrote back telling him about a concert he had given in a place called Tanglewood. Pira liked the name Tanglewood a lot. It sounded mysterious and dark like the woods in Hansel and Gretel, but it was light and real because David had been there.

*

Several times a week Martha played string quartets with three Hungarian men, Ferenc, István, and Sándor.

Sometimes they came to Pira's house to practice, but usually they met at Sándor's. Sándor was the first violinist, Martha the second. Ferenc played the cello, and István the viola. They were known as the Ferenc Sándor Quartet. Every few months they played in Mexico City, Guadalajara, Juárez, and other big cities. Once they played a piano quintet in New York with Pira's first father David playing the piano. But that was a long time ago.

Sándor was Bruno's best friend, and a Hungarian friend of Sándor's, Valéria, was also a good friend of Martha's.

They both spoke German, like Bruno, as well as Hungarian. Sándor came to the house often, to talk and smoke and drink with Bruno, to laugh and sing with Martha, sometimes even dance with her to the sound of a record, and to do magic tricks for Pira. He could tear paper money and bunch up the pieces and then unfold a smooth, untorn bill. He could pull off half his thumb and stick it on again. He could slide cigarettes into his nose, one after the other, and they would be gone. He could blow smoke rings. Sándor was fun.

*

On the radio sometimes a man sang: "Porqué me llamas, si no me quieres? Porqué me escribes, si no sé leer?" Why do you call me if you don't love me? Why do you write me if I can't read?

Martha thought the song was funny. It wasn't funny for the man who wasn't loved, but Martha said she wasn't laughing at him.

Every few days a letter from Zita's novio Federico arrived, and Martha read it to Zita. Pira liked to hear the letters too. They told stories about Federico and his family—about who was sick or getting better, who had a novio and what the novio did for a living, who had a job or was out of it, whose children were learning how to read, and greetings from all of them, a long list of names—and also about Federico's union and their plans to go on a strike to help all the railroad workers earn more money, and about Federico's love for Zita. Especially the parts about planning a huelga sounded exciting.

But listening was only part of his pleasure. The other part was watching Zita as she listened. When Federico said he was "feliz," the meaning of the word shone in her smile and her eyes—she was happy with him. And when he spoke of tristeza or soledad, Pira saw sadness or loneliness in Zita's face and felt those feelings with her. Martha had told him once that poems were like music made only with words. Federico's letters were like that. But the words weren't even all his, because Federico didn't know how to write. He had to dictate his letters to a letter writer in Mexico City, and according to Martha that writer changed his words and added new ones to make the letter more beautiful. So who was making the music?

In the same way, Zita dictated her letters to a man who set up his typewriter on a small table near the bandstand on the zócalo. Pira was with her sometimes when she did that. "Tell him I miss him," she once said to the man, and he typed for a while. Later, when she asked Pira to read her the letter before she sealed it inside an envelope, it sounded different: "My dearest, most beloved Federico. Life without you is only half a life, but your love sweetens my sorrow."

"That is true," Zita said then. "That is how I feel."

*

Every two months Federico came to visit Zita. Each time he arrived on a Friday morning after traveling for a long time. She would meet him at the bus station, and together they would walk to Pira's house on the Calle Humboldt. Always Federico would carry a small valise, while Zita held the flowers Federico had brought her. Sometimes they held hands as they walked. Federico's jefe let him take

Friday and Saturday off, and the following Monday too. That was nice of the jefe, Federico said. Federico would lose three days' pay, but then he would work longer hours and Sundays to earn back the money he'd lost, and also to earn more money that he could put in a bank. It wasn't hard, he said, because as a reward he could spend three full days with his novia. Pira saw how happy it made Zita to hear Federico call her his novia.

Once Martha told Zita that Federico's sacrifice proved how much he loved her. Sacrificio, she said, and enamorado. It wasn't clear to Pira which of those two words made Zita's eyes widen, as they always did when Martha said something big. He figured it was sacrificio. That certainly was the bigger sounding word.

Pira knew what a sacrifice was from reading about the conquista. There was one book in particular with pictures that showed how the ancient Mexicans sacrificed people to their gods. A priest cut the victim's heart out of his chest with a knife and held the heart up to the sun. Other priests held the victim's arms and legs so that he couldn't move. The victim's head was thrown back with his mouth open. Some of the victims were children. Maybe the victim was screaming, and maybe he or she was already dead.

Sometimes the victims were prisoners who didn't want to be sacrificed, and sometimes they were athletes who had competed with other athletes in sacred ball games for the honor of having their hearts cut out for Huitzilopochtli or some other god who liked the taste of human hearts. Why would anyone want to have his heart cut out? He would have to ask Bruno. Bruno knew a lot about things that had really happened and that were happening now anywhere in the world. Martha knew a lot too, but not so much about real things long ago and in the world.

For Pira, Federico's visits were always exciting. Federico was strong, probably stronger than Bruno. Once, when Pira and Bruno wrestled in the garden, Bruno struggled to pin Pira's wrists to the ground, and then Pira pushed hard and suddenly Bruno rolled over on his back and Pira pinned him to the ground. Bruno said, "You're strong!" and Pira felt proud, but then he didn't like being stronger than Bruno. So he asked Martha: "Why is Bruno weak?" and Martha said he was just pretending and actually he was really strong. But once when Bruno was sitting on the lawn, Martha and Sándor's friend Valéria snuck up on Bruno from behind and grabbed his arms and pinned him to the ground. They were all laughing, it was just a game, but Pira could see that Bruno wanted to sit up again and couldn't until they let him. They were two against one, but still, Bruno was a man, so it wasn't clear.

But with Federico there was no question. Federico was strong. He could lift Pira way up and lower him back to his feet fast as if he weighed nothing at all. When Pira tried to wrestle with him, Federico would whirl him and flip him around in any direction he chose. He was like a giant. He could make a round hard mountain of muscle appear on his bent arm, like Popeye. He also combed his hair in a special Mexican way. He needed both hands to do it, and he needed a mirror. First he would sprinkle something on his head from a bottle and rub it into his scalp. Then with one hand he would slowly run the comb through his shiny black hair while with the other hand, carefully, he followed the comb to make sure with his fingers that the hair *felt* combed and didn't just look it. If the part wasn't straight, he would start all over again. Only when everything was perfect would he add the finishing touch, which was to push his hair from the top of his head toward the front on one side just a bit to make a wave over his forehead. Also, his shoes were special. They were pointed and decorated with many little holes in the front.

*

Zita had two gods in her room. They stood on night tables, one on each side of her bed: an ídolo made of greenish-gray stone, with squat legs and a wide smiling face, holding a square tray, and a metal crucifix like the ones in Arón's mother's house. Zita told Pira a lot about el Señor Jesús and almost nothing about the ídolo, who didn't even have a name.

"He's just for decoration," she said. "I don't pray to him. I pray to el Señor Jesús. He is the god of love. No other god is needed."

"What about La Virgen de Guadalupe?"

"I pray to her too. She's not a goddess, though. She's the mother of God. She's also the mother of all índios, but she's not a goddess. Jesús is the only true god."

El único Diós verdadero.

But often she put something on the little statue's tray—usually a flower, sometimes food, like a piece of chile, and once a picture of Federico—so Pira suspected that Zita was lying, and that the ídolo wasn't just for decoration but special in the same way that el Señor Jesús was special, a god.

He told Martha about this: "I think Zita lied." Not that he really minded. Zita wouldn't lie to be mean. He just wanted to know.

"That's not a lie," Martha said. "It's a secret."

He knew the difference. Secrets were things you didn't tell anyone. Sometimes when his penis got big and he was alone and in bed, he would hold it upright with one hand and with his other hand make a little man with two fingers. The man would come walking along the sheet and climb up Pira's body, which to the man was a steep hill, and keep walking, and then the penis would hit him. Except it wasn't a penis but a giant. The man would wrestle with the giant. Sometimes he won and sometimes he lost. That game was secret. Only Pira knew about it.

So Zita too had a secret. But he knew about it.

*

There was another word, "private," that meant something similar to "secret." When Pira walked into the bathroom while Bruno was peeing, Bruno asked him to leave until he was finished because for him peeing was private.

Martha didn't mind Pira's being there when she was peeing, but she minded his opening the top drawer of her dresser to see what was in it because those were her private things. Bruno's peeing and the things in Martha's drawer weren't secrets, because he knew about them and they didn't mind his knowing. If you had a secret, it was also private, but private things weren't necessarily secret. That was the difference.

Bruno and Martha received letters that had both their names on the envelope. Those letters were for both of them. But there were also letters addressed only to Bruno or only to Martha, and these they read separately and then told each other about them. Sometimes they gave each other these letters to read, but still they were private. Pira learned this one day when Martha got angry at Bruno for reading a letter that Pira's first father, David, had written to her only. "I don't keep secrets from you," Martha said, "it's just private," and Bruno, who was hurt at first, understood and apologized. That made it really clear.

Zita's letters to Federico and Federico's to her weren't private, but that was because they couldn't read or write and needed other people's help. But Zita herself was "a very private person," according to Martha. Did that mean she had secrets besides the one Pira had discovered? He didn't think so. He didn't know what Martha meant when she said that.

2

Before Pira learned how to write, he learned how to write poems. He did it with Bruno's help. That is, Bruno did the writing and Pira spoke the words. Then Bruno read them back to him. Usually Pira's poems were in English, but one day he wrote one in Spanish. When it was finished, Bruno read it back to him, and Pira didn't like it.

"Why not?" Bruno asked.

"It's silly." He was embarrassed.

"Is there any part that you like?"

"Yes, the part that comes back."

"I like it too," Bruno said. "It's called a refrain."

The refrain was "Cuando canta la verde rana": When the green frog sings.

"Sometimes poems don't come out perfect right away," Bruno said. "But if you work on it, it can get better."

Work.

Pira felt honored and surprised. Never in his life had anyone told him that he could work. From the music room, he could hear Martha practicing the violin. She too was working.

"How can I work on it?"

"By trying out different words. Different feelings."

"But how?"

"Start with the part you like. Your refrain has a magical feeling."

Magical.

"See if you can bring that feeling into the other parts."

"How?"

"By thinking about it. Take your time."

He gave Pira the piece of paper with his poem written on it in capital letters.

"Read what you have and ask yourself how you could improve it."

How can I ask my own self? Pira wondered.

"Be patient," Bruno continued. "It will come. If you think of any changes, you can dictate them to me tomorrow."

It will come.

All afternoon, on and off, Pira thought about his poem. He sat on his perch in the zapote tree murmuring words. Canta turned into cantaba. When the green frog sang, not sings. It sounded more magical that way, like something from long ago. But then he liked canta after all, because of the rhythm: Cuando canta. Rana, he realized then, rhymed with mañana. Mañana reminded him of the birthday song Las Mañanitas, and then it occurred to him that if it was just one mañanita it could rhyme with Zita. He couldn't wait to finish his poem. But when would it be finished? When it was perfect.

He came down from the tree and threw sticks for Tristan in the garden. But he was distracted. He was thinking about the poem. Tristan let out a little bark, impatient for another toss of the stick. Pira had to say "No más" several times before Tristan understood and went to the tall grass near the zapote tree and lay down with his chin resting on his paws.

Pira went into the house to look for a pencil and came back outside and tried to write MAÑANA on the back of the sheet where his poem was written, using the patio floor for a support. He couldn't picture the word clearly enough to copy it from his mind onto the page. He thought of looking for it in a book and copying it from there, but that seemed too much trouble, so he gave up.

He lay down with one hand on the page where his poem was written, so that the wind wouldn't carry it away, and pressed his ear to the cool, smooth surface of the tile and listened. Through the stone, he could hear Zita's footsteps in the house. With his other ear he heard Martha practicing and, farther away, Bruno tapping on his typewriter. But beneath those sounds, all the way down and down through the stone, there was silence. Into that depth, he sent his words—not speaking them, but in his mind they were loud, like a call:

Cuando canta la verde rana . . .

. . . and listened. He could almost believe that the stone would answer, like an echo, but it didn't.

He repeated the phrase. There was a tune in it, he could imagine it. It was sung by mariachis with guitars. They kept on singing, and there were moments when Pira thought he heard new words in the song. He wanted to run to Bruno and tell him, but Bruno was working, and he had said tomorrow. And now the words were forgotten again. For a moment he felt on the edge of tears. Then Zita called him to dinner.

He was still distracted. Zita said something as she put a bowl of soup in front of him, and then Martha said something. He heard them and saw that they were speaking to him, but it was as if they were far away. Finally, Bruno called his name sharply, and Pira said, "Yes?"

"You must answer when you are spoken to," Bruno said. "It's rude not to do that."

Bruno rarely spoke to Pira like that. Pira was always surprised when it happened. Zita was on her way back to the kitchen, so he couldn't say "disculpa." He looked at Martha. She was looking at Bruno. Bruno was frowning at his soup. Martha looked at Pira and said, "You weren't really rude, Peter. It just looked that way." That felt better, but Pira wasn't sure. Bruno thought he had been rude, and Bruno was usually right. Pira's hand lifted the spoon, put it into the bowl, brought the soup to his mouth. His own hand felt far away from him. Again he felt that sadness, like distant tears behind his eyes.

*

Bruno came to sit on the edge of his bed that night. "I'm sorry I scolded you," he said. "Martha was right. You weren't rude."

"You weren't either," Pira said.

Bruno was silent. Then, tenderly, he stroked Pira's hair.

"I want to be bald," Pira said.

"Why?"

"I want to look Mexican."

"Like the boys you play marbles with?"

"Yes."

"Do you know why their heads are shaved?"

"No."

"To get rid of lice."

"What are lice?"

"Little insects that live in a person's hair. They suck blood like mosquitoes, but it itches much worse. You don't have lice."

"I wish I did."

"I'm glad you don't."

Pira still wished he was bald, but he didn't want to argue. They were silent for a while.

"Isn't it good," Bruno said, "that two people can have opposite wishes and still love each other?"

Maybe it was good. But it was confusing to Pira, and this time tears came and rolled down his face.

"I'm sorry," Bruno said, wiping Pira's tears with a handkerchief. "Did I hurt your feelings?"

"I don't know," Pira said. "I don't think so."

After Bruno kissed him good night and left the room and Martha came in to kiss him good night and left, Pira thought: *Tomorrow I'll finish my poem.* Then he prayed to La Virgen de Guadalupe for Bruno, asking her to make Bruno happy. Usually he prayed to God, but this time he thought of La Virgen and as soon as he started praying to her he felt that she liked it and that felt good to him. After praying for Bruno he prayed to La Virgen for Martha and Zita and Arón and Tristan and Chris and Arón's mean mother and Federico and Chris's father Mr. Riley and the charros who worked for him and their horses and the boys Pira played marbles with and David his first father and all the people and all the animals, asking La Virgen to make each and all of them happy, and when he was finished, he felt wonderfully content.

*

When Pira woke up the next morning, he knew how his poem would begin. He jumped out of bed and ran into the bathroom, where Bruno was shaving.

"I have the beginning!" he said.

"Of what?"

"Of the poem. Can you write it for me?"

"Let me finish shaving first."

"Can I tell it to you?"

"All right. How does it go?"

"Cuando canta la verde rana, en la mañana, la mañanita."

Bruno turned toward Pira, one side of his face still covered with shaving cream.

"That is very good," he said.

It was so different when Bruno praised him. Martha always said "beautiful" or "wonderful." Bruno used different words: "Nice" and "I like it." Never before had he said "very good."

"Beautiful," Bruno added.

Then he smiled to let Pira know that he really meant it, and turned back to the mirror.

"How will it go on?" he asked, shaving again.

"I don't know. Mañanita will rhyme with Zita."

"Excellent idea."

When Bruno had finished shaving and put eau de cologne on his face, he went to his study with Pira and wrote Pira's words with his typewriter, using capital letters and centering the lines on the page so that they looked like printed lines in a book:

CUANDO CANTA LA VERDE RANA
EN LA MAÑANA, LA MAÑANITA

As soon as Pira read them (they were still in the typewriter), he had an idea of how the poem could continue, and spoke the new words out loud. Bruno whistled through his teeth and asked Pira to say the words again and typed them under the first two lines, centering them:

VENÍA CON GRACIA LA MADRE DE DIÓS
QUE SE LLAMABA GRACIELA ZITA.

"Really good," Bruno said. "Who is Graciela?"

"No one. It's just a name. I read it in a book."

"A beautiful name. Why is she the mother of God?"

"I don't know."

"It's good."

"I'll show it to Martha."

"Why don't you wait? It's not finished yet."

"Why not?"

"I don't know. It feels to me as if something else needs to happen. What do *you* think?"

It was true. Pira was disappointed.

Bruno stroked his head, smiling. "The fact that it's not finished doesn't mean it's not good. It's very good. It's just not quite finished."

"You mean it can get better?"

"Well, yes, in a way. It can get more complete." He described a round form with his hands.

"Like perfect?"

"Yes, in a way."

"Can I show it to Zita?"

"You could, but it would be a shame. It needs more work."

"OK. I'll tell you when it's finished."

He ran out of the office and into the garden. Never before had he felt this kind of excitement.

Shortly before dinner, after he had made up some new parts and thought the poem was finished, he recited the new parts to Bruno, but from the way Bruno said "nice," Pira knew they weren't good enough. Even so, Bruno asked Pira to dictate the whole poem to him, complete with the first part, and typed all of it out with the lines neatly centered on a new sheet of paper, and handed it to Pira.

Then Pira sounded out the words in his mind, moving only his lips.

"What do you think?" Bruno asked.

"It needs more work."

Bruno smiled: "I think so too."

Before going to bed, Pira crossed out all the new lines. Then he crossed them out more thickly. No one should read them. They weren't good.

*

The next morning the bell rang and it was Arón. He wanted to look at the big green book with the woodcuts showing the end of the world and heroes being executed and criminals cutting their victims' throats and the mother who burned her daughter all over her body with a red-hot poker. He had seen that book many times, and now he wanted to see it again. So Arón and Pira looked at it together, and then Pira thought of another book Arón would probably like and brought it out from the bookshelves next to his father's office. It was a book with many words for grown-ups that Pira had never read, but in the back were photographs of dead people. Dead people lying in the street, singly and in dark clumps, several bodies at a time, and rows of dead people lined up by the side of a road, and pictures of dead children. Someone had piled them up in a big heap, boys and girls. Some of them were naked, with their behinds showing, but they were dead, so they had nothing to be ashamed of. Others wore short pants and dresses and had shoes on. Their arms and legs were entangled. Some were buried under the bodies of others, some lay on top with no one on top of them. A few had their eyes and mouths wide open. These children, Pira explained, had been killed by bombs. It happened in Spain, he said, in a war that was over now.

"They kill children?" Arón asked.

"Yes. In a war they kill everyone."

"Why do they kill children?"

"To make the grown-ups sad."

Arón became still.

They played a little with trucks and then with soldiers, and then Pira brought out his Superman doll and Arón tipped all his soldiers over without any shooting.

"They're all dead," he said, but that was ridiculous, it was like they all fainted, and where was the fun in that?

Then Arón decided that one of them, the General, was still alive. He put him in the back of a truck, lying down, and drove him far away across the lawn, all the way to the garden wall, and there he put the General in a crack between the stones, standing, and put a clump of grass in front of him so he would be hidden.

"No one can see him here," he said, "not even El Superhombre," and Pira accepted that.

"I'm going home now," Arón said. "I'll see you tomorrow."

He always said that, "hasta mañana," but it didn't mean he would come back the next day, it was just a grown-up way of talking.

After lunch, Bruno and Martha and Zita and Pira all had a siesta, Martha and Bruno in their bedroom, Zita in her room in the back of the house, and Pira in his room with the window facing the Calle Humboldt. The window had no glass, nothing dividing his room from the street except five iron bars, so when he closed his eyes and listened, it was almost like lying on the street with people and mules and dogs and horses passing his bed right and left. Anything could happen at any moment.

"Mantequillaaaaaa!"

That was the man with the butter cart.

"Chicleeeeee!"

A Chiclet vendor.

The clatter of a mule's hoofs, a muttered "Ándale!" from its owner, and the light smack of a stick on the animal's rump.

Men and women walking, the sharp trill of a bicycle bell, a laugh, a curse.

There was stillness between the sounds. In the stillness, he heard distant voices, and then, very far away, a radio.

The singing of the caged bird across the street. Now and then, a car passing.

A horde of children ran by, panting, giggling, pattering on their bare feet. Pira wondered if he knew any of them from playing marbles, and if Arón was among them, and then he thought about being bald again.

"Tejocoteeeee!"

Martha always bought a couple of the sweet yellow fruits from that boy because he needed the money.

Gradually, as the sounds came and went, he descended.

He wouldn't sleep—he never did during siesta—but he would doze in that delicious balance between sleeping and waking. Always before he arrived there, little rainbow-colored spheres appeared before his eyes and clustered together in quivering stacks or in rows. He liked them, even though he found them scary too. He would watch them for a while and then pictures would appear. This time it was a frog. He laughed.

He recited the first four lines of his poem several times, murmuring the words and feeling a glow of completeness and pride.

CUANDO CANTA LA VERDE RANA
EN LA MAÑANA, LA MAÑANITA
VENÍA CON GRACIA LA MADRE DE DIÓS
QUE SE LLAMABA GRACIELA ZITA.

Why couldn't the poem just stop there? It would be perfect. But the poem wasn't finished. It needed more work. How would it go on?

"Venía con cariño," his mind said. She came with kindness.

"Venía con amor." She came with love.

"That's good!" he thought. He imagined Bruno saying it. "Really good!"

Then more words came: "Venía cantando por todos los niños."
She came singing for all the children. Except "por" was bigger than
"for." More like "for the sake of." It sounded more special.

Now he was excited! He jumped off his bed and went outside.
Tristan was glad to see him and looked around for his throwing
stick. But Pira wasn't in the mood for throwing. He was listening
to the poem, sounding it out in his mind and listening:

CUANDO CANTA LA VERDE RANA
EN LA MAÑANA, LA MAÑANITA
VENÍA CON GRACIA LA MADRE DE DIÓS
QUE SE LLAMABA GRACIELA ZITA
VENÍA CON GRACIA Y CON AMOR
VENÍA CANTANDO POR TODOS LOS NIÑOS

All he needed now was a rhyme for "amor." "Flor" would fit.
So would "calor" and "señor" and "mejor" and "peor." But "flor"
was best. What would la Madre de Diós do with a flower, when
she's already singing for all the children? Is she carrying the flower?
Bringing it? Wearing a flower maybe, the way Zita sometimes wore
flowers in her hair. He tried many sentences ending with flor. None
of them fit. What if he couldn't find one? The whole poem would
be ruined, it wouldn't be good at all.

He went to the wall to check on Arón's General. He was still
there, of course, hiding behind his clump of grass.

Pira thought of making him climb the wall. What if he climbed
up, crevice by crevice and brick by brick, all the way to the bottle
shards on the top? That would be heroic. From up there he could
survey the garden, the patio, everything. But the wall was too
high for Pira. And besides, it was Arón's General, so Arón had
to decide.

He went to the patio. There, next to his soldiers, lay his best marble, the one with the blue swirl. Usually it was a big cannonball, but right now he needed it for rolling.

He lay down on the cool flat tiles and stretched out his arms before him so that they lay like the long curving walls of the bay where, last year, he had caught a small silvery fish, and with a tap of a finger he set the marble rolling. There it went with a dark, hollow sound, wobbling slightly, until the palm of his other hand stopped it like a barrier. Then, with a gentle push, it was sent back across the wide bay, rolling slowly like a wandering wave, maybe, or a fish, and rolled back again with a tap of a finger. The way out to the sea was open, but the fish didn't know it. All it could do was swim back and forth, maybe remembering the big sea without walls but not seeing it, and wondering if there was a way out. The little fish, when Pira caught it, was just like that. He was sorry that he caught it, he wished he hadn't, but back then when he saw it dancing and glittering on the hook, he was proud.

His parents suggested that he put it back in the water but he didn't want to, it was his fish now because he had caught it, and he wanted to eat it because that was what big boys did with fish after catching them. So his parents filled Pira's pail with seawater and took the little fish off the hook and put it in the pail and there it swam. Back in the beach hotel his mother took him to the kitchen and showed the cook Pira's fish and asked him to fry it for Pira. The cook was big and had a white cook's hat. He laughed "Ha ha ha!" and his teeth were big and yellow. He had a moustache like Zapata. He took a knife and cut a piece of butter and put it in a pan and turned on the flame of a stove and swooshed the butter back and forth until it melted and turned the flame down. Then he reached into a bag of flour and strewed some flour on a cutting board. His hands were enormous. Then he reached into the pail and took Pira's fish in one hand. It was wriggling again as it had on the hook, but this time the man was holding it delicately between two fingers, and with his other hand he brought the blade of his knife to the fish's mouth, which was opening and closing. Then he held the hand with the fish and the hand with the knife close to Pira's face so that he could see, and with two or three slicing movements cut the fish in half and tossed the half fishes into the flour. There they leaped around separately. The cook turned the half fishes a couple of times in the flour with his fingers and then dropped them into the pan. They were still wriggling. Then Martha took Pira by the hand and led him to the dining room, and there they waited. "It all happened so fast," she said, looking sorry for Pira. When a waitress brought the two half fishes on a plate with some lettuce and tomato and a piece of lemon, they were no longer moving and didn't much look like the fish he had caught. Martha squeezed some lemon onto both of them. Now, lying on the patio, still rolling his marble, he couldn't remember what the fish tasted like or even if he ate it at all.

He stopped the marble and held it in his hand and put one side of his face on the floor and closed his eyes. The stone was cool and hard and flat, but it was also deep, like the sea. It was always like that when his eyes were closed. Always at first when he sensed this soft depth it scared him, and then he would feel the hardness of the tiles supporting his body and knew he wouldn't sink down. But this time he wasn't afraid and thought that as long as he held the marble it would keep him safe on top of the patio while in his feelings he sank down. As soon as he thought that, it was already happening. He was sinking slowly and it wasn't like falling at all, it was more like being held and slowly let down. He still felt the marble in his hand, so he wasn't scared, even though in a way he was nowhere near the hand with the marble. He was sinking in an ocean of stone. It was soft, soft as air. How could that be? It wasn't possible. Yet it felt familiar, as if he had done this before many times and knew how to do it. Then Zita came out of her room onto the patio.

"Pira, mi amor," she said, laughing. "Why do you sleep on the hard stone?"

"It's not hard," he said, opening his eyes.

"Really?" She bent down and knocked on the tile with her knuckles. "It feels hard to me!"

"Not to me," he said, conscious that he was keeping a secret from Zita and that he would keep it from his parents as well. As for Chris and Arón, they wouldn't understand or even be interested, so not telling them wasn't a secret.

*

Chris came for a visit a little while later. A driver brought him in his father's shiny blue car. They climbed the zapote tree and played pirates, and Pira decided they were Mexican pirates because "pirate" in Spanish sounded a lot like his name. Then they played marbles on the patio. Then they played war with the soldiers. Pira showed Chris Arón's General and Chris said that didn't make sense, Generals don't hide. He wanted to take the General back to the other soldiers, but Pira told him the General had to stay in his cave as long as Arón wanted him there. Then they decided to wrestle on the lawn. Sometimes Pira was stronger than Chris and sometimes he wasn't. It was different from wrestling with Arón, which Pira had done only once. Arón was too timid and gentle for wrestling. Chris was tough. He didn't give up. Arón gave up. His whole body gave up.

When they were done with wrestling they pretended to be giants in Lilliput, lying on their backs with their shirts off and waiting for ants to crawl over them. But there weren't many ants, so they decided they were hungry and asked Zita for something to eat and she gave them mangos, Pira's favorite fruit. Then they let Tristan lick the sweet sticky juice off their faces and hands and chests until Martha came out and pulled Tristan away by his collar and asked Zita for a damp cloth and washed the boys with it.

Then Martha gave them watercolors and brushes and paper and they painted battleships for a while until the driver came to take

Chris home for dinner. That was how the day passed, and Pira still hadn't found the line ending with "flor."

But the next day he found it, and it wasn't anything like what he had expected:

Y para la única blanca flor.

The lady didn't bring a flower. She didn't bring anything. She came with grace. Grace wasn't something you could bring, it was just a slow, tall way of walking, the way Zita walked when she balanced something on top of her head. Walking, walking, down from the sky, singing for all the children *and* for the only white flower, the flor that rhymed with amor. Immediately he felt happy because he knew the poem was finished. It was finished because it couldn't go on. It was perfect.

He was afraid, then, to tell the new lines to Bruno, especially the last one. What if he liked it a little but not a lot? That would be too disappointing. He didn't want to think about it. It would be like not getting any presents for Christmas.

He climbed the zapote tree and thought about other things. He thought about Christmas, which was a long way away, but still, it was worth thinking about. He wanted roller skates and a Superman costume. He wanted a curl on his forehead like Superman, but you couldn't really wish for that. He thought about having a little brother. At first he would be a baby, then he would get bigger. But Pira would always be the older one, the big brother. He would protect his little brother. He would teach him things that he knew. What would his name be? David. Or Robin. Robin was Batman's friend, who also had a curl. And it was the name of a little boy he remembered from long ago when Bruno left Martha to live with another woman and Martha went to New York with Pira and Pira went to The Little People's School in Greenwich Village, where he met Robin.

Robin had red hair. Martha sang Pira a song back then about "Little Robin Redbreast," and because of that song Pira thought of Robin as a bird. He loved Robin's name and his red hair as much as he loved Robin himself. He also remembered meeting his first father in New York. His name was David and that was all Pira knew about him at the time until later, when he and Martha were back in Mexico with Bruno after Bruno left the other woman because he loved Martha more and because he loved Pira more than anyone in the world, and because Martha loved Bruno and also because David loved another woman. It was then, one night after singing Pira his bedtime song, that Martha told him he had a second father and that he was David, the big nice man who visited her and Pira when they were in New York, and that she hadn't told him then because he was little and she didn't want to confuse him, but now he could understand. In a way he already knew it because David had let him know, without ever once saying the words "father" or "love," that he loved him.

It was nice having two fathers. Most children only had one. Arón didn't have a father at all. Chris had no mother. Which was worse? If you had a mother like Arón's, it was better not to have a mother. But only if you had a father, which Arón didn't. There were children like that, orphans. Like the kids who begged every day by the Hotel Juarez until someone shooed them away, and on Sundays outside the Cathedral. Was there a Padre de Diós? He would have to ask Zita. Not Bruno. Bruno didn't believe in God. But Zita—what would she say when he told her the poem and she heard the part about la Madre de Diós? Maybe she wouldn't like it. She would ask why the Mother of God's name was Zita. "It's not Zita," he said to her in his thoughts, "it's Graciela Zita." "But that's not her name," she replied. He didn't know what to say about that. And Bruno? Even if he loved the poem, he wouldn't just love it. He would think about it. "Why is it the only white flower?" He could ask that. He probably would. There were many white flowers. How could there be "the only white flower"? It didn't make sense. Maybe I'll tell it to Martha, he thought, before I tell it to Bruno. There she was, in a deck chair beneath the banana tree, reading. He would go down the ladder and say, "Martha?" She would look up from her book. "I finished the poem." "Really? Can I hear it?" Then he would recite it from the beginning and she would love it. But Bruno would be disappointed if he did that. Pira felt tears behind his eyes. It was too hard, making this poem. He wished he hadn't ever started it. Why did it have to be perfect? The first four lines were really good, Bruno had said so.

He leaned his cheek against the green, smooth, soft bark of the tree. It smelled good, but he liked especially the way it felt. Maybe the tree liked his touch too. Once, sitting on this same branch, he had seen a leaf creeping toward him slowly on spidery legs. The leaf had a head with two round black shiny eyes and long feelers, and it was walking. It frightened him. Later he told Bruno about it, and Bruno said that what he had seen was called a Walking Leaf, but it wasn't a leaf, it was an insect pretending to be a leaf to protect itself from birds. Then Bruno showed Pira a picture of a Walking Leaf in a book, and under the picture were words explaining the picture, and one of the words was "mimicry." That was the name for this kind of pretending. Pira was always told not to mimic people because it could hurt their feelings, but it was obviously different with bugs.

Now he felt sleepy. He wished he had a tree house. In a tree house he would be able to see everyone and no one would see him. Not even Tristan. Tristan would smell him, though. That would be good. He would have a pulley for Tristan. Like an elevator. He would pull him up and let him down, but nobody else could join him.

At that moment Bruno came out of his office and saw him. He smiled and waved. Pira waved back.

"How is your poem coming along?"

"It's finished."

His heart leaped when he said that.

"Can I hear it?"

Pira swung a leg down to set foot on the ladder.

"Careful," Bruno said.

"I know." But he was hurrying.

*

Nothing happened as Pira had expected. Instead of asking to hear the new lines first, Bruno invited him into his office, rolled a fresh sheet of paper into the typewriter, and asked him to dictate the whole poem from the beginning.

CUANDO CANTA LA VERDE RANA
EN LA MAÑANA, LA MAÑANITA
VENÍA CON GRACIA LA MADRE DE DIÓS
QUE SE LLAMABA GRACIELA ZITA
VENÍA CON GRACIA Y CON AMOR
VENÍA CANTANDO POR TODOS LOS NIÑOS
Y PARA LA ÚNICA BLANCA FLOR

He didn't say anything as he typed, but when the poem was finished on the page, he looked at Pira and said:

"Peter, it's wonderful. This is a truly good poem."

For a moment Pira puzzled over the meaning of "truly good." He had never heard those words put together like that. Was the poem good in a way that made it true? Then Bruno reached out and drew him close, and Pira felt Bruno's stubbly cheek brushing against his cheek and thought there was no one, ever, in the whole world, whom he loved more than his father. Then he remembered Martha and said with excitement, "Let's show it to Martha!" They went out together and Pira ran over to where Martha was reading beneath the banana tree, and said, just as he had imagined before: "Martha?"

"Yes?"

"I finished the poem!"

"I heard you when you told Bruno. I can't wait to hear it."

"You can read it."

He handed her the page with the poem and she read it silently, smiling as she read, and then she said, "It's beautiful," and then, looking at Bruno, "really beautiful." Then, after reading it again, she said, "I love the whole thing but also parts in it, like the singing frog and especially la unica blanca flor, that's so beautiful," and Bruno agreed.

Zita was out shopping, so Pira had to wait for her to come home. Then she wanted to start making dinner, but Martha told Zita that dinner could wait because Pira had something to show her. He felt shy reciting the poem to her in Bruno's and Martha's presence, so Zita smiled and said, "Ven, mi amor," and took him by the hand, which was something Martha and Bruno rarely did any longer because he was no longer little, but he liked it when Zita did it. She led him by the hand to her room and said, "Por aquí estaremos solitos," which means "here we will be alone," except "solitos" sounds so much friendlier than that. She sat down on her bed, and he said he had written a poem that was in a way for her (he was surprised when he said that) because her name was in it, but it wasn't really her name because he had made it "Graciela Zita" and that in the poem this was the name of la Madre de Diós, which of course it isn't really either, and could he tell it to her? She smiled and said, "Claro que sí," and he recited the poem, and as he spoke, it sounded bigger than it had before, maybe because Zita listened so seriously, as if Pira's words were something one could believe, not just like or love. When it was finished, she said, "Que hermosa canción," and her calling it a song was the most surprising and suddenly true thing anyone had said about it.

*

Arón came the next day. The first thing he did was check on his General. There he was in his cave, still hidden, still standing. Arón turned to Pira and smiled. Then they went into the house to look at books with pictures, and Pira read to Arón from a picture book for children about ants: how there are worker ants and warrior ants and an ant queen, how the pregnant ant queen sheds her wings and creeps into the earth to lay eggs, how an ant hive is like a city where everyone has different work to do, how the worker ants help each other carry things and the warrior ants fight side by side against enemies, how all those thousands of little bodies running around in all directions stay in touch with each other, as if there were a brain telling everyone what to do, but there isn't.

That made Arón wonder: What happens if you kill one ant? Do the other ants notice? They don't, Pira said, though he didn't really know. And if you kill ten ants? They still don't. A hundred? Maybe then they notice, Pira said.

They decided to go to the anthill and watch the ants. They were fantastically busy, as always, running in streams away from the hive and back to its opening on the top.

"Are there baby ants?" Arón asked.

"There must be," Pira said.

"But where are they?"

"Maybe they're inside, getting bigger."

"I'm going to put the General on the anthill," Arón said. And he did. He put him on top of the hive, next to the entrance. Several ants inspected him right away, felt him with their feelers, crawled up his body and over his blue cap and down again. They didn't seem to mind his being there.

"He's their General," Arón said. "They're his soldiers."

The General held a sword up over his head, looking brave.

3

Sometimes Pira and Martha played the What If game. Either he would begin, or she would.

"What if flowers wore sombreros?" Martha asked once.

"They would sing Las Mañanitas," he said. Martha was delighted.

"And what if they wore huaraches too?" she asked.

Huaraches were sandals that men with sombreros wore in the streets.

"They would be drinking pulque," he said. "The whole garden would be drunk."

They laughed together at that. To Pira, it was hilarious: hundreds of flowers dancing and reeling, wearing sombreros and singing Las Mañanitas.

Then it was his turn: "What if Zita was my mother?"

"*Were* my mother."

"What if Zita were my mother?"

"Then I would be a criada."

"And what if she spoke English and played the violin?"

"Then I would have a boyfriend named Federico."

"No, you wouldn't, because Federico would be my father. You would have a boyfriend named Bruno."

"True," she said.

"Bruno would work for the railroad," Pira continued, "and you would wash the clothes while Zita played the violin. I would like that!"

"You would, would you?" She said that in a joking way, but she looked thoughtful too. "Why would you like that?"

"Because it would be upside down but still the same."

"Would it?" his mother asked. "Would Zita's love be the same as my love if she were your mother? Would my love be the same if I were the criada?"

That stopped Pira's imagination. The funny upside-down world was no longer funny, and almost sad.

But his mother continued to imagine it: "You would see Bruno only every two months," she said.

"You too," he said quietly. "You would only see him every two months."

Two months were such a long time. They both stopped talking, and they both noticed that Pira's eyes had filled with tears. Martha wiped his eyes with her fingertips. He pressed his wet face into her soft cotton blouse, smelling her skin through it, feeling her hand caressing his hair and wrapping his arms around her body, pulling himself close to her.

"I don't like this game anymore," he said.

"I know," she said. "We can play something else."

*

Pira tried to play the What If game with Chris and Arón, but they didn't like it. They liked games with robber masks and a Superman cape and toy soldiers and trucks, but not with words. So Pira played the game by himself.

Sometimes while he was drifting off to sleep or sitting on the zapote tree, a What If thought would happen, and then he would start imagining things being different or even opposite from the way they were in reality. Sometimes he returned to What Ifs he had already thought of, and that made them feel real. One he returned to several times was:

What if children didn't grow up but down? What if they got smaller and smaller? Eventually the grown-ups wouldn't be able to see them. The children would be like ants. They could even get stepped on. But they wouldn't get stepped on because there wouldn't be any grown-ups, there would only be grown-downs! Tiny little people. But even an ant-sized person could get smaller—smaller and smaller, tinier and tinier, until eventually he would be nothing at all. Nothing! He could imagine being small and getting smaller, but he couldn't imagine nothing.

So he asked Bruno: "What is nothing?"

"Nothing is nothing," Bruno said.

"Yes, but what is it?"

"It isn't anything. It's nothing."

"So nothing isn't anything?"

Bruno laughed. It seemed Pira had made a joke.

"How could nothing be something?" Bruno asked. "Think about it."

Pira thought about it.

"Nothing is nothing," he said.

"Exactly," Bruno said.

"There is no nothing."

"Exactly."

Later the thought of nothing came back. It seemed to still be something. What was it? Nothing! Maybe nothing was an imaginary thing that didn't really exist, like a dragon. But you could imagine a dragon, while nothing was something that couldn't be imagined because it didn't look like anything.

*

When Pira told Chris that his parents still read stories to him and sang songs before he went to sleep, Chris said he would hate that, it would be like being a baby again. So Pira told his parents that he was big enough to go to sleep by himself, and they said, "Of course you are, you're six and a half." But then he missed being with Bruno and Martha in that way and told them he would like it if once in a while they sat with him the way they used to, and they said they would like it too. So they did—not every night, but once in a while. Bruno read him bedtime stories even though he could read by himself, or he would make up new stories. Sometimes he sang German songs. Martha sang to him too, accompanying herself on a guitar: Mexican songs like "Malagueña" and American songs like "Oh Katie dear." Other times she played the violin.

On one of those evenings, Pira asked Martha if there was real magic, not just magic tricks like Sándor's or make-believe magic like in fairy tales. Martha said music was real magic. Why? Because it had the power to remind people of their happiness.

"You mean people forget?"

"Yes, and then music reminds them. Like this." She played something, and it made Pira feel happy.

"Sometimes music can be sad," she said.

"I know," he said.

"But sadness in music is beautiful, so it doesn't make people unhappy."

Pira wasn't sure about that. He didn't want Martha to show him what she meant, but she did anyway.

"Like this," she said.

The tune she played was almost too sad.

"And sometimes it's both at the same time," she said.

She played the beginning of the Springtime Sonata, which Pira had heard many times on the record where she was playing with his first father, David.

"Did you hear it? I mean, that it's both? Sad and happy, happy and sad?"

He wasn't sure. But he nodded.

"It's so beautiful," she said. "Would you like to hear it again?"

He did. She played it again.

"I'd better stop," she said, laughing, "or else you won't be able to sleep."

She bent down to kiss him and pressed her lips against his, and he could smell her perfume. After she left the room, Pira thought that the difference between Martha and Bruno was that she never forgot her happiness. She liked to have fun. When guests came, she would sing and play the guitar. She liked to laugh. She liked to dance. She liked to go to concerts and plays and parties. Bruno was different. He liked to be by himself. Sometimes in the evening he would lie on a deck chair beneath the zapote tree, smoking and looking up at the sky.

*

One day Pira asked Bruno what he was writing.

"I'm writing a story," Bruno said.

"What's it about?"

"It's about a dog."

"About Tristan?"

"No. It's about a dog we had when you were little."

"What was his name?"

"It was a female. Her name was Tonta."

"Tonta!" Pira laughed. "That means silly!"

"She *was* silly, but then she became crazy. It was a sickness. I didn't know she was sick when I named her. I called her Tonta because she seemed silly in a funny way."

"A happy way?"

"Yes."

"Like Cantinflas?"

Cantinflas was a clown who made movies. Everyone loved Cantinflas.

"Sort of. She seemed foolish. But lovable. But then she became crazy. So it's a sad story."

"What happened?"

"I had to put her to sleep."

"Why is that sad?"

"I mean I had to put an end to her life. Because she was suffering, and there was no cure."

Pira thought about that.

"La mataste?" He said it in Spanish. "You killed her?"

"Yes, but very gently. She didn't know that she had to die. It was like going to sleep."

"Como la mataste?"

"With a pill."

*

Pira told Zita about Tonta and how Bruno had killed her with a pill. "Con una píldora."

"Una píldora!" Zita said, laughing. "Era una pistola!"

"My father said he did it with a pill."

"Píldora, pistola—the words are similar. You must have heard it wrong."

"I didn't. We were speaking English. The words are different in English. 'Pill' and 'pistol.'"

She smiled. "They still sound similar. Believe me, he did it with a pistol. It couldn't be helped. I remember. It was a sad day."

*

Pira asked Martha, "Did Bruno kill Tonta with a pill or with a gun?"

Martha looked surprised, and then annoyed.

"Who told you about that?"

"Bruno."

"What did he say?"

"He said Tonta was crazy in a sick way and no one could help her, so he had to kill her."

"With a pill?"

"Yes. That's what he said. But Zita says he did it with a gun."

"Oh," Martha said.

"Which was it?"

Martha said nothing. She seemed to be thinking, or else she was waiting for Pira to speak. But he was waiting for her answer.

"I think you need to talk with Bruno."

"Now?"

"No, later. He's working now."

Suddenly Pira realized that Bruno had not told him the truth. Then he thought he couldn't be sure because Martha hadn't said anything. Did she know how Tonta had died? Why had no one ever told him about Tonta? There weren't any pictures of her either. Was it a secret? He looked into his mother's green eyes, and for a moment he was frightened because she was looking at him as if she didn't see him, like a person in a painting. But then she reached out to stroke his hair, and her face was full of kindness.

"Don't worry, Peter. You'll talk to Bruno later. He'll explain everything."

*

That evening Bruno sat at Pira's bedside and confessed that he had lied about Tonta's death.

"It was wrong of me to lie. Please forgive me."

"I do."

"It was wrong because when we lie to those we love, we damage their trust, and without trust there can be no love."

"Damage?"

"Yes, in the same way that you can damage a thing. Sometimes damaged trust can be repaired, and sometimes it can't."

Pira nodded.

"That's what we're doing," Bruno said. "Repairing trust."

Pira nodded and smiled.

"And now I'll tell you why I lied. Maybe you've guessed it already."

"You didn't want me to know that you have a gun. Because it's forbidden."

"I don't have a gun. It was someone else's. No, I didn't want you to know that I would do something like that."

"But you did it to help her."

"I did."

"Why didn't you give her a pill?"

"I didn't have one. And she was dangerous because of her sickness. The sickness made her angry and frightened. If she bit a person, that person would die. So I borrowed a gun from a friend and took her to a field and shot her there."

"Did you shoot her in the heart?"

"No, behind the ear. That way the bullet went into the brain. She was dead right away."

"Did it hurt her?"

"I don't think so. It happened so fast, she didn't even notice."

"Did you cry?"

"Yes."

"Did Martha cry?"

"Yes. Zita too. But they didn't see her die. I told them afterward."

"Poor Tonta."

"Yes, poor Tonta."

There was a big silence then. It was bigger than the room they were in. They sat in the silence together and listened to the sounds outside: footsteps and voices, near ones and distant ones, gentle and mean voices, laughter.

The caged bird across the street made its clear fluting sounds. It did that every evening at sunset. Then there was a baby crying far away. A car rumbled past.

The stillness was no longer sad.

"What if someone lies," Pira asked, "and the other person doesn't know they're being lied to? Then there's no damage!"

"I think there is. The damage is invisible, but it's there."

They were silent again. The color of the walls had turned a soft dark violet. It was so comfortable, talking with Bruno at night. The way silence and words were both good. The way you could rest in silence as long as you wanted, a silence to which you both listened together.

Then, when either of them spoke, the words sounded quieter than the way most words sounded during the day.

"You and Martha used to lie to me about Santa Claus," Pira said.

"That's true. Lying to children is an old custom. But I don't think it's right, even though we did it too."

"There was no damage."

"There was, a little. But we mended it."

They were silent again.

"Arón lies to his mother sometimes."

"I'm glad to hear that. Lying is his way to protect himself. She's strong and he's weak. It's completely unfair."

"But she's his mother. You said we shouldn't lie to the people we love."

"When she's kind to him, she's his mother, but when she beats him, she's his enemy. When a person has enemies, he may have to lie."

Pira thought of Arón, who was so timid and weak, and thought that in a way Arón was a hero. Just coming home from his errands or from playing with Pira or children in the street took courage. Every day. And what about Bruno? He had fought in a war.

"Do you have enemies?"

"Not right now. But there were times when I did."

"Who?"

"Hitler and his followers. Many people."

"Did you lie to them?"

"Yes."

They were silent again. Then Pira said: "You will never be my enemy."

"No," Bruno said, "that can never happen."

Pira turned over on his side and closed his eyes and Bruno tucked him in and kissed his cheek and remained sitting on the edge of his bed, and Pira felt happy knowing that his father would stay until after he was asleep.

*

Bruno sometimes spoke with Pira in German, just for fun. Pira didn't understand most of it, but he liked the way it sounded. Some of the stranger words he learned how to pronounce. Spazierengehen was one of them. It meant "going for a walk." That was something Bruno liked to do by himself after his work was done.

One day Bruno asked, "Willst du mit mir spazierengehen?" Pira said, "Ja." They walked down the steep, curving slope of the Calle Humboldt, past houses and huts that got poorer the farther they walked, until they reached the edge of the town. Dogs were barking in the valley, some of them very far away. Somewhere a mule was braying. They sat down on a flat stone near a shallow pond and watched long-legged flies walking on the water.

"Zita said Jesus could walk on water," Pira said.

"I've heard that story too," Bruno said, "but I don't believe it. People can't walk on water."

"So she lied?"

"No, Zita doesn't lie. Somebody told her the story and she believed it. You mustn't tell her that it's not true. She wants to believe it."

"I want to believe it too."

"Hmm," Bruno said, and that was all he said.

They watched the insects darting around on the surface of the pond.

"How do they do it?" Pira asked.

"I don't know. Maybe they have oil on their feet. Oil floats on water. It's an interesting question."

"If I put oil on my feet, would I be able to walk on water?"

"No. You would be too heavy. You would sink."

"Even lots of oil?"

"Even lots of oil. You would sink."

"What if the story about Jesus were true?" Pira said. "Even though you don't believe it? That could be, couldn't it?"

"Not really," Bruno said. "But it's a nice thing to imagine."

"It's a What If story," Pira said.

Bruno didn't know what that was, so Pira explained it to him.

"You're right," Bruno said. "It is a What If story. As a What If story, I like it."

"Me too," Pira said.

"Some What Ifs turn out to be true, and some don't," Bruno said.

"You never know?"

"Most of the time you do know."

They sat for a while, watching the insects on the water.

"I like this What If game," Bruno said.

"Do you want to play it?"

"Not right now. But I'm going to think about it."

They talked about other things on the way home. But that evening, after Pira was in bed, Bruno came and sat on the edge of the bed for a while without talking, holding Pira's hand.

"I've been thinking about the What If game," he said. "It's a good game. Grown-ups play it too. When an artist makes a painting or I write a story, that's a What If. Before there was an airplane there were two brothers who asked themselves, 'What if people could fly?' Then they invented the airplane. Before anyone does anything special, first they ask what if, and then they do it. Some What Ifs are playful, just for fun, and some are serious. The playful ones become real very quickly, unless they're too silly to be real. The serious ones can take a long time. That's what I've been thinking."

"What's a serious What If?"

"There's one I've been thinking about for many years," Bruno said. "What if everyone had enough food to eat, so there wouldn't be any beggars? What if everyone treated everyone kindly?"

"What if no one hit their children?" Pira said.

"Yes, for example."

"What if no one threw stones at dogs?"

"Yes."

"What if no one ever died?"

"That, for me, is not a serious What If because I don't believe it. People will always die. But I believe it's possible that someday there will be no more beggars, and no one will beat their children or throw stones at dogs. So, to me, that's a serious What If."

Pira liked that and thought about it. He was still holding Bruno's hand. He loved his father's seriousness. Bruno rarely laughed. Once Pira and Bruno went to a movie with Cantinflas and Bruno laughed so loud that someone in front of him turned around to laugh with him. When Pira told Martha about it later, she was moved: "Really? He laughed out loud?" It surprised her and made her happy. She thought Bruno was sad because he was so serious most of the time. But now Pira, holding his father's hand, thought that being serious was Bruno's way to be happy. Then, in his thoughts, he saw insects walking on water, running forward and drifting back, forward and back.

*

Not long after that, Pira heard Martha say to Valéria: "Bruno is homesick." He didn't know the word but it sounded like a feeling, and not a good feeling.

"They're all homesick," Valéria said. "Not me. I love Mexico."

Pira didn't care who the other homesick people were. He cared about Bruno. He didn't want him to be homesick.

Later, alone on his listening spot on the patio, he thought about Bruno some more and about the word, and he didn't understand it. Maybe it wasn't a feeling. Zita's mother in Oaxaca stayed home a lot because she was sick. Bruno was home most of the time. Maybe he was sick. Why didn't he talk about it? Why didn't he go to a doctor?

That evening, when Bruno sat with him before he went to sleep, Pira asked him what "homesick" meant, and Bruno explained:

"It means you're far from home and you want to go home but you can't, and that makes you sad."

So Bruno *was* sad after all. The sadness was hidden. Maybe it was a secret.

"You dream about your home," Bruno continued, "and even if the dream is a happy dream, when you wake up you realize you're not home at all, and the sadness is back. It's hard to make it go away. That's why they call it a sickness."

"How do you cure it?"

"By finding a way to go home."

"But how can you be homesick? You're home already."

"Who says I'm homesick?"

"Martha."

Now Bruno understood Pira's question. It took a while for him to explain that he wasn't homesick all the time, just sometimes. That the home he missed wasn't the house he lived in. That it was Germany. That he needed to go there, not only because he was homesick but because Germany was in ruins and he wanted to help rebuild it. That he would never go to Germany without taking Pira and Martha with him. That the three of them would go together. It would be an adventure. Pira would learn German. He would go to school there.

"When will we go?"

"Not for a while. Maybe two years."

"Will I go to first grade before then?"

"Of course. First grade begins in three months."

That put Pira's mind at rest. Later it occurred to him that if he left Mexico he would be leaving his friends. And that maybe in Germany he would be homesick for Mexico. But two years was far away.

*

Sitting on the big branch of the zapote tree, Pira thought: "I'm going to climb down. Right now I'm up here, then I'll be down there. But when I'm there, there will be here, and then will be now. And where I am now will no longer be now, it will be then."

The more he thought about this, the stranger it seemed. Did now really become then? And then now? Were both true? How could that be?

He climbed down the ladder and stood on the grass, and it was now. He felt the coolness of the grass beneath his bare feet. He hadn't imagined that earlier. There were smells too, from the purple flowers spilling over the wall from the neighbor's garden, and the thick dark smell of rotting zapote fruits under the tree. Someone was playing an accordion somewhere.

He looked at the tree. He remembered sitting up there a short while ago, and thought: "That was then. This is now. Later this now will no longer be now, it will be then." He was going to climb the tree again. He pictured himself sitting on his lookout post. He wasn't there yet, but he could see the future. He was going to sit there and look at the volcanoes, and it would be now. He climbed the ladder and swung his leg over the big branch, feeling the warm smoothness of the bark against his skin. He settled into his post and looked at the volcanoes.

Now.

It was different from the way he had imagined it. There was a small cloud over Popocatepetl, white against the blue sky. It looked like a speech bubble in a comic book, as if Popocatepetl were saying something to Iztaccihuatl. Something that couldn't be heard, so the speech bubble was empty.

Later the cloud would go away. When that time came, it would be now. Time was so strange. He wanted to experience the moment when later turned into now. He waited. But the cloud wasn't moving. It was taking too long. He turned his head and saw that Bruno had left his office door open, maybe to let out cigarette smoke. Then he forgot about time.

4

Martha and Pira were going to go swimming at the Hotel Zapata and Martha invited Zita to come along, even though Zita couldn't swim. She wouldn't have wanted to swim in the pool anyway because, she said, "They don't like índios there," but Martha said it was wrong of the people who owned the hotel to make someone like Zita feel that she didn't belong there. She said it so firmly it sounded as if it would be wrong of Zita not to go. Zita shook her head, lowering her eyes. "Señora, no vale la pena," she said—it's not worth it—which sounded to Pira like a polite way of saying "I don't want to." But Martha, who didn't like not having her way, said: "You could come as Peter's niñera. That way no one will mind." Then Zita looked at Pira and, seeing that he really hoped she would come, said, "All right, I'll be your niñera." It was funny because Pira was too big to have a niñera, but even so they would all pretend.

So they went to the hotel, and as they walked through the swinging door into the lobby with the big chandelier and the flags and rifles and sombreros on the walls and the big gold-framed painting of Zapata hanging over another swinging door that led through the garden to the swimming pool, Zita pretended to be Pira's niñera by holding his hand and holding the beach bag with the towels and bathing suits and suntan lotion slung over her shoulder. Martha paid the man behind the reception desk for the use of the swimming pool, and Pira, feeling too tall for the part he was playing, had a hard time suppressing a grin over the trick they were playing, because nobody seemed to think anything of this índia walking into a place where people didn't like índios.

They walked through the garden, still pretending. It was like making believe they were people they weren't.

Pira looked around to see if there were any índios and realized immediately why there wouldn't be any. Never in his life had he seen índios sitting around tables smoking and drinking, and that was what everyone here was doing. He had been in the Hotel Zapata before and never noticed the absence of índios, but now it was obvious. All the while Zita held his hand, and he liked it. She didn't let go of his hand until they reached the swimming pool and it was time for Martha and Pira to change into their bathing suits and fetch a swimming tube for Pira. When they came back, Zita had put two lounge chairs near the pool and was sitting a little apart from the chairs in the grass. She sat the way she often sat in the garden at home, straight-backed on her haunches with her knees together and her hands on her thighs.

"Siéntese con nosotros por favor, Zita," Martha said, and put another lounge chair next to the other two. Zita shook her head. She was comfortable on the grass, she said. Martha insisted: "Please, Zita, you are with us, you have a right to sit with us." Again Zita shook her head: "Thank you, Señora Marta. I like it here. Don't worry." Martha said: "It's embarrassing to me if we don't sit together." Then Zita stood up and sat down in one of the lounge chairs and Martha sat down in the other.

"Go swim a little," Martha said to Peter. "I'll follow you later."

In the pool, Peter met a little American girl who asked him what his name was and then told him her name was Dorothy. She was here with her uncle Harry, she said, pointing at a very big man with hair on his back. It looked almost like fur. Would they call a man Harry because he was hairy? No. He must have had that name as a baby.

"My father's name is Bruno," Pira said.

"Oh," Dorothy said.

Pira thought she was awfully pretty. He had read that combination of words in a book, "awfully pretty," and they really fit this girl. She had freckles and blue eyes. He couldn't tell what color her hair was because she was wearing a bathing cap.

Dorothy, too, was looking at Pira. They were both examining each other's faces and treading water, held up by their swimming tubes.

"You're cute," she said.

"Cute" was a word for babies. It didn't sound nice, calling him cute. He wondered why she did that. He didn't know what to say, so he turned to paddle back to where Martha and Zita were sitting.

They were talking and smiling and sipping bright yellow drinks through straws. Pira decided he wanted one too, and if it had alcohol in it he'd have Coca-Cola with ice, that would be good. He climbed out of the water, leaving his swimming tube by the edge of the pool, and suddenly noticed Chris's father, Mr. Riley, approaching the two women with a drink in his hand that looked like whisky. He was wearing a narrow-brimmed straw hat, white shorts, and a red and green shirt with pictures of parrots on it.

The top three buttons of his shirt were unbuttoned. Martha stopped talking when she saw him, and Zita pulled a towel from the beach bag.

"Ven, Pira, sécate," she said, handing him the towel.

Pira took it, remembering their game, and started drying himself like a good little boy.

"Hope I'm not interrupting," Mr. Riley said.

"You're not," Martha said. "How are you?"

"Just fine, just fine. It's always a pleasure to see you. And you," he added, with a wink to Pira. He didn't greet Zita.

"I'm surprised to see you here," Martha said. "You have a big pool in your house, don't you? Peter told me."

"Oh, the pool. No, I'm here on business. Always on the job, wherever I am. Driven, I guess is what you might call me. But I like it that way, it suits me just fine. How about you? Giving any concerts?"

Pira had seen Bruno drunk a few times, and when he was drunk he spoke a little like Mr. Riley, as if trying to remember what he was going to say next.

"Not anytime soon," Martha said, "but I'll send you a notice when we do."

"I've always wanted to ask you something . . . It's a sincere, honest question, it's been on my mind."

"Dame la toalla," Zita said. Pira realized he was staring at Mr. Riley. He gave her the towel. Zita draped it over the armrest of her chair.

"My question is . . . Here you are, Martha . . . That's your name, isn't it? Martha?"

Martha nodded. She didn't look happy.

"Martha . . . Look, my name's Bill. No reason why we shouldn't be on more familiar terms. Our sons are buddies, that counts for something. Buddies don't last forever."

Pira had never thought of Chris as his buddy. It was a book word, a cartoon word. But he liked it. He liked having a buddy. At that moment Pira liked Mr. Riley even though he was mean to almost everyone, including Chris. He had never been mean to Pira.

"My question, Martha . . . My question is simple, no point beating around the bush, I hope you don't take it amiss. What's a pretty, sweet, talented, smart American girl like you doing with a goddamn . . . well, strike the goddamn from that sentence . . . with a German? Can you explain that?"

"I don't owe you an explanation, Mr. Riley."

"Please . . . Bill . . ."

"And you've had too much to drink." She was frowning. She looked mad.

Pira was shocked. Why didn't Martha explain to Mr. Riley that Bruno had fought against Hitler? He was just asking for an explanation. Why didn't she tell him?

"I apologize," Mr. Riley said. "Sincerely. I sincerely apologize. I meant no offense."

Zita opened a bottle of suntan lotion.

"Ven, Pira, te pongo bronceador."

She did this often at home. It always felt nice when she did it. But here she was the niñera taking care of her niñito, and that made him almost laugh with pleasure as she rubbed the cool liquid onto his back.

Martha and Mr. Riley were watching the performance.

They had stopped speaking. Then Mr. Riley said: "Do you always bring your nigger along?"

Right then Martha decided that it was time to leave.

Pira didn't want to, but Martha insisted.

On the way home, still holding Zita's hand because that was how they had left the hotel, Pira asked Martha why she got so mad at Mr. Riley. He asked it in Spanish so Zita could understand.

"Not now, Peter," Martha said in English. "I'm too angry to talk. I'll tell you later."

"Was it because of—"

"Not now. I mean it."

Pira looked up at Zita. She was staring straight ahead. She looked hidden. A pregnant dog trotted past them with her pink teats dangling beneath her. She was very thin, except for her belly. Pira watched the dog getting smaller as she zigzagged down the road with her nose to the ground.

"Martha, what does nigger mean?"

"It's a really bad word. He shouldn't have used it. That's why I'm mad at him."

"What does it mean?"

"I don't want to talk about it."

The way she said that, Pira realized that "nigger" was one of those expressions that were so bad that no one would explain them to a child. They walked on silently. Then Pira remembered that he wasn't little anymore. He pulled his hand out of Zita's hand. A little later he thought of doing something that men sometimes did. He turned to Martha, who was carrying the beach bag, and said in English: "Can I carry that for you?"

"*May* I carry that for you," Martha said with a smile. "Yes, you may," and she gave him the bag to carry.

*

After that day Pira knew that Martha didn't like Mr. Riley at all. Even so, when Chris had a birthday party and Martha drove Pira to Chris's house and Mr. Riley met them at the door smelling of whisky she was friendly, or at least polite, and Pira was glad about that.

"So good to see you, Martha," Mr. Riley said, peering into her eyes as if looking for something inside them. "Come on in."

"I'm sorry, I can't."

"Won't you stay just a little while?"

"I'm sorry, I have something . . ."

"I'd like you to meet some friends of mine."

"Mr. Riley . . ."

"Please, call me Bill."

"Who's minding the children?"

Mr. Riley seemed surprised by her question. Then he laughed. "Oh, not *me*! Don't you worry! I hired a professional staff."

She nodded, smiling, and, waving goodbye to Pira—"Have fun!"—she walked off to her car.

Chris had said it would be a Super Party, and it was. First a lady named Concha directed games like pin the tail on the donkey, blind man's buff, and hide and go seek. Some of the children hid behind the big machine gun pointing at the entrance. Pira and Chris hid inside a large crate behind the stable, so near the horses they could smell them and hear them breathe. Nobody found them there.

Then six mariachis appeared with guitars and a trumpet and sang Las Mañanitas. All the children were shown where to sit around a long table. The mariachis kept playing and singing: "Rosita Alvírez," "La Malagueña," "Jalisco Jalisco," and Pira's favorite, "Traigo Mi Cuarenta y Cinco," about a charro with his forty-five and its four cartridges. Two waiters in white suits brought a huge chocolate cake with six candles for Chris to blow out over a secret wish. Then the waiters served the children ice cream and chocolate cake and brought them mangos or Coca-Cola or whatever they wanted.

A little girl waved at Pira from the other side of the table: "Hi!"

He waved back. He recognized her. It was Dorothy. He had told Martha about the girl who had been mean to him in the swimming pool and Martha had said that when a girl says to a boy that he's cute it means he's handsome, and that he could have said "You're cute yourself" and it would have meant she was pretty and she would have liked it.

So he waited for a moment when Dorothy would look at him again from across the table, and when she did, he said, "You're pretty."

"Thank you," she said, tilting her head and smiling with her mouth full of cake.

After the ice cream and cake were eaten, Concha told the children to sit down by the edge of the garden and stop talking. There was going to be a show. Everyone waited. A ball came bouncing out through the open door of the parlor and down the steps and rolled onto the lawn. A clown with red hair, a red nose, and enormous red shoes followed it, tottering a little like a baby. He tried to pick up the ball, but his feet were so big they touched the ball before his hands could. He tried it again, and the same thing happened. And again. Martha always said jokes were only funny the first time, but this one kept getting funnier.

After seven or eight tries the clown just stood there scratching his head. He decided to sneak up on the ball, pretending not to be interested, and now the ball started looking as if it was waiting for him. But when he got near it he moved too fast and kicked it again, this time all the way to the other end of the garden.

"Walk slowly!" somebody said. So he walked slowly. But he walked so slowly it would take him forever to reach the ball.

"That's *too* slow!" somebody else said.

He moved his feet faster, but his steps were so short it would still take a long time to get there.

"Make long steps!"

"No, stop!"

And of course he knocked the ball away again.

Then Dorothy offered to help him: "Here, I'll give it to you."

She went to the ball, picked it up, and brought it to the clown. Didn't she understand that he was just pretending?

For a moment the clown, or the man playing the clown, didn't know what to do. But then he looked delighted. He stretched out his arms, his hands, his fingers. Dorothy put the ball in his hands without letting go of it. Now they were holding the ball together.

"Careful!" she said, very sincerely.

The man looked down at his feet. They weren't in the way anymore. He was glad.

"Are you ready?" Dorothy said.

He nodded, holding the ball firmly.

"I'm letting go now," Dorothy said.

The clown nodded again.

She let go of the ball.

He was holding it.

He turned around and carefully carried the ball through the open parlor door into the house and was gone.

When Martha returned to pick Pira up, Mr. Riley was quite drunk and Pira was worried that she would be mean to him, but she wasn't. She thanked him for the party and asked him if he too had had a good time. He said, "Well, yes, Martha, yes, can't you tell?" and she said "I guess so" without smiling, and he laughed. Then, as she and Pira were leaving, Mr. Riley said, "I've registered Chris in that school you told me about," and Martha said, "That's great. Did you hear that, Peter? You and Chris will go to first grade together."

On the way home, Pira asked Martha: "Will Arón go to school with us too?"

"I don't think that will be possible. The school you're going to is a private school, and Arón's mother won't be able to pay for it."

"What's a private school?"

"A school that costs money. Arón will go to a public school, where his mother won't have to pay anything."

"Can't I go to the public school with him? And Chris?"

"We've thought about it. The private school you'll go to is very nice, we like the teacher, and you'll learn how to ride a horse, it's lovely. The public school isn't so nice. It's too big, and there aren't enough teachers."

"Can't you pay for Arón to go to the nice school?"

"I would if we could afford it, but we can't, it's too expensive. I'm sorry."

"It's not fair."

"I agree. It's not fair to Arón."

"It's not fair to me either."

"Why not?"

"Because he's my best friend."

"I'm sorry. But you know, Arón will continue to be your best friend. He'll come to visit just as he does now. You'll have stories to tell each other. He'll tell you about his school and you'll tell him about yours."

"I don't want to go there."

"I understand. We'll talk about it. We don't have to make a decision now. School starts on the first of September. It's still the middle of summer. Lots of time to play with Arón and with Chris."

"We'll talk about it?"

"Yes, we will."

*

A few days later, Chris brought a magnifying glass to Pira's house. It was one of his birthday presents, part of a chemistry set. Arón was there too. He and Pira were shooting marbles on the patio, but Chris said the magnifying glass would be more fun. You could kill ants with it. His father had shown him how.

"Una pistola de rayos!" he said—a ray gun!

He would show them how to use it. He told Pira to go into the house and bring a handkerchief, which Pira did. Chris spread the handkerchief on the ground and held the magnifying glass at the right distance and angle to make a bright point of light appear on the white linen and held it in place until the cloth started to smoke. Chris moved the light to another place on the handkerchief and produced more smoke. Then he showed Pira and Arón how to hold the glass and move the point of light around, keeping it always the same size.

"This is training," he said. "I'm training you. Then we'll fight a war against the ants."

Finally, when they all knew how to use the ray gun, he said, "OK. Now we can fight the ants. You'll see."

They killed ants on the patio. Chris said that was the best place because it was flat with no grass for the ants to hide in. There weren't many ants, but enough. Most of the patio was in the shade, where the ray gun wouldn't work. So you had to zap the ants in a strip of sunlight between the shade and the edge of the patio. They took turns pointing the ray at ants, one at a time, as they wandered across the strip of sunlight. It was a little like hunting because some of the ants felt the heat and ran. The lucky ones ran into the shade or over the edge of the patio. Most of them couldn't get away. It was easy to follow them with the bright spot until the little body burst into flame and shriveled into a piece of ash with a couple of legs or feelers still sticking out. Some ants didn't notice the danger and didn't even run. At one moment they were going somewhere, at the next they flared up and were dead.

After killing a few ants, Pira didn't want to play the game anymore. It wasn't like killing toy soldiers. The ants were alive. But

Chris and Arón were having fun. Arón in particular was excited: "Let's go to the anthill, we can kill hundreds there!" Chris thought that was a good idea. That made Arón proud. "Vámonos!" he said, as if he were the leader. But Chris thought of something even better: "Let's get two more ray guns. Does your mother have one?" Arón shook his head, his pride gone. "How about you, Pira?" Without hesitation Pira ran into the house and knocked on the door of Bruno's office even though he wasn't supposed to and asked if he could use Bruno's magnifying glass. "Yes," Bruno said, "just don't lose it." He didn't ask what Pira needed it for, which Pira was glad about because he was pretty sure Bruno wouldn't like his using it to kill ants. Chris tried the new ray gun on the ants on the patio and it killed them faster than the one he had brought. "It's more powerful," he said—"màs poderoso"—and now Pira was proud.

They went to the anthill. The first thing they saw there was not the ants, it was the General. Even though Pira and Arón knew he was there, they hadn't expected to see him. Neither had Chris, of course.

"He's the General," Arón said, as if to introduce him.

"What's he doing there?" Chris asked.

"He's their leader."

"Whose?"

"The ants. They're his soldiers."

"Good. We're soldiers too."

Chris crouched down by the edge of the anthill, where hundreds of ants were streaming back and forth between the anthill and the garden like cars on a highway, and focused his weapon. Arón, who was holding the other ray gun, hesitated. He wanted the General to have a say.

"He doesn't want us to do it," he said.

Chris looked up, surprised.

"Who?"

Arón, too, was surprised by the words he had said.

"The General. He doesn't want them to be killed."

The way the General stood there on top of the anthill, holding his sword high up in the air, he looked almost real. But Arón had to speak for him, so it was up to Arón.

Chris looked puzzled: "Do you want to kill ants or not?"

"I do," Arón said, "but the General . . ." He was confused now.

"He's their protector," Pira said. He meant the General, but it sounded as if he meant Arón too. But Chris knew what he meant.

"How can he protect them?" he said. "He can't. We have ray guns."

Arón looked at the General, and then at the magnifying glass in his hand. Right then, the General lost his command. You could see it in Arón's face. Arón shrugged and crouched down next to Chris, holding up his ray gun at a slant to the sun. Pira crouched down also to watch them shoot ants even though he didn't feel like watching anymore. There were so many ants running so close together, you didn't have to hunt them. Just joining the two points of light into one and pointing that brightness onto their path was enough. The ants ran into it steadily. Not all the ants who passed through the beam died, but many did. Little clumps of charred bodies formed. Live ants kept running over them and around them. When several ants caught fire at the same time you could hear a fine crackling sound, like tiny explosions. More ants kept coming. Arón was excited again, he was having fun. Pira was feeling a little sick.

He finally thought of saying that his father needed his magnifying glass back, and that put an end to the game.

*

Later Pira told Martha how they had killed ants with a magnifying glass.

"You shouldn't have done that," she said.

"I know."

"It's called killing for sport."

"What's sport?"

"It's a game. Killing as a game. It's cruel. You shouldn't do it."

"I know."

He was ashamed. He didn't tell her how many ants they had killed. When he thought of that he was more ashamed, even though Chris and Arón had done most of the killing. He wanted to forget it, and after a few days he did.

*

"I got a call from a man named Harry Taub," Bruno said to Martha at dinner. "He says he's a film producer. Have you ever heard of him?"

She shook her head.

"He says he's Dorothy's uncle," Bruno said to Pira.

"Oh, I know him. His name is Harry, and he *is* hairy. He has hair all over his back."

"How do you know?"

"I saw him without his shirt on."

Martha translated this for Zita, explaining the play on words as best she could, and then they all laughed together.

"How did he get our number?" Martha asked Bruno.

"He got it from Riley. Riley's investing in one of his films."

"What else did he say?"

"He said Dorothy took a shine to Peter. What does that mean?"

"It means she has a crush on him."

Bruno didn't know that expression either.

"It means she's in love with him."

"Oh."

Martha explained to Zita in Spanish that the little girl Pira had told them about after Chris's birthday party was enamorada de Peter.

Pira didn't like the way they were smiling. He wasn't a baby. But he liked that Dorothy loved him. That was even better than being liked.

The next day, Bruno, Martha, and Pira met Uncle Harry and Dorothy and Uncle Harry's wife Louise on the big lawn behind the swimming pool at the Hotel Zapata. Pira had brought a bag with a towel and his swim trunks.

Dorothy said "Hi!" just as she had at Chris's party. No one Pira knew ever said "Hi!" in that bright happy way. It was either "hello" or just "hi," or something in Spanish.

"Hi!" he said.

The grown-ups introduced themselves in the usual grown-up way, shaking hands and smiling and nodding a lot. They ordered drinks and sat down around a table in the shade of a giant palm tree. Then Uncle Harry said to Dorothy, "Why don't you and Peter go upstairs and put on your swimsuits and bring down the swimming tubes and have some fun in the pool." And he gave her the key.

"Are you sure you'll be able to open the door?"

"Oh, yes!"

Everything Dorothy said was delightful. The way she said "Oh, yes!" Who spoke that way? Nobody he could think of. Only she.

Up they went in the elevator. "I'm glad we're not on the eighth floor," she said. "I wouldn't be able to reach the button." That too was delightful.

Dorothy led Pira around the apartment.

"This is the master bedroom," she said.

That sounded important, and the room looked that way. It was big, with a big puffy bed and a desk and a chair and a liquor cabinet (Dorothy explained what it was) and a big radio and a painting of a muscular Prince Popocatepetl carrying the dead Princess Iztaccihuatl on the wall above the bed. A glass door led onto a balcony.

"Look," Dorothy said, "what a marvelous view."

Pira knew the word "marvelous," but he had never heard anyone say it. Next to the master bedroom, and almost as big, was the bathroom, white with a huge tub on golden lions' feet.

"And the living room?" Dorothy said, lifting her voice at the end of the phrase as a sign that the list would continue.

But the sight of the couch distracted her.

"I *like* this couch a *lot*," she said. And she jumped onto the couch and bounced up and down on it.

"I'm not supposed to do this with my shoes on, but . . ."—she smiled—"they're not here!"

Then she ran through a door and said, "And the kitchen-*dining* room?"

Pira followed her, dragging his towel bag behind him, wondering why she was showing him all the rooms, and liking her, and feeling a little dizzy.

"And *my* room!" she said with finality, and plopped herself down cross-legged on a short, narrow bed with a flower-patterned cover.

He looked around. All the toys, all the things that were Dorothy's and not the hotel's, were girls' toys, girls' things. A Little Lulu comic book on her pillow. A Raggedy Ann doll at the foot of the bed. A baby carriage on the floor, with a doll in it. Some paper dress-up dolls, also on the floor. A watercolor of a girl in a blue dress taped to the wall. Dorothy must have painted it.

She bounced off the bed, hurried to the dresser, opened a drawer, pulled out a blue, shiny garment.

"Let's swim!"

Pira felt shy about taking off his clothes in front of her, but once she started undressing, he had to do it too, and it wasn't embarrassing. This too she did differently. She put her socks in her shoes and placed the shoes neatly side by side at the foot of the bed. She folded her dress instead of tossing it onto the bed the way he did with his shorts and his shirt. She even folded her underpants. And she had a vagina—naturally, but it was the first time he saw one, and it didn't look anything like what he had imagined.

"Wait!" she said, just as he was about to put on his bathing suit. "We need to pee first. It's a rule."

She ran into the bathroom, leaving the door open, sat down on the toilet, and smiled as they both listened to the sound of her peeing.

"Now it's your turn."

She stepped aside to watch him pee. He lifted the seat of the toilet and peed. He liked that she was watching him. She didn't have a penis. That was why she was interested.

"Outside, I can squirt pretty far," he said, still peeing.

"How far?"

"Like a garden hose, sort of."

When he was finished, she flushed the toilet and lowered the seat and the lid. Then they put on their bathing suits.

"Oh, look, we're both in blue!" she said.

She ran back to the bathroom and came out with two swimming tubes.

"You take one, I'll take the other."

On the way down in the elevator, each holding a towel and a swimming tube, they looked at each other and smiled.

"I want to marry you," she said.

*

Listening to Bruno talking with Martha on the way home, it seemed to Pira that Bruno had taken a shine to Harry.

"He's intelligent, progressive, well read, a friend of Chaplin, an admirer of Cantinflas. What's a man like that doing in Hollywood?"

"The same thing Chaplin is doing," Martha said.

"*Charlie* Chaplin?"

"Yes, Peter."

Pira imagined Charlie Chaplin, Cantinflas, and Harry together and wondered what they had in common. The only funny thing about Harry was his back.

"You should take him up on his offer," Martha said. Bruno said nothing.

"Is Dorothy friends with Charlie Chaplin too?"

"You're interrupting," Martha said.

Pira was sure he had not interrupted.

"I liked Louise too," Martha said. "Even though she's a little affected."

What's that, Pira wondered, but he didn't ask. Usually his parents didn't mind his asking questions, but this was not one of those times.

Their conversation continued, but Pira was no longer listening. He was thinking about Dorothy. Her tears, her wails when Harry and Louise said their flight was booked and there was no way they could stay a few days longer. "A regular tantrum," Louise said. He had felt sad about having to part from Dorothy too, but he would never cry like that in front of everyone. He wouldn't cry like that alone either because someone could always hear it. Once he had heard Martha say about someone she knew: "I think it's admirable to show one's feelings like that." Maybe, but Martha herself didn't always show her feelings. Bruno even less. Sometimes he was sad and you could tell, but if someone asked what was the matter, he would say, "Nothing, nothing's the matter." Pira thought *that* was admirable.

Some feelings weren't good, it was better not to show them. And some feelings were private. But when Dorothy said, "I want to

marry you," that was so nice. He loved her for that. Even though it
didn't make sense. Children couldn't marry. And now she was leaving. That was really sad. If he thought about it too much he would
cry, and he didn't want to, not here in the street.

Near the Vogelsangs' house, five boys were crouching around a
circle they had scratched in the sand. They were shooting marbles.

"Can I play with them?" Pira asked.

"*May* I play with them. Of course," Martha said. "I'll call you
when dinner's ready."

He ran inside to get some marbles, and made sure to bring his
favorite, big one with the blue swirl in clear glass. It was worth
twenty of the smaller clay marbles. Anyone joining a game with
a marble like that was welcome, even a gringo. Pira risked that
marble often but never lost it because he was good at the game.

*

Shortly after she left, Dorothy wrote Pira a letter with her mom's
help. Martha was sure Dorothy's mom had written some of the letter and made it sound fancier than the way Dorothy talked, sort of
the way the letter writer on the zócalo changed Zita's words when
she wrote to Federico.

"No child would mention bougainvillea in the garden," she said.

That was probably true. But there were parts of the letter that
Pira was pretty sure came straight from Dorothy. A list of the
rooms in her house in Hollywood, for instance, among them a
master bedroom, a French room, and an Italian room. Behind the
house was a tennis court where Dorothy's dad played tennis with
Uncle Harry, who was Dorothy's mom's brother.

When Pira dictated his reply, he asked Martha not to change
anything. He wanted her to write his own words and nothing else.
As a result, his letter turned out shorter than Dorothy's:

Dear Dorothy,

I miss you too. I wish we could play together. Someday I
want you to meet Arón. Arón is my best friend. We have
a lot of fun. When you visit, I'll show you the things in
our garden. An anthill, a zapote tree you can climb. I also
have books and comic books.

                                        Love,
                                        Peter.

Another letter came from Dorothy, shorter than the first one.
She mentioned two friends, Lucy and Rachel. She said sometimes
she wished she had a brother and that if she had one, she hoped he
would look like Pira.

Then Pira wrote again, and this time it was hard to think of
anything new to say.

"Tell her about Tristan and Paco," Martha said, so he did.

Then for a long time there was nothing from Dorothy and Pira
was almost glad, because writing letters had become difficult. Then
a postcard came with a picture of palm trees and some words and
"Love, Dorothy." Then Pira sent back a postcard of Popocatepetl
under a red cloud with some words of his own and "Love, Peter,"
and that was the last they heard from each other.

5

"Isn't life strange?" Martha said to Bruno. "It's like a miracle."

They were sitting at the table on the patio, smoking and drinking. Pira, who was lying on the floor of his room drawing cowboys and Indians, stopped and listened through the open door. He liked hearing about miracles.

Bruno said nothing. He often answered with silence. "Look at that hummingbird," Martha continued.

"I see it," Bruno said.

"Don't you find it strange?"

"No, I don't find it strange. What do you mean?"

"I mean, how is it possible? Like jewels. But no one can make a jewel like that. And they're alive!"

"Yes, that is a miracle," Bruno said. This time Martha was silent.

"That there's life," Bruno said. "That there's anything."

Pira felt as if he was hearing something he wasn't supposed to. Bruno always said there were no miracles and there was no magic either, just magic *tricks*, but now he was saying something else.

*

Near the zócalo there was a café called El Rincón del Sosiego where they served ice cream sundaes. The Vogelsangs sometimes went there with Pira. Often there was a man sitting there, reading a newspaper or just sitting.

He wore a white suit and had straight black hair brushed over one side of his forehead and a little square moustache. Pira thought he looked like Charlie Chaplin, but his parents said he was trying to look like Hitler.

"But Hitler is dead," Pira said.

He knew about Hitler. Hitler had told the Germans—people who spoke German like Bruno—to attack the world. But Bruno hadn't listened to Hitler. He ran away. He even fought against Hitler in Spain. Then the whole world fought back. Many German cities were destroyed. In the end Hitler shot himself. That was why Bruno was now trying to earn enough money to go back to Germany with Pira and Martha.

How could this man make believe he was Hitler, when Hitler was dead?

"Some people who liked Hitler want to believe that he's still alive," Bruno said. "So I think this man dresses up like Hitler because he wants people to think he's Hitler."

Once the make-believe Hitler waved at Bruno, but Bruno didn't respond. Martha said the man was crazy and Bruno agreed. Pira thought he was funny, but his parents said there was nothing funny about crazy people or about Hitler or about a man who tried to look like Hitler.

So it was surprising when German friends of Bruno's came to the house to rehearse a play that Bruno had written in German and Bruno played a character who looked a lot like the man on the zócalo. He wore a white suit and had his hair brushed like Hitler and had a Hitler moustache pasted under his nose. The only difference was that he walked with his feet sticking out to the side like Charlie Chaplin, which the man on the zócalo probably didn't, since he wasn't trying to be funny.

One of the other actors was Bruno's best friend Sándor. All he did in the first part of the play was smoke a cigar and choke Bruno. There were also two women, a fat one and a thin one. There was a lot of shouting. At one point Sándor choked Bruno and Bruno fainted and fell back onto a chair, looking dead. The thin woman threw a glass of water in his face. He stood up, turned to the fat woman, said something, she slapped him, he fell backward into Sándor's arms, Sándor pushed him toward the thin woman, who slapped him again, and he fell back into the chair. Then everyone laughed, and Bruno dried himself with a towel.

Then they did it again. It was fun to watch the moment when the make-believe ended and people were their real selves again. It was always the moment when they laughed and Bruno dried himself, but there were also moments in between when they stopped to discuss something and started again. After a while Bruno's cheeks were red from being slapped. Pira thought his father was very brave to allow himself to be slapped like that, over and over.

There was another scene they repeated several times.

Sándor knelt down in front of the thin woman and hugged her knees and looked up at her, looking desperate as he spoke. She stroked his hair and spoke slowly, without looking at him, as if in a dream. Then Sándor stood up and folded his hands in front of his chest and shouted something and ran out of the room, leaving the door open. The thin woman went to the door and closed it quietly.

*

After the rehearsal, Bruno and his German friends went out for drinks, leaving Martha with Pira in the garden.

Pira asked, "Why was Hitler funny in Bruno's play?"

Martha said, "It wasn't really supposed to be Hitler."

"Who was it supposed to be?"

"Bruno was playing a crazy man who believes he is Hitler."

"Like the man in El Rincón del Sosiego?"

"Sort of. That's where Bruno got the idea."

"But you said that man wasn't funny. You said there's nothing funny about Hitler or about a crazy man who pretends he is Hitler."

"That's true. You're such a clever boy, Peter. You remember everything."

She was praising him but her eyes looked watchful as if his being clever was maybe not altogether a good thing. But she was smiling.

"So he *is* funny!" he said.

"I still don't think that man in the café is funny. But the crazy man in Bruno's play is not the same man. In the play, he actually believes he's Hitler, *and* he's funny."

"That doesn't make sense."

"I know. It's confusing. It confuses me too. Maybe the man in Bruno's play isn't really funny. Maybe he just looks funny. I don't know any German, so I can't tell. Let's ask Bruno."

They asked him when he came home. His answer was surprising:

"He *looks* funny, he *seems* funny, but he's a lost soul. So he's to be pitied. We laugh at him, and then we're ashamed of laughing."

Pira didn't understand that. Was he funny or not funny? It would be good to know.

"Why does he think he's Hitler?"

"Because secretly—without even realizing it himself—he wants to be Hitler."

"Why?"

"Because Hitler is evil, and this poor crazy man thinks that evil is the most powerful force in the world. Which it isn't. And he's not evil at all."

"What's evil?"

Martha and Bruno looked at each other as if they didn't know what to say. Or was evil a secret, or not for children?

"Evil means bad," Bruno said then. "But it's worse than bad. An evil person isn't just bad, he's really *really* bad. There's nothing good about him."

"That's not possible!" Pira said. Bruno looked surprised.

"I think you're right," he said.

Pira felt proud, though he didn't know why he had said what he said. But later he realized what evil meant, and it scared him. He remembered seeing Snow White and the seven dwarfs. The witch in that movie, the Queen who turned into a witch, was the scariest person he had ever seen, so scary he didn't want to think of her ever again. She was evil. So he knew what evil was. His fear knew.

*

Usually when Bruno's friends came over, there were only men. Their wives stayed home or went somewhere else. The men would sit in the garden and take turns speaking German and listening and nodding their heads.

Sometimes they got excited and interrupted each other. Then they would calm down and get serious again and take turns speaking and listening. Pira knew he was not to disturb them. They were having a discussion. Martha, too, stayed away, until at some point she decided they had discussed long enough.

As soon as she joined them, their talk turned to English and everything changed. There were smiles, there was laughter.

It wasn't just Martha who made people feel good that way. Sándor did too.

Sometimes Sándor and Martha made music together. He would play a guitar while she played the violin, or they would sing Mexican songs in harmony.

Once Martha was in the kitchen with Zita preparing food while Bruno and his friends were having a discussion. Then Sándor took

Martha's guitar and went to the patio and with one foot on the patio and the other on the lawn he started strumming melancholy Mexican chords like a mariachi, and then he sang:

"Come out my darling . . ."

But she didn't come out. He strummed some more chords. "Come out my duck . . ."

Pira could tell it was going to be a joke. Just calling his mother a duck was funny.

"Come into the garden . . ."

She appeared in the doorway smiling and holding a tray with sandwiches.

"I'll give you a flower . . ."

Everyone laughed very loudly and Martha opened her mouth, looking shocked but amused, and said, "That was naughty, Sándor," and then Pira saw that her face had turned red.

Later Pira asked Martha what was so funny about that pretty song and she said it was grown-up humor, hard to explain. He remembered the words and spoke them to make her laugh again. But she didn't. She just watched him as he spoke.

"Funny," he said, to remind her.

"Not anymore," Martha said. "It was only funny the first time."

"But the song was pretty, wasn't it?" Pira said.

"It *was* pretty," Martha agreed.

"Why did you tell Sándor that he shouldn't sing it?"

"I didn't."

"You said he was naughty."

"Calling me a duck was naughty."

"And funny?"

"Well . . . yes, but naughty too."

"I think it's funny," he said, and started reciting the poem again.

She interrupted him: "Once is enough. No more." Clearly Martha did not like being called a duck.

*

Sometimes when Bruno and Martha discussed serious things and Pira was nearby, he heard the word "party." At first he thought it meant the times when Bruno's German friends got together to talk and drink whisky, but this wasn't that kind of party.

He wasn't curious about it until one day he heard Bruno say to Martha: "That's because you're not in the party."

That made him wonder.

"Martha, why aren't you in the party?"

She didn't know what he meant at first, but then she laughed.

"No reason. I like the people who are in the party, that's enough for me."

"Is Bruno in the party?"

"Yes, he is."

"Where is the party?"

"It's not anywhere, it's . . . Good grief, Peter, you want to know everything! I don't think I can explain to you what the party is. Ask Bruno."

So he asked Bruno.

"It's called the Communist Party," Bruno said. "We believe that there shouldn't be rich people and poor people. Everyone should have enough. Some people—some rich people—don't want that. They don't want to share what they have. They consider us their enemies. And we consider them our enemies."

That was a good explanation. But one day Pira heard someone talk about "enemies in the party." That was confusing. So he asked Bruno:

"How come there are enemies in the party?"

"Peter, this is not something children can understand."

"Why not?"

"It's too complicated."

It did sound complicated. But something didn't make sense.

"Your friends, are they all in the party?"

"Yes."

"Sándor too?"

"Yes, he too."

"Are any of them enemies?"

Now Bruno was annoyed: "They're friends, Peter. They're not enemies. I wouldn't bring enemies into our house."

So Pira stopped wondering about enemies in the party.

It was too confusing.

*

When Pira and Chris or Pira and Arón played together, they played as equals, but when the three of them played together, it sometimes happened that Chris became the leader and the two other boys followed. They would follow even when one or the other of them didn't really like the games Chris was inventing.

Once when Pira and Chris and Arón were playing with toy soldiers and Indians, Chris decided that Arón should have only Indians because he was an índio himself, and that Pira and Chris would have the soldiers. Arón thought that wasn't fair because there weren't that many Indians. Pira thought so too, but Chris said he had seen it in a movie.

According to the movie, the Indians fought brave battles even when they were outnumbered. "That's how we'll play it," he said. "You'll see. It's a good game."

They set up their men in fighting positions, some of them half hidden behind a wooden block or next to a pillar. They couldn't be completely hidden, otherwise they couldn't be shot.

The Indians were surrounded on three sides by soldiers. Behind them was a wall. They couldn't escape. They had to kill all their enemies or die one by one. Most likely they would fight to the death. That was Chris's expression: "Hasta la muerte." Pira and Chris always spoke Spanish when Arón was there.

The shooting was done with marbles by flicking them with one's thumb over the crook of an index finger. It was an exciting game at first. Arón thought so too because he liked having brave índios to fight with and because he was good at shooting marbles. But it soon became clear that no matter how well his men shot, they didn't stand a chance because Pira and Chris had more men and they were fighting together. It was no fun being brave if you couldn't win. So Arón complained again that this game wasn't fair.

"Don't be a llorón," Chris said. "This is war. War isn't fair. And besides, in a war, Indians fight to the death."

Arón looked close to tears.

"What if some of our soldiers take sides with the Indians?" Pira suggested.

"That's not possible," Chris said.

"Why not?"

"Because they're enemies. It's a war."

He sounded so certain. He knew something. At this point, neither Pira nor Arón were enjoying the game, but they didn't know how to stop it. So they shot at each other's men, without pleasure, until the last Indian was dead and the soldiers had won.

*

That evening, after Pira was in bed, Bruno came into his room. They talked a little and then Pira asked, "When the Indians lost against the Spaniards, did they fight bravely?"

"Yes, they did."

"Why were they brave? Why didn't they run away?"

"Some did run away. But others fought bravely."

"Why?"

"Because they had hope. They hoped they would win."

"But when they knew they couldn't win, did they still fight?"

"A lot of them did."

"Why?"

"Because they would rather die as brave men than live as slaves to the Spaniards."

"Hasta la muerte."

"Yes."

"They were macho."

Bruno nodded.

A drunken man walked past the window, cursing: "Me cago en la leche!" I shit in the milk! The voice was shockingly near. The man walked on, scraping the street with his sandals.

"Why did he say that?" Pira asked.

"Because he's angry."

"What is he angry at?"

"I don't know."

Farther down the street, the drunk cursed again: "Me cago en la leche de la Madre de Diós!"

Pira giggled: "He's *really* angry!"

Bruno agreed. Pira wondered about the man cursing the Mother of God with such bad words. Would God punish him for that? And the Mother of God, did she punish people? He didn't think so.

"Are women brave too?"

"Yes, some women are brave."

"Women aren't macho."

"No, but they can be brave."

"Is Martha brave?"

"Yes."

"Always?"

"Yes, always."

"Are you brave?"

"Not always. Sometimes I'm not brave."

"When?"

"When I'm afraid."

"What are you afraid of?"

"I'm afraid of pain."

"Then you're not macho."

"No, I'm not macho. But sometimes I'm brave."

"When?"

"When people I love are in danger. Then I'm brave. I fought in a war to protect people I loved. That was brave. If you were in danger I would protect you."

"Would you hit someone to protect me?"

"Yes."

"Would you kill him?"

"If necessary, yes. But only if it were necessary."

"Like if someone wanted to kill me?"

"Yes."

"That's brave."

"I think so too."

"Sometimes I'm not brave."

"When are you not brave?"

Then Pira told Bruno about the way Chris had made Arón fight a losing war with a few Indians, and how Pira had helped Chris do that with a lot of soldiers, even though it made Arón feel bad, and as he described how it happened, a tear ran down one of his cheeks, and that was the proof, it really didn't need saying, but he said it:

"I'm not brave."

Bruno pulled a handkerchief from his pocket and dried Pira's cheek with it.

"Peter," he said. "You're a very brave boy. You're braver than many men I have known."

They were silent together. Why am I brave? Pira wondered. It didn't make sense. But because Bruno had said it, he believed it. Still, the question remained. He didn't want to ask it out loud. He didn't want to speak at all.

6

One of the five bars in Pira's window had an electric current running through it. When his hands were sweaty and he wrapped his fingers around it, the vibration ran through his arm like a fast-wriggling snake. It didn't hurt.

Sometimes he touched the bar just to feel the vibration. Bruno said the bar must be touching a live wire somewhere in the wall, but it wasn't dangerous.

One day, for no reason, Pira put his tongue to the bar and a violent quivering shock went through his body. It hurt a lot, but it happened so fast that he was more astonished than hurt. It took a while before he dared to do it again. Carefully he put his tongue to the bar, and again the shock ran through him and his head flew back right away. He touched the other four bars with his tongue, but nothing happened. His heart thumping, he touched the first bar again with his tongue, and this time he held it there for a little while, until it was too much.

The next day he did it again. By the seventh or eighth time it was easy. Pain was no longer pain, and there was no fear. It was like an adventure each time: danger, daring, and immediate safety.

After lunch one day, during his naptime, he heard children play-

ing in the street and went to the window to look. They were playing tag. Arón was one of them. The moment he saw Pira, he waved
and came to the window.

"Come on out," he said.

"I can't."

"Why not?"

"My parents say I have to sleep."

Arón understood. He knew about rules.

"I want to show you something," Pira said. "Come closer. Put
your tongue here. Just touch it. You'll see."

Arón rose on his toes and touched the bar with his tongue and
jumped back with his hand on his mouth, staring at Pira.

"Disculpa," Pira said. "Excuse me."

Arón stepped back a few steps and kept staring with his hand on
his mouth. Then he turned around and walked away with long steps.

Pira threw himself face down on his bed, wishing desperately
that he had told Arón it would be scary at first but it would change
after a few times and that he could do it. Arón would have done
it and would have been proud. Together they would have shown it
to Chris. And Pira wished that when he said "disculpa," Arón had
said "no te preocupes." But Arón didn't even know that Pira hadn't
meant to hurt him. He had to tell him. But how? Arón wouldn't
believe it. He probably hated him now.

He cried, hoping Martha would hear him, but at the same
time he muffled his voice with a pillow because he was ashamed
of what he had done and afraid that Martha would not understand, that she would think he was bad because he had been mean
to his friend for no reason. "Why did you do it?" She would ask
him that. What could he say? He had an explanation—that he had
only wanted to show his friend the strange thing that happened
when you put your tongue there—but somehow that didn't feel
true, because when he told Arón to lick the bar, he knew it would

hurt him and he didn't tell him. It was like a trick, a mean trick. It hurt a lot. What would Bruno say? And Zita? He didn't want to think about that.

What about Chris? Would Chris understand? Maybe he would. Chris could be mean, and his father was very mean. Martha said he sometimes told his charros to beat someone up. And they were cruel to their horses and Chris's father didn't care.

Then Pira remembered el Señor Jesús. Zita always said that he forgave everything and that he was muy poderoso.

Pira didn't like thinking of Jesus because he was nailed to a cross, but now he did. Silently he spoke to Jesus in Spanish, shaping the words with his tongue and his lips.

"Perdóname. Forgive me, please. Make me good again. Don't let anyone know that I was bad. And please tell Arón that I didn't mean it."

Then he listened. No answering word or touch or feeling let him know that he had been heard. He turned over on his back and folded his hands the way Zita had taught him. If she knew that he was praying to el Señor Jesús, it would make her happy. But he wouldn't tell her. He wouldn't tell anyone. It was a secret, not a lie, just like Zita's belief in her ídolo. What he had done to Arón was a secret too, but it wasn't a good secret, it felt terrible.

"I'm sorry," he said to Jesus, in English this time. "I'm sorry about what I did. Please let Arón be happy. Please tell him I'm sorry."

*

That night Martha came into Pira's room before he went to sleep and sat down by his bedside.

"Did you have a good day?"

There was that watchful look in her eyes. Maybe at dinner she had noticed that he was keeping a secret. Was it the one about Jesus or the one about Arón?

He thought about her question. That was something Bruno did sometimes—think before answering a question—and now Pira was doing the same thing. He thought, and Martha waited.

Had he had a good day? The day was so big. So many things had happened, most of them good. Paco had whistled at Zita. That was funny. Zita had pushed Pira way up high on the swing. That was fun. Bruno had taught him two new German words: "Wunderbar" and "Dankeschön." He had read a good story in Spanish about how Cuauhtémoc surrounded the Spaniards with ten thousand warriors and how later the Spaniards remembered that black moonless night as La Noche Triste. Not "the scary night"—they were too brave to be scared—but "the sad night." Then he thought that this night would be his Noche Triste.

"What happened?" Martha asked. Her gaze looked softer now.

"I did something bad."

"What did you do?"

He wished she had said "What happened?" again. He didn't want to tell her. But he had to. So he did. He told her everything: what he had done and how Arón was hurt and how Pira apologized and Arón just walked away fast, thinking that Pira had hurt him on purpose, even though he hadn't. Her gaze was watchful again, as if she was seeing something that he couldn't see.

"I didn't . . . I didn't . . ." His voice was catching. He couldn't talk. "I didn't want . . ." He was sobbing, trying not to cry like a baby.

"I know," she said, cradling the side of his face now. "I know. But it happened. And that's why you're sad."

"Yes," he said, crying freely now. Her warm hand was still and knowing, like the look in her eyes, and he felt safe and no longer afraid.

"What you did wasn't bad," she said. "It was a mistake."

"I know."

"But you have to tell him how sorry you are."

"I already did! I said disculpa!"

"It wasn't enough. If it were enough, you would know it."

He knew that was true. Maybe he should have said "lo siento."

Martha stroked his cheeks dry.

"Go to sleep now."

He felt quieter.

"Good night." She kissed him on the lips.

"Good night," he said.

After she left, he was glad he hadn't told her the other secret, the one about Jesus. It was a good secret. He asked el Señor Jesús to make everyone happy who wasn't and to keep everyone happy who was, and then he asked him to do that specifically for Arón, and Martha, and Bruno, and Zita, and Paco, and Tristan, and Chris, and Chris's father, and Chris's father's charros, and their horses, and Federico, and Arón's mother, and Bruno's friend Sándor, and the man who thought he was Hitler, and several others, each in turn, until he fell asleep.

*

Pira didn't want to apologize to Arón the next day. "I can't . . . I know he hates me . . . I'm too ashamed . . ."

But Martha insisted that he had to, and that it would be cowardly not to do so.

"What's cowardly?"

"Not brave."

So he went to Arón's house, slowly, feeling brave and anxious at the same time, half hoping Arón wouldn't be there. For a moment he imagined telling Arón's mother that he had been mean to Arón and that he was sorry and her saying that she would tell Arón when he came home, but of course that could never happen. The best thing would be if Arón's mother let him in and he told Arón he was sorry and Arón forgave him and that was the end of it. That would be so nice. It would be perfect.

But Arón's mother wasn't at home when he came to the house, and Arón was. The front door was open. Arón was sweeping the floor with a large broom. When he saw Pira, he turned his head away and kept sweeping. Then Pira spoke with his heart beating high in his chest.

"Lo siento."

Arón continued sweeping.

"What I did . . . I'm sorry. I just wanted to show you . . . I didn't want it to hurt."

Arón was still sweeping. He was building up a small pile of dust, adding to it with each sweep. The broom was too big for him, but he knew how to use it.

"I swear."

No answer.

"Let's play in my house."

Finally Arón spoke, still sweeping and still not looking at Pira: "I can't play. I have to work."

Pira heard pride in his friend's voice and thought, "I know how to work too," but he realized that the kind of work Arón was doing was not the kind Pira had done when he wrote the poem. It was different, so he didn't say anything.

Arón took the broom into the kitchen and came back with a dustpan and a hand broom. He swept the dust onto the dustpan and carried the dustpan to the door, looking at the dustpan as he walked. Pira stepped aside and watched Arón empty the dust onto the street. Then Arón went inside and put the brooms and the dustpan in a closet and took a feather duster that was hanging from a nail in the wall. He took a chair and put it underneath a big wooden crucifix that was hanging on the wall and climbed up on the chair and carefully dusted the sculpture. Then he stepped down and put the chair underneath another crucifix and climbed onto it to dust that one. There were four others. Next to them hung the belts Arón's mother used to punish him. There were several of them, of different lengths and widths.

Sometimes she made the belts wet, Arón had told him, so that it would hurt more.

"Can I help you?"

Arón was startled by the question. He looked at Pira from where he was standing on top of the chair. Then he shook his head and continued dusting the crucifix.

"Why not?"

"I don't want to say."

He climbed off the chair and carried it to the next crucifix. "I have to clean all the dust in the house. If she finds any dust, she'll punish me more."

"I could look for dust."

"You should go. If she comes home and you're here, she'll get mad at me."

"I'm sorry I hurt you. I'm your friend."

Arón halted with his back to Pira. He was holding the brightly colored feather duster, staring at the feet of the crucified man. Then he turned around and with tearful rage, staring into his friend's eyes, shouted—never before had Pira heard Arón shout:

"Go away! I'm telling you, go away!"

And Pira went home.

*

Pira had never felt sad for so long before. Martha said he was mourning and that it was natural. At first he was confused because the word sounded like the early time of day and it didn't make sense. Then Bruno explained that it meant being sad because someone has died. "But Arón didn't die," Pira said, and Bruno said, "No, but it feels like that when you lose a friend." The truth of that echoed in Pira's mind for a while, and he wished Bruno hadn't said it.

Chris came to visit, and while Chris was there Pira didn't think of Arón, or at least not in the same way. They climbed the zapote tree and pretended to be pirates. They threw sticks for Tristan, they tried to get Paco to say "cabrón," which he refused to do. Then Chris remembered the General, who was still standing on top of the anthill, and wanted to stick him headfirst into the entrance so the ants wouldn't be able to get in. Pira said, "No, he has to stay there. Arón put him there. Even though he's not my friend anymore."

"Why not?"

So Pira decided to tell Chris about what had happened. He told the whole story, and as he told it, he teared up a little and was embarrassed because Chris was tough and might not understand. But Chris was more interested in the electric bar than in Pira's sadness. He wanted to try it out for himself. So they went to Pira's room and Chris put his tongue to the iron bar and jerked his head back when he felt the shock. He laughed. He did it again. He did it several times. Then Pira did it too. It was easy, even though it hurt. "It's like lightning," Chris said, and then Pira thought of saying "Arón is stupid" but didn't because he knew it wasn't true.

Later, after Chris left, he thought that thinking that Arón was stupid was being mean to him all over again. He was sitting on the patio with his back to the house, so he didn't notice Zita approaching him until he heard the soft tread of her huaraches on the tile floor. She halted. He didn't turn his head. He wanted to be alone, but he was glad she was there.

"Pira," she said. "Mi Pirito. Todavía estás triste?" He nodded.

She stroked his head. He closed his eyes to feel the sweetness of her caress.

"Pide al Señor," she said, pray to the Lord, and went back into the house.

Which Señor? Why didn't she say el Señor Jesús? "El Señor" could be any Señor, like Señor Nuñez, the plumber. That thought made him giggle: Pide al Señor Nuñez. For a moment he forgot his sadness. Then he thought of Zita's ídolo and his heart leapt because suddenly he knew that her secret belief in the ídolo was not like his secret belief in Jesus, it was a forbidden secret, and his knowing it was forbidden too. How did he know? He just knew. Did she pray to the little green man? Did she call him Señor? No, he was too secret, too hidden for that. What did she ask him for? What could he give that the god of love or the Virgen de Guadalupe would not give?

Pide al Señor.

He had already done that, and Jesus had not answered. Maybe he should try again. But he couldn't. To pray to Jesus you had to fold your hands, otherwise it wasn't real. He couldn't do that here on the patio. He wasn't alone enough. Even though Bruno was in his office and Martha was visiting a friend and Zita was cleaning the house, he could still imagine a person coming into the garden from the street, seeing him holding his hands like that and wondering why the little gringo was praying. They would laugh at him. Or if Bruno came out of his office or Martha came home and saw him praying, that would be embarrassing too. Zita would like it, but he didn't want her to know. It had to stay secret.

He went to his room to pray there, but he couldn't because the bars on the window reminded him of the mistake he had made with Arón. It was almost like having another person in the room, a person who reminded him of what he had done and didn't think he should be forgiven. Where could he go? He could climb the zapote tree. He went back outside. But the moment he saw the tree and pictured himself on his lookout post, he remembered sitting there with Arón, side by side with their arms around each other's shoulders. It was too sad.

He didn't go to the tree. He just stood on the patio. Without thinking, then, as if he already knew what he was going to do, he pulled out of his pocket his favorite marble, the clear one with the blue swirl, felt its weight in his hand, and began to feel sleepy. He lay down, put one side of his face against the cool tile floor, and began to roll the

marble slowly from hand to hand, listening to its dark stony voice as
it rolled, and closed his eyes. The rolling sound came from close by
and from far away, deep, and already he was sinking into the stone
world, so soft, so much softer than anything else. How could that
be? His eyes opened. Everything was as it always was. The blue swirl
inside the marble turned as it always did when the marble rolled, and
the marble made a little bump as it always did when it crossed the
seam between two tiles. He waited until it rolled into his open palm
and took it into his hand and closed his fingers around it and shut his
eyes. Again he was sinking, and this time he drifted down and down
without stopping, trusting that there was a bottom. And there was.
It was soft, like mud, but softer than mud. He couldn't see anything,
but he could sense that something was there, something or someone,
and now he felt a little afraid. "Ayúdame," he said. He didn't know
whom he was asking for help, but saying the word helped him feel
safe again. He stretched out his hand and touched something hard
and cold. It was a sword, and the hilt of the sword was in his fist.
How strong he felt, and brave. Was it a magical sword, like King
Arthur's? Excalibur! All around him were rocks, and cactuses. There
would be danger. He knew it, yet he wasn't afraid.

Then he heard Martha coming in through the garden gate, and
his eyes opened.

*

After a while, when Pira thought of Arón it wasn't so much with
sadness and guilt but more with fear of meeting him in the street.
When he imagined it, his body felt cold and rigid. What could he
say? He would almost rather not see him at all, ever. But Arón lived
nearby. It was strange that they hadn't met already.

7

It never rains but it pours," Martha said, and when Pira asked Bruno what that meant (because Bruno could explain words better), he said it meant different kinds of trouble all happening at once, the way lots of raindrops together make for a downpour. That made sense, because Martha's and Bruno's talk had been about different kinds of trouble for days. Bruno was drinking more whisky than usual, and Martha didn't like it. Sándor was going to go to Hungary, where he had lived before Hitler chased him out, and if no one was found to replace him as first violinist there would be no Ferenc Sándor Quartet and Martha wouldn't be able to earn any money. A book of Bruno's that was supposed to be published in Germany wasn't going to be published because the publisher wanted him to change something in it and Bruno didn't want to. The lady Bruno had loved more than Martha when Pira was four had written some poems and sent them to Bruno and Bruno was helping her to get the poems published, and Martha was angry about that. The nice lady running the school where Pira and Chris were going to go to first grade had a boyfriend who had left the party because he liked a bad man with a funny name who was dead but it still was a problem. Federico, who was supposed to visit on Friday, wasn't coming because the bosses of the Mexican Railway didn't want to give the railroad workers the money they needed, so the unión was going on strike, which was the English word for the much tougher-sounding word huelga, which meant that none of the railroad workers would go to work, so the trains wouldn't run, people wouldn't buy tickets to use the trains, and the owners would lose a lot of money. Bruno thought the strike was a good idea but it could turn into a big fight with enemies of the unión and with the police. That made Zita sad because her novio wouldn't be spending the weekend with her, and more than being sad she was worried that he would get hurt and that he could lose his job if the jefe got mad at him, because then he wouldn't be able to earn enough money to visit her at all. A couple of times she put her hands to her cheeks and said "Diós mio," as if this time she couldn't be sure that Jesús or the Virgen would help her.

Tristan was having trouble too. He was in love with a little white dog in a distant neighbor's house, and it wasn't a happy love, he whined and yelped pitifully and tried to stand on his hind legs in order to be nearer to her when she looked out of a high window in her house.

Martha asked the neighbor to let the dogs meet because her dog was suffering, but the neighbor said no because he was afraid his dog would get pregnant.

Only Paco was happy. Every once in a while, from his favorite perch on the banana tree, he whistled the way men whistled when they saw a pretty girl. Martha said she sometimes thought he was making fun of Tristan.

*

Pira went with Zita to buy a cactus for Bruno's birthday because Bruno loved cactuses. On the way they ran into Arón. He was walking toward them, carrying something heavy in a large paper bag. The moment Arón saw Pira, he stopped, and Pira, still walking, felt his heart thump high into his throat. Arón started walking again, but turned his head sideways to avoid looking at Pira. Then Zita held out her arm as if to pull him in toward her but also barring his way. Arón stopped and looked up at her, his eyes wide with fear. Zita crouched down to bring her face level with his, smiling, and brought her hand to his cheek and stroked it tenderly, and said:

"Aroncito, listen to me. We all love you. Pira too."

Arón looked at Pira from the corners of his eyes and looked away again.

"Tengo que irme," he said, "I have to go."

But before he walked on, he looked at Pira again and Pira managed to mumble "Hasta luego," see you later, so quietly Arón couldn't possibly have heard it, but maybe he saw his lips pronounce the words.

They walked on. After a few steps Pira turned his head to see if Arón would look back at him, but Arón was walking away quickly, pressing the bag to his chest.

*

Two letters from David, Pira's first father, arrived. One of them was for Martha, and the other one was for Pira. It was addressed to him, with his name on the envelope, instead of being included as a note in a letter to Martha. That alone made it special. He decided to open the envelope in the zapote tree, where he could be by himself. The letter was folded, with two sharp creases, and when he opened it, he saw that it was written with a typewriter on onionskin paper, which made it look even more special:

My dearest Peter,

Your mother sent me the poem you wrote, with a translation to help me understand it. It's beautiful. But

that does not say anything near to what I feel about it,
and what I feel for you. So let me try again. Your poem
touches me the way music does, and you know how much
music means to me. I just want to tell you how proud I am
to have a poet as my son.

With all my love,
David

"With all my love." Pira had never heard those four words put
together like that. He repeated them in his mind. He imagined
speaking them. Then he imagined feeling them as he spoke them.
The "all" was so big. "*All* my love." How much love would that be?
It was almost scary.

Even though David's other letter was addressed to Martha,
some of it was about Pira and his poem. Through the door of his
room after he went to bed, Pira heard Martha read it to Bruno in
their bedroom. He couldn't hear most of the words, but what he
heard filled him with such pleasure that he could barely hold himself back from shouting out loud. So he shouted in his mind: "I'm
happy! I'm so happy!" Now he wanted to write many more poems
for David and for Bruno, for Martha and for Zita. They would
be in English and Spanish, and if he learned German someday he
would write poems in German.

The shouting joy in his mind subsided, and he listened again to
his parents' conversation. Their voices were low. There were long
pauses after each one of them spoke. They sounded serious.

*

The next day, sitting in the zapote tree, Pira went over in his mind
everything David had written to him. That his poem was beautiful,
but that calling it beautiful wasn't enough. That the poem was like

music. Zita had said the same thing when she called it an hermosa canción. But David said more. He said Pira was a poet, and that having a poet as his son made him proud.

Proud! Now Pira felt proud too. He felt tremendous.

He imagined David reading the poem for the first time and being surprised. By what? By the singing frog maybe, or by the rhymes. Those *were* surprising. And maybe reading it a second time he would be surprised in a different way, because there were things in the poem that surprised even Pira still now as he sounded out the words.

*

A few days later, Bruno left his fountain pen on a bookshelf outside his office and Pira found it and opened it and tried it out. He had seen Bruno write with this pen many times. He knew it was special to Bruno because Martha had given it to him as a birthday present and because it was a Parker Pen and Parker Pens were expensive. Once he had asked Bruno if he could draw with it and Bruno said no, it wasn't the kind of pen that children could use, and when Pira asked why not, Bruno said: "Because it could break." But Pira was older now, and he was learning how to write.

Martha had given him a chart of the letters from A to Z, show-ing how each letter looked in print or written with a typewriter and how it looked in what Martha called "cursive." She also gave him a box full of special pages with lines for copying the letters out. He had been practicing with a pencil and already knew how to write any word once he knew how to spell it, though the words still looked crooked and not really right. And here was Bruno's pen in his hand, black and shiny with a gold clasp. Just holding it gave him the feeling that with this pen he would be able to write, really write, like a grown-up. The lines would flow in the same shiny way they did on Bruno's pages. He would make the words small, the way Bruno did, and the letters of each word would connect instead of standing separate and much too big the way they did when he practiced writing with a pencil. It was easier to write with a pen. He was sure of that.

But Bruno wouldn't like it. Not if Pira used the pen without permission. But he couldn't ask him now—he wasn't supposed to disturb Bruno when he was working. He would have to wait. But if he waited and asked later, Bruno would say no again. So why wait, and why ask? It was really very simple and obvious. If he just used the pen while Bruno was in his office and put it back on the shelf before he came out, Bruno would never know.

The moment he thought that, he felt excited, guilty, and brave, all at once. What he was going to do was not bad but it was forbidden and it would be a secret. He went to Martha's desk—the one she called her secretary—and took out two sheets of her special pale blue paper for writing letters. Then he took the big green book of woodcuts by Posada for a support and went to his room, closing the door behind him, and sat on his bed with the book on his lap and the paper on top of it and pulled off the cap of the pen and pressed it against the bottom end, where it fit perfectly, and held the pen the way he had learned to hold a pencil properly, and made a short straight downward line on the left side of the page near the top, the first line of a capital D, which would be the first letter of "Dear." He was going to write a letter to his first father, David.

*

Writing complete words wasn't as easy as he had imagined. They looked good in a way because of the ink, but the sentences didn't run straight and the letters were crooked and not all the same size. Still, he was writing complete words and complete sentences, and by the time he was finished it would be a complete letter. He couldn't wait to put it in an envelope with a stamp.

It occurred to him that in order to answer David's letter, he needed to read it again. He had left the folded onionskin page in the box with the special lined paper Martha had brought him. He put the pen on top of his pillow and went to get the letter and went back to the bed, reading as he walked, and sat down, still reading, and noticed too late that the pen was rolling off the pillow onto the sheet, where it made a dark blue stain. That worried him for a moment, but then he thought that Zita would be able to wash out the stain, and that, anyway, she didn't know about Bruno's pen and that he wasn't supposed to use it. He put the big green book on his lap and the page on the book and reread David's letter from start to finish. Then he put David's letter aside and slowly and carefully continued writing his own.

A few words further on, he stopped at the word "tree," unsure of how long the three sideways lines on an "E" had to be, so he put the pen on the floor where he wouldn't step on it and went to get the chart for copying the letters from A to Z and took it back to the bed and picked up the pen and sat down with the green book on his lap and his letter on top of it and the pen in his hand. But as he put his left hand on the page to hold it steady before he wrote "tree," he smudged one of the words he had already written and had to start over again on a fresh page from the beginning. That turned out to be fortunate, because the new lines came out straighter than before and the words looked pretty good. Slowly, with great carefulness, he spelled out his message until he reached the last word, which was his own name, and read what he had written one more time:

Dear David,

It made me hapy that you love my poem. I red your letter
in a big tree. Its a tree in our garden. Its called a zapote
tree. Im proud of you too.

> With all my love,
> Dearest Peter

"I did it!" he thought, and with the next thought—"I'll show
it to Martha!"—he leaped off the bed, and the pen, which he had
placed, still open, on top of the book he had used for support, slid
off and dropped to the floor.

When he picked it up—"Oh God!"—he saw that its gold point
was bent. "God!" But the pen was broken, not even God could fix
it. He sat with both fists pressed into his mouth, biting his knuckles,
his eyes pressed shut. He wanted to cry, but he couldn't.

Then he thought of something, a desperate possibility. He pressed
the bent point against the hard cover of the book, and the point
became straighter. It was still bent at the tip. He pressed the point
down on the book again and lightly, gently bore down on it with the
tip of a finger, and looked to see if the point was straight now. It was.

Hardly daring to believe in his luck, he drew a straight line on
the smudged sheet of his first draft. The pen didn't glide quite as
smoothly across the page as it had earlier, but the line was good.
He drew lines up and down and sideways and then in circles.
The pen wasn't broken, it worked! He drew a capital D next to
the D in "Dear." It looked just as good as the first one. Thank
God! He put the cap on the pen. It closed with a satisfying click.
Thank you!

*

He went to the bookshelf and put the pen where he had found it. Bruno was still in his office. Then Pira went to the kitchen, where Martha was helping Zita make dinner.

"Look, I wrote a letter to David," he said, and Martha and Zita burst out laughing.

"What happened to your face?"

He couldn't see his face.

"Is that ink?"

He nodded.

"Where did you find it?"

So he told her that he had written the letter with Bruno's pen.

"You shouldn't have done that," she said. "Bruno loves that pen. He doesn't want anyone else to use it. Not even me."

That surprised him. So it wasn't about his being a child.

"I'm sorry," he said. "I'll tell him I'm sorry. But I wrote a whole letter. Look."

"Really?"

She took the letter and looked at it and looked at Pira, smiling and shaking her head from side to side to show him how unbelievable it was that he had written a whole letter by himself and how much she admired him. Then she showed Zita what he had done—"Mira, Zita—aprendió a escribir por sí mismo!"—and Zita looked at Pira with admiration. Martha sometimes pretended that look but Zita wasn't pretending, she was really impressed, because she could neither read nor write.

"Read it," Pira said to Martha.

"I'll read it. But you go to the bathroom and wash your face and hands with soap. Use the washcloth and keep rubbing until the ink is all off. Get up on the footstool so you can see yourself. Be sure to use soap. Wash the sink when you're finished. And wring out the washcloth when you're done and bring it back to me. I'll read your letter meanwhile."

Those were a lot of instructions. He hurried off to the bathroom. At that moment Bruno came out of his office.

Their eyes met, and Pira froze.

"I'm sorry," he said.

Bruno smiled: "Is that paint on your face?"

"Ink."

"You used my pen?" The smile was fading.

Pira nodded.

"Where is it? I've been looking for it."

Pira pointed at the shelf where the pen lay.

"You shouldn't have used it."

"I know. I'm sorry."

"I'll buy you one of your own. Would you like that?"

That was so unexpected that Pira's "yes" didn't come out. He just nodded. Of course he would like it!

"I wrote a letter," he said then.

"Really? To whom?"

"To David."

"Oh."

Bruno looked thoughtful, or maybe surprised. Pira too was surprised. Why did Bruno not think it was wonderful that he had written a whole letter all by himself?

"Wash your face and hands now. With soap. And please don't use my pen again."

Bruno's voice sounded cold. He was angry after all. He hardly ever talked to Pira that way. Sometimes, very rarely, he would scold

Tristan in that tone of voice when he peed against the doorpost or something like that.

"Schlechter Hund," he would say, and Tristan would tuck in his tail and fold back his ears and lower his head, looking so sorry and guilty that no one could stay mad at him, not Bruno either.

As Pira cleaned his face and hands with the washcloth, he watched the soapy water turn a paler and paler blue, and his hurt feeling faded as well. When he stood on the footstool and saw that his face was clean, he was glad.

Martha called from the living room: "Bruno?"

"Yes?"

"Come and see what Peter wrote."

＊

The next morning Pira and Martha were in the garden. He was on the patio drawing cowboys and Indians, and Martha had set up her violin stand in the shade of the zapote tree and was practicing her scales. Paco was talking to himself among the dark leaves above her. Tristan was sleeping by her side. Zita had gone to the stream to wash clothes with the other women.

Suddenly Bruno came out of his office, walking fast, and spoke to Pira in a stern voice: "Why didn't you tell me that you broke my pen?"

"I didn't break it."

Martha stopped playing.

"You damaged it."

"But I fixed it."

"You knew I didn't want you to use my pen, so you used it behind my back. You dropped it, I can tell. Then you put the pen back where I left it and said nothing. If I hadn't seen you with ink on your face, you wouldn't even have told me that you used the pen. I'm very angry at you."

Pira's mouth was open, but he didn't know what to say.

He was frightened. He had never seen Bruno so mad.

Martha spoke for him: "That's not fair, Bruno. Before you saw him, he came to show me the letter he had written, he wasn't hiding anything. He was going to apologize to you."

"For what?"

"For using your pen."

Bruno closed his eyes. His chest was moving up and down as if he had been running. Then he turned to Pira. His voice was quieter now.

"Did you tell Martha the pen was broken?"

"No. It wasn't broken!"

Now Bruno raised his voice again: "I want you to go to your room! Right now! I want you to stay in your room until I tell you that you can come out!"

Pira stood up. He was trembling.

"Bruno, stop it!" Martha said. "Why are you so angry? He's just a child. He meant no harm. And it's just a pen, for Christ's sake!"

"And I'm just his father! All right?"

What happened then happened very fast. Bruno lunged toward him, his hand getting bigger as it came close. The hand grasped Pira's shirt, lifted him off his feet, and swung him under Bruno's other arm, where he hung with his head down. The next moment Bruno was sitting on the edge of the patio with Pira upside down on his lap. Pinning him down with one hand, he pulled off Pira's pants. Then he pulled off one of his sandals. Only after the third stinging slap did Pira begin screaming, with rage more than pain, and when Bruno still didn't stop hitting him, he roared, "YOU'RE NOT MY FATHER!" and at the same time Martha's voice sounded from the far end of the garden, "Stop!" and a second time, louder as she came closer, "BRUNO, STOP!" Bruno stopped and Pira ran into Martha's arms. Then he heard and felt her anger flying out at Bruno with all its claws out:

"DON'T YOU EVER TOUCH HIM AGAIN!"

Those words frightened Pira. Their meaning was too dangerous, too terrible. But even more terrible was the silence that followed. When would Bruno answer? Why didn't he march across the lawn to take Pira back and say "He's my son too"? Pira opened his eyes and saw that his father's face was white. His mouth was open. His arms hung by his sides as if he had lost all his strength. Nothing felt more urgent then than to make Bruno happy, to let him know that he was the father he loved, that Pira loved him more than his first father, much more, that he was sorry about what he had said, that it wasn't true. But Bruno went back to his office and closed the door behind him.

*

Martha sat on the grass with Pira on her lap. They were both crying. Her weeping was silent, but as her tears fell, he could feel their wet warmth on his neck. That was even more comforting than her embrace and the touch of her hands on his skin. His grief became soft and wide, like darkness or like falling asleep. Then the thought of Bruno alone in his room pierced him like a knife. More than anything in the world he wished he could make those words he had said disappear, so they would have never been spoken.

"Peter?"

"Yes?"

"We have to talk to Bruno."

"Yes."

"Right away."

Together they walked across the lawn and up the patio steps to Bruno's office. Martha knocked. There was no answer.

"Bruno?"

No answer.

She opened the door. There he was, sitting on the cot where he sometimes lay to think about what he was writing. He had one sandal on, his other foot was bare.

The moment he saw Pira, he held out his hands to him and Pira walked into his embrace. Bruno kissed his forehead and pulled Pira's head close and pressed his cheek against Pira's cheek. Martha sat down next to Bruno and put her arms around them both, touching their foreheads with hers.

"I'm sorry," Pira said. The words turned into a moan.

Bruno pulled Pira closer. Martha relaxed her embrace to make room for them. Then Bruno broke into sobs. Pira had never heard a man cry. It was sadder than hearing a woman or a child cry. He wanted it to stop.

Bruno gently held Pira away from himself, just far enough away to look into his eyes, his own pale blue eyes full of tears.

"My dear boy," Bruno said. The tears brimmed over and ran down his cheeks. "There is no one in the world I love more than you."

"I know," Pira whispered.

"I will never hit you again."

"I know."

They brought their heads together again.

"I'm so sorry, Bruno," Martha said.

"I know," Bruno said. He looked at her. "But you were right." She nodded.

Then Martha reached out to take one of Pira's hands in hers.

"Peter?"

"Yes?"

"Why don't you bring Bruno his sandal? He looks silly with just one sandal on."

So Pira ran out to fetch Bruno's sandal. When he returned, Martha and Bruno were sitting with their four hands one on top of the other on Bruno's leg, like in the sandwich game. Their faces were wet and they were smiling.

*

A storm broke out that night. It started with wind rustling in the treetops. Then a hard rain came down. Then a burst of thunder exploded so close that Pira jumped out of bed and ran into his parents' room and leapt onto their bed. There they lay together listening to the downpour. There were more claps of thunder, and the sound of rain pouring, pouring onto the roof.

"Doesn't it feel good," Martha said, "to be together, safe and dry, on a night like this?"

After a while the storm calmed down and Martha said, "You can go back to your bed now, Peter."

*

"I will never hit you again."

Pira believed that. But the memory of Bruno hitting him wouldn't go away. It came back that same night and the next day and the day after, always when Pira was alone.

When he was with Bruno he wasn't afraid, but alone he didn't feel safe with his own thoughts. Always they showed him the moment when Bruno asked, "Did you tell Martha the pen was broken?" and Pira said, "No. It wasn't broken!" It wasn't true. He knew it wasn't true, and he said it anyway. It was a lie, and Bruno knew it, and that was why Bruno got so mad and hit him. Each time he remembered that moment he wanted to go to Bruno and tell him he was sorry for using his pen and breaking it and then lying about it, but then he would remember Bruno's rage and how he had picked him up as if he weighed nothing, exactly like Federico but not for fun but to hit him SO HARD, and the moment he remembered the hitting and the pain there was also something else that frightened him almost more than anything he remembered in his whole life. It was a feeling. He didn't know what it was and he didn't want to know. But that feeling, each time, stopped the wish to tell Bruno he was sorry. It was as if telling him that would bring up the other feeling, and it was too scary.

A few days after the spanking Martha saw Pira frowning and asked him if he was all right and he said he was. It wasn't completely true but it wasn't a lie either. The bad memories were becoming less.

*

"Bruno had an idea," Martha said. "We should do something every day, the three of us, that we all enjoy. So I thought, why don't we paint together? We'll do that for an hour after siesta."

She went and bought three sets of watercolors and special watercolor paper and brushes of different thickness. Every day after siesta they painted on the patio and in the garden. At first Martha copied plants and flowers and Bruno copied cactuses, while Pira drew índios shooting arrows and throwing spears at conquistadores on horseback, dressed in armor and shooting guns, and then colored them in. Bruno said one of Martha's plants looked wise because its leaves were like elephants' ears. Martha thought he was teasing her but he said he meant it. Then Martha copied a photograph of a young Lacandón Indian with long hair she liked a lot, and Pira and Bruno were amazed by how similar the man in her picture looked to the man in the photograph. Both Martha and Bruno praised Pira for painting from his imagination. Martha said that was the best way to paint if you could do it, but Bruno said all ways were good, and Martha agreed. Then Bruno started painting from his imagination too, and Pira thought those pictures were better than either his or Martha's. First Bruno painted dragons with fire coming out of their mouths and knights who looked like Pira's conquistadores but with lances instead of guns and riding horses that were a lot better drawn than his. So Pira tried to copy Bruno's horses. Now his pictures were partly from his imagination and partly copied. Bruno said, "That's what artists always do, it's a little of both. I'm imagining dragons and I'm also copying from my memory of pictures I've seen." That made sense.

A few days later, Bruno painted a picture of a man leaning way out over the edge of a boat with both arms stretched out to a rose-colored woman with bare breasts, long blond hair, and a fish's tail who was rising out of blue waves with her arms stretched out to him. He painted her hair with the finest of all the brushes Martha had bought. He put tiny white dots into her blue eyes to make them sparkle.

"A mermaid!" Martha exclaimed. "She looks German."

"She *is* German."

"He's going to drown."

"It can't be helped."

"Can't he swim?" Pira asked.

"She's stronger than he is," Bruno said. "She will pull him underwater."

"Why?"

"Because she wants to hold him in her arms forever."

"Why?"

"Because she loves him."

"Does he love her?"

"He does."

"Is he scared?"

"No. He wants to drown in her love."

"That doesn't make sense. If he drowns he'll be dead. And then he can't love her. And she won't love him either. She won't want to hold him in her arms."

Then he thought of the painting of Popocatepetl carrying the dead Iztaccihuatl in Dorothy's master bedroom.

"At least not for very long," he added.

"You're so right," Bruno said.

Pira loved being right.

They painted every day and pinned their favorite pictures to doors and walls in the house.

*

Martha hummed a tune while she was painting.

"What is that?" Bruno asked.

"Don't you remember?"

"Vaguely."

She sang the words: "Happy days are here again, the skies above are clear again, tadadá, tadá, tadá, tadá, happy days are here again! Do you remember?"

"I do."

"The song just came to me. It's not just a memory."

Bruno smiled.

"You're thinking about it, Bruno. It's not for thinking!"

"I know. But I like to think."

Pira knew what he meant. Sometimes Martha didn't understand Bruno.

*

The little white dog Tristan was in love with had noticed him and was barking at him from her high window. Every day she sent bright little yelps in Tristan's direction. Tristan raised himself up on his hind legs, pawing the air and making sounds that were almost like talking: "You! You! I want to be with you, play with you! Come down!" It was too sad.

Finally, Martha could bear it no longer. She went to the man who owned the little dog and asked him to please let them meet at least once. He wouldn't do it. Instead he would keep his dog out of the room with the window. That way they would soon forget each other, and all would be well.

Pira thought that was mean of the man, and he was sorry for Tristan. So were Bruno and Martha and Zita. For a while Pira petted Tristan while they listened together for the little dog's voice. If she ever barked in another part of the house, they might hear her. But there was no sound.

Maybe she had forgotten Tristan. But Tristan remembered her. Every day he sat looking up at the distant window, which was closed now.

*

A mirror in Zita's room dropped to the floor. The frame fell apart, but the glass didn't break. Pira found the frameless mirror leaning against the stone tub behind the house. He picked it up and saw himself reflected from below. It made his face look weird. His chin and his mouth looked too big for the top of his head. He could see the inside of his nostrils. His eyes were staring down. He looked like a giant. He opened his mouth and saw the inside of his mouth. Behind his tongue he could see the two holes where the air and the food went. He tried looking down at the top of his head but that wasn't possible because he had to look up to see the mirror and that put the top of his head behind him. Looking down at his feet with the mirror made them look far away and tilted. Everything looked tilted if you tilted the mirror. Even without tilting, things looked different and strange in the mirror. Why was that? The boards connecting the roof of the house to the wall looked like slanting oars on a Viking ship. The side of a garden pail was a tall curving windowless wall of a prison, maybe. Lifting the mirror just a little revealed that it wasn't a prison but a pool in a fancy hotel, the clear water itself reflecting reflections of grass and flowers in the mirror. The General in his blue uniform raising his sword on the ant heap was taller in the mirror and more like a real person. Everything in the mirror was a piece of the world lifted out of the world, the same and yet different and separate from everything else. Watching the ants scurrying in and out of their house was exciting because it was like being with them in their own world. A hummingbird hovered in front of the mirror, darted away, and came back for a second look. That was funny.

Pira walked backward in the garden while looking in the mirror. Walking while looking into his own eyes was strange. If he looked at his eyes for too long it was almost like being blind, because he lost sight of everything else. But on either side of his reflected face he could see enough of what was behind him to steer himself across the lawn, up the patio stairs, and into the house, around the dining room table into the kitchen, where Martha and Zita were making dinner.

"Cuidado!" Zita said, laughing. "Te ves como un loco!"

"It's a method for walking backward," he said.

"That looks dangerous," Martha said. "What if you fall and the glass breaks?"

"I won't fall. I can see everything. It's like having eyes in the back of my head."

He was leaving the kitchen backward as he said this.

"If the glass breaks, don't pick up the pieces. Call me. Will you promise me that?"

"I promise."

He steered himself toward the patio steps and walked down the stairs backward, holding the mirror above him so he could see his feet. Back on the lawn, he tried walking forward while looking in the mirror. That was more difficult. By watching the reflection of what was behind him he could half remember, half guess what was in front of him. It was a little scary. After a while his toes felt as if they were trying to see.

The mirror became one of his favorite toys. There were always new things to look at from different angles, and revisiting the old ones was fun too.

Once when Bruno and Martha were watching him playing with it, Pira heard Bruno say, "He's an artist." That made him proud, though he didn't understand why an artist would look at things in a mirror.

*

A letter from Harry Taub, Dorothy's uncle in Hollywood, came. It was addressed to Bruno. After Bruno read it he called Martha and read it out loud to her, and Martha was even more delighted than Bruno. Pira came out of his room.

"What happened?"

He had to ask three times before Martha and Bruno told him, they were so excited. Harry said someone had told him about a story Bruno had written. He thought it would make a good movie. He wanted Bruno to translate it so he could read it himself, and if he liked it, he would ask Bruno for permission to turn it into a movie. Then, if Bruno said yes, Harry would send him money, maybe enough to pay for the trip to Germany. And if that happened, they would be able to leave soon.

This wasn't good news for Pira. Nothing about it made him feel good. But Bruno assured him that it would be at least a year before they left, maybe more. He would have to find work in Germany first, and that could take a long time.

"Will I still go to first grade?"

"Of course."

"When?"

"In a month. Four Sundays."

That wasn't very soon, but not long either.

"With Chris?"

"Yes."

"And Arón?"

Bruno shook his head. It wasn't possible. Pira knew that, but he liked to imagine the possibility: all the new children sitting behind desks, two by two, and one desk for three children, himself in the middle and Chris and Arón on either side. All bad feelings were forgotten. It was the first day of first grade.

8

A few days before Sándor left for Hungary, the Vogelsangs drove
to the house of a friend of Sándor's who was giving him a farewell party. The friend's name was Agnes. She lived far out of town
in the mountains, so the drive was a long one. Martha was driving because Bruno didn't know how to drive. Pira sat in the back,
watching the trees get bigger until they slid past the car, and the
fields turning slowly farther away, and the much slower turning of
distant mountains. Above the mountains hung the moon, pale and
almost full, even though it was still daytime.

On and off, Martha and Bruno talked. Martha was sad. She
was sad because Sándor was leaving, and because there would be
no more Ferenc Sándor Quartet. She would have to get a job in the
city. But doing what? She didn't know. Couldn't Bruno write something that would bring in more money?

Bruno got annoyed, as he always did when she said things like
that. "I don't write for money," he said. "Of course not," Martha
said, "but you don't have to compromise. Look at Chaplin," and
Bruno said nothing.

A little later they talked about Agnes, and the word "party"
came up in that other meaning Bruno said was too complicated
for children to understand. Agnes had friends in another party, the

one given by Trotzky, the bad man who was dead. Bruno hoped Agnes's friends from the other party weren't invited to the party he and Martha and Pira were going to.

"She wouldn't do that to Sándor," Martha said.

Pira returned to watching the landscape turn around him.

High up in the sky there were big birds. Maybe they were eagles.

*

There were more guests at the party than Pira had ever seen inside a house. In addition to Pira and Bruno and Martha and the three other members of the quartet and Sándor's friend Valéria, all of Bruno's German friends were there, and American friends of both Bruno's and Martha's, and Mexican friends who had come from as far as Juárez, and Hungarian friends of Sándor's, and all these people were friends of Agnes, the hostess.

Everyone was wearing fancy clothes, the women long shiny skirts and pretty blouses, earrings, and necklaces, the men suits and ties. One of the Mexican women sat on a chair with wheels underneath. A young man rolled her around so she could talk to different people. Pira had never seen anyone so magnificent. She looked like a queen. Her black hair was piled above her head like a crown with many bright flowers woven into it like jewels. Her eyebrows swung out from the bridge of her nose like wings of a large black bird. Her lips were painted dark red. Her long skirt was red too, but brighter than her lips, almost the color of blood, and over her shoulders hung an orange rebozo embroidered with green parrots.

Agnes was blond and old and she smelled good. She shook Pira's hand as if he were a grown-up.

"Peter," she said. "I love the name Peter. Do you know what it means?"

What could it mean? It was a name.

"It means stone."

He didn't believe it.

"I'm not fooling you. Peter means stone. It's a good name. Stone is good. Stone is honest and strong."

Pira smiled at the description, but he didn't believe that his name meant stone.

There were a few children at the party, most of them younger than Pira, and two older boys who were dressed alike and looked the same too, brown-skinned and oval-faced with black hair reaching down to their shoulders, almost like girls, but they were boys.

Pira tugged at Bruno's hand and whispered: "Are they twins?"

"They're identical twins."

"What's identical?"

"Identical means the same."

Later he learned that the boys were Agnes's adopted sons, and that they had Nahuatl names: Cuauhtémoc and Huitzil. He wished he had a name like that.

People hugged and shook hands. Some of them hadn't seen each other in a long time. Everyone was happy to be there. Martha too looked happy and no longer sad. Maybe she was happy for Sándor. He looked happiest of all. Pira remembered what Bruno had told him about homesickness. Sándor was happy because he had been homesick and now he was going home.

A man in a black suit shook a bell and announced that dinner was going to be served in the garden. Everyone went outside and looked for their seats around several white-clothed tables that stood under three big trees. The tables were lit by lamps that hung from the branches above them.

The lamps gave off a scent that repelled mosquitoes. It was getting toward evening. The guests' names were written on cards that were placed in front of the dishes, and you had to sit where your name was. Fortunately, Pira was seated next to Bruno. Martha sat opposite Bruno. Sándor sat between them at the head of the table.

Sándor's friend Valéria was also nearby, and Ferenc and István, the two other members of the quartet, and Agnes. At the other end of the table were two other Hungarian men and a Mexican woman whom Pira did not know.

"We seem to have the table of honor," Bruno said, and Agnes said, "Yes, that is because everyone at this table is a close friend of our guest of honor."

Pira had never thought of himself as a close friend of Sándor's. It felt nice but almost too big. He looked around for Cuauhtémoc and Huitzil. They were at another table with people he didn't know. The meaning of honor wafted through him, raising him up like wind in a sail.

Waiters in white suits came with food on silver platters and looked around for empty wine glasses to fill. The sound of loud happy talk and laughter filled the garden. A peacock and two pea-hens wandered from table to table, looking for food. Agnes had asked her guests not to feed them, but people fed them anyway.

Sándor murmured something in a waiter's ear. The waiter went away and came back with a large white paper napkin and gave it to Sándor, and Sándor started folding the napkin over and under, inside and out, creasing, flattening, indenting, turning, and pressing it into a delicate, growing form with his long fingers. Little by little, a flower developed. It was a white rose.

"This is for Peter," he said, handing the flower to Pira. Did Sándor know about the white flower in his poem? Maybe he had read it.

*

Then dinner was served—duck breast, roast potatoes, brussels sprouts, carrots and peas, stewed cherries on the side. The waiters kept coming to refill the glasses. Pira drank Coke.

Everyone at the table was talking, mostly in English or in Hungarian. One of the Hungarian men at the far end of the table translated for the Mexican woman. The conversation was too grown-up for Pira to follow. He was bored and hoped the party would end soon.

Agnes smiled at him from across the table.

"Do you like the food?" she asked him.

"I do," he said. "I like everything except the peas."

Several people laughed. Bruno patted Pira's hand. The people who had laughed looked at Pira kindly. It was all right.

Every once in a while, someone stood up and clinked a spoon against a glass until several people said "Toast, toast," and everyone stopped talking. Then the person, still standing, would speak.

"Why do they say toast?" Pira asked Bruno.

"A toast is a speech people give at a party."

So toast meant two things, just like party meant two things.

All the toasts were about Sándor, and they all had words like "victory" and "glorious" in them, which gave the speeches a kind of hurrah feeling Pira liked a lot. After each toast, people drank and shouted and clapped their hands.

The queen-like lady with the flowers in her hair gave a toast in Spanish. She didn't stand up. Instead she held her glass high above her head. The young man who had rolled her around earlier translated her words into English:

"To Sándor—to music—to life and to love. When you go back to Hungary, do not forget Mexico, Sándor. Remember our sad and beautiful land."

Then everyone shouted: "Viva México! Viva la revolución!"

Now Sándor stood up, holding his glass with red wine in it, and everyone quieted down.

"How could I forget Mexico? That is not possible. I would sooner forget my own mother, or a woman I love. Of course, strictly speaking, Hungary is my mother and Mexico . . ."

He stopped talking and rubbed the top of his head.

"Mexico was a kind stranger who welcomed me into her home."

Pira could tell by Sándor's slurred speech that he was drunk.

"But that is not right, is it? Mexico, Hungary . . . I think they are sisters."

He halted again.

"But that would make Mexico my aunt. No, no."

People were laughing. Laughing *with* him, Pira assumed.

"What I mean is . . . the heart of Mexico and the heart of Hungary are not different . . . even though they are not the same."

Again he stopped talking. He rubbed the middle of his forehead with his fingertips.

"This is impossible to say in words. . . "

He turned around and went to where his violin case stood leaning against the trunk of the tree whose branches stretched over their table and came back to put the case on his chair. He opened the case and took out his violin and bow.

"István, can you help me?"

On the grass behind István stood a large square suitcase made of black wood. István opened it and took out a foldout table with four slender legs. The table turned out to be hollow, with tight rows of metal strings stretched across the top. István tapped the strings several times with two long black rods that had something white wrapped around their curved ends, and a deep singing sound came out, DUN durudun-dun-dun-dun, while Sándor plucked the strings of his violin, tuning them to the sound István was making, and tested the tuning with a few strokes of his bow. István tapped the strings of his instrument rapidly upward and downward and out to the sides too, so quickly it made a single long smooth sound made of many parts, grand, rich, and full, like an organ.

"What an instrument," Bruno whispered, and Pira was filled with pleasure at Bruno's saying that to him alone.

István held the rods poised over his instrument, looking at Sándor and waiting.

"Even though it's evening," Sándor said. "And not a birthday party." He tucked the violin under his chin and started playing Las Mañanitas.

István joined him with strumming chords. The tune climbed its gently rising path step by step and then wended its way down, dancing as it walked. Pira always liked the moment when the words, if someone was singing, would say, "Ya viene amaneciendo ya la luz del día nos vió," and the music would pause as if to listen. Sándor and István played it that way. They made a pause: there was only the sound of the crickets. Then the song went on to the end, and began again.

One of the peahens screamed. It sounded like a miserable child. But it just wanted food. Pira dropped peas on the grass, and the peahen ate them.

Sándor was changing the tune. It was still Las Mañanitas but it didn't have a glad feeling the way Las Mañanitas was glad about dawn and the flowers. It was more like wanting something so badly you would leave everything and everyone to find whatever it was. István was changing his part of the music too. His rods were hammering so fast they made a blur in the air. The guitar-like strumming turned into a drone that rose and fell like long slow waves.

This music was different from other music. It didn't come back to where it started the way tunes usually did. It just went away and away, as if it wanted to escape. Like that bird Pira had seen once trying to fly away from a boy who held a string that was tied to its leg. But this wasn't a bird, it was a voice, it was crying. It was like nothing he had ever heard. It soared, it sailed, it wanted only to go far away. Tears were streaming down Pira's cheeks. Now Sándor was plucking the strings and making the bow skip.

Agnes and the other Hungarians at the table clapped their hands to the beat. They were happy, the music was happy. Martha was clapping too. Then the sadness began again, the wanting, Sándor drawing the bow across the strings in long arcs. Pira saw that Agnes's blue eyes were wide open, she too was weeping. And again the music changed. It was no longer flying away. It was that sweet, gentle tune again, Las Mañanitas. Everyone was clapping. Someone shouted "Bravo!," some people were singing along. And then the music stopped, and there was more applause. Pira felt proud of being Sándor's friend. One of his *closest* friends.

More food and drinks were served, and after a while people were getting tipsy and talking and laughing at the same time without listening.

Pira liked being with grown-ups, but not for so long. He pulled Bruno's sleeve: "When are we leaving?"

"After dessert."

"Can I walk around a little?"

"Sure. I'll call you when they bring the dessert."

Gratefully, Pira left the table and walked past the other tables, feeling strange because some people were looking at him and maybe wondering where he was going or whose child he was. He walked past the tables and kept walking until he could no longer see the people, but he thought he could feel their looks on his back as he walked away from them. Then he saw the place where two of the high brick walls that surrounded the garden met, and now he knew where he was going. He went there and turned around and sat down, and right away he felt content.

Once in the Little People's School in New York the teacher had called him a bad boy and made him stand facing a corner after he hit a little girl. All the children could see him standing there but he couldn't see them. That was a bad memory, very bad. Sitting here was the opposite. The corner was behind him. He could see and hear everyone. He wasn't alone, but he was by himself. That felt so good he was smiling with pleasure.

He sat there and thought how nice it would be if he and Arón were still friends and Arón were here with him. They would share this feeling of being by themselves and separate from all the others. It was like that when they sat side by side on the biggest branch of the zapote tree with their legs dangling, giggling about something funny one of them had said, talking or not talking. It was perfect. With Chris it was different. Chris was always starting new things, or changing things. There was never any quiet time with Chris.

A large white butterfly fluttered around him and settled down on his knee, sat for a while, fanning its wings, and flew away.

From among the many chattering, laughing guests clustered around the five tables, the twins, Cuauhtémoc and Huitzil, came walking toward him. They were wearing long blue pants and white pleated shirts. Their shiny black hair hung down to their shoulders. They were the same height and their arms swung in unison. They looked exactly the same.

They stopped in front of him and one of them asked in Spanish, "What are you doing?"

"Nothing."

"What's your name?"

"Pira."

"What kind of name is that?"

"It means stone."

The moment he said the word "piedra," he recognized its similarity to "Pedro" and realized Agnes had told him the truth when she said that Peter meant stone.

"My name is Cuauhtémoc," one of them said. "His name is Huitzil."

"I know," Pira said.

Cuauhtémoc thought that was funny.

"How do you know? No one can tell us apart. Even our mother can't."

"Well, now I know."

"Yes, because I told you. But turn around for a moment. Face the wall."

Pira hesitated.

"Go ahead. It's a test."

Pira stood up and turned around. He didn't like facing the corner.

"Now turn around again."

He turned around.

"Which one of us is Cuauhtémoc and which one is Huitzil?" one of them said.

"You are Cuauhtémoc," he said to the boy who had stood on the left before and was now on the right.

They laughed.

"You're wrong," the boy he thought was Cuauhtémoc said. "You can't know unless we tell you. And even when we tell you, you can't know if we're telling the truth."

They watched him as he thought about that. They were right. He didn't know what to say.

Cuauhtémoc and Huitzil laughed. One of them did a cartwheel.

"Our mother told us to tell you we're having dessert," the other one said.

They had their own separateness, and they liked it.

*

The dessert was warm chocolate pudding with cream and chocolate chips. "Qué sabroso!" the Mexican woman at the end of the table exclaimed. Everyone else at the table praised it too. Martha was especially enthusiastic: "Absolutely delicious!"

"But you don't like chocolate pudding," Pira said.

"That's not true, Peter. I love chocolate pudding."

"But at home you always say—"

Bruno's foot knocked against Pira's ankle. Pira lifted the tablecloth: "Why are you kicking me?"

Everyone was laughing. What was so funny? They laughed and laughed. It wasn't the "laughing with" kind of laughter. Were they laughing at him? Martha was laughing too, but differently. She was laughing into a napkin. Her shoulders were shaking. She was blushing. Pira had never seen her face look so red. Bruno too was laughing and looking down at his dessert.

Sándor clinked his glass with a spoon until everyone at the table was quiet and looking at him.

"There's something I forgot to remember," he said. "Peter, may I borrow your flower?"

Pira handed him the white flower. Sándor held it up like the bowl of a wine glass.

"This is for Martha."

What did he mean? Everyone was looking at the flower.

Nothing happened. Then a faint reddish glow appeared in the center of the flower. Slowly it spread through the petals, deepening and darkening until the whole flower was a dark glowing red. It really looked like a rose now.

"Oh, Sándor, that's marvelous!" Martha said.

The color faded and flowed back to the center of the flower, rested there as a faint pink glow, and then it was gone.

Sándor gave the flower back to Pira, drew a cigarette lighter from his pocket, and handed it to Bruno.

"Now Bruno," he said. "I know you don't believe in magic. But you and I believe in justice. You light the fire, I'll provide the flint."

Bruno lit the lighter and held out the flame. Sándor stretched out his hand and very slowly lowered his open hand to the fire.

"To the revolution," Sándor said.

As his palm touched the flame, a brilliant flash of white fire burst out from beneath his hand, crackling and sparkling, and immediately vanished.

Bruno laughed and closed the lighter and gave it back to Sándor, who put it in his pocket.

*

Before leaving, the guests hugged and kissed and shook hands and a lot of people crowded around Sándor to wish him a safe voyage. Both Bruno and Martha hugged him for a long time, as if they didn't want to let him go. Martha was crying.

Agnes was next in line. She patted Sándor's cheeks with both hands and said something in Hungarian. Then she held his head and stood up on her toes and kissed him on the mouth.

Then Bruno asked people to please step to the side so that Pira could say goodbye too. Sándor tried to lift him by his armpits. He had to let him down.

"Carajo, you've gotten so big!"

Pira laughed because Sándor, whose Spanish was not very good, had said a bad word.

"I wonder how tall you will be when we meet again," Sándor said, holding Pira with his gaze. Often grown-ups said, "How big you've gotten," but this was different. It made him feel bigger than himself.

"Farewell," Sándor said. Pira knew this solemn word but had never heard anyone say it. He gave Sándor his hand and wanted to say "Farewell," but the word didn't come out.

Sándor turned to someone else who was waiting to say goodbye. That took a while, and then there were others. By now Pira was bored and sleepy. He practiced handstands until his parents were ready. Sometimes he could hold a handstand to the count of four.

Suddenly he heard Martha's voice: "Come on, showoff. It's time to go home."

Why did she say that?

9

Pira and Zita went to pick up Federico at the bus station. To get there you had to walk through the market on the Calle Mazatlán. Why was it always so still here? People were talking, laughing, bargaining, but their voices were quiet. So was the sound of the many birds whistling in their cages. It was a little like the stillness at the river when Zita and the other criadas washed clothes there and talked while Pira sat near them reading in the grass.

Zita stopped to talk with a friend who had just bought some pigs' feet and was putting them in her basket. The feet were wrapped in newspaper, but Pira could see the hooves sticking out. He turned his head and saw the pig's head right next to his, pink and blue-eyed in a red crate, looking up and a little to the side. The corners of its mouth were curled as if it were smiling. Pira looked away and saw the feet again, four feet bundled together. He reached for Zita's hand.

"Qué quieres, Pira?"

He couldn't speak. He felt dizzy. He pressed his face into her belly and closed his eyes.

"Está bien, mi amor. Nos vamos ahorita mismo."

She stroked his head and he clasped his arms around her waist, still with his face buried in the softness of her belly. They stood like that until Zita finished her conversation. Then they walked on, holding hands.

*

The first thing Federico did after getting off the bus was put down his little suitcase and place the bouquet he had brought for Zita on top of it and lift Pira as high as he could:

"That's how big you will be one day!"

Pira didn't believe it but he loved the idea. Federico lowered Pira back to the ground and then kissed Zita on the lips, holding her head between his hands and shaking his head:

"Qué hermosa eres!"

And not just beautiful, he added, but more beautiful than any other woman in sight.

"I don't want to insult anyone" (lowering his voice to a near whisper), "but Pira, look around, is there anyone here more beautiful?"

Pira looked around and shook his head. Federico and Zita laughed. For a moment it seemed they had laughed at him, but their smiles were kind. Then Federico gave Zita the bouquet. She smelled the flowers and said they were pretty. Then Zita asked Pira if he would like to carry the flowers, and he did. Then the three of them walked together through the farmer's market and past the pig's head, which Pira avoided looking at, Federico carrying his suitcase in one hand and holding Zita's hand in the other, Zita holding Pira's hand and Pira carrying the bouquet. He didn't always like holding hands on the street, but he did now. It was like pretending they were a family, even though everyone could see he wasn't their child. His blue eyes gave him away. People always praised his blue eyes, but to him they were the most obvious sign that he wasn't Mexican. He wished they were black and shiny like Zita's and Federico's, and like Arón's eyes too. Still, it was fun pretending.

"Zita told me you're teaching yourself how to write," Federico said.

Pira nodded proudly.

"I'm learning how to write too," Federico said. "But I have a teacher."

"You do?" Zita said.

"Yes. The union is providing classes. Soon I'll be able to write my own letters. I'm reading now too. It's not hard."

"I can read a little now too. Señora Marta is teaching me. And I teach her Spanish. We're reading a book. I'll show it to you."

*

"I love Federico. His visits are like holidays for all of us. We're so lucky to know him."

Martha said that, and it was true. Federico was fun. He played badminton with Martha in the garden, which was something Bruno rarely did. He played better than Bruno, which Bruno knew because Martha always tried to win and Bruno never won when he played against Martha, which was probably why he didn't like to play. Federico sometimes won and sometimes lost, so the game was fun for both of them.

Bruno didn't mind that Federico played better than he did. He admired Federico. He said so. And not just for how he played badminton. He admired his character, he said. Once when Pira asked what character was, Bruno said it was a combination of being honest and brave—being brave enough to be honest and honest enough to be brave. Pira didn't understand that, but it sounded a lot like Federico, so he remembered it.

That afternoon after Zita and Federico had taken their siesta, Bruno and Federico talked and drank beer at the table on the patio while Zita and Martha cooked dinner.

Pira was throwing a stick for Tristan when he heard Federico say the words "huelga general," and a little later the same words coming from Bruno's mouth. He knew what a huelga was, but huelga general reminded him of generals like Zapata or Cuauhtémoc, so he said "basta" to Tristan and listened.

"There won't be a huelga general," Federico said. "The other unions are weak. They won't join us. That is the reality."

"I'm sorry," Bruno said. "I was hopeful."

"It's not possible," Federico said.

"But your union is strong," Bruno said. "That too is reality."

"We will strike, without the other unions. Unless the bosses change their mind, but they won't."

"How much of a raise are you asking for?"

"Sixteen centavos an hour."

"It's not much. They can afford it."

Federico laughed bitterly: "What they can't afford is to give us dignity."

He paused.

"I'm ashamed it's so little."

They both fell silent.

"When are you making the huelga?" Pira asked. The two men were surprised that he had been listening.

"Probably next week," Federico said.

"Can I go with you?"

He knew they wouldn't let him. And they didn't. Both Bruno and Federico said no firmly.

*

While they were eating dinner Bruno asked Federico if he had heard about the death of Manolete.

"Of course I heard," Federico said. "The whole country must have heard about it. At the railroad we even stopped working for a little while. The foreman called for a minute of silence. We took off our hats to remember Manolete."

"Who is Manolete?" Martha asked Bruno, but Bruno looked at Federico, waiting for him to speak.

"Manolete was the greatest matador de toros who ever lived," Federico said. "They called him El Monstro. We saw him two years ago in the Plaza de Toros, Señor Bruno and I. We went together."

"I remember now," Martha said.

"Manolete was hurt," Pira said. "But he won anyway. Federico told me about it."

"Híjole! What a memory! This boy is tremendous!"

"He is," Zita said in her slow, gentle way. "But he's not eating his tamales."

The grown-ups laughed. Zita put her hand on Pira's arm to let him know she wasn't making fun of him, or else to apologize for her joke. But he himself thought it was funny.

"He was killed by a bull," Federico said.

"There's justice in that," Martha said. Zita agreed.

"I remember that day," Martha said to Bruno. "I never understood why you went there. You hate bullfights."

"It's true I disapprove of bullfights." He used a Spanish word Pira had never heard: tauromaquia. "But I respect the toreros. They're almost always poor boys, and it's one of the few professions they can practice with any hope of escaping poverty. It takes courage to be a torero. It also takes skill, because the public wants to see it done well, with grace . . ."

"Con gracia" was how he said it in Spanish. Pira's mind lit up at the sound of that word. But some of what Bruno went on to say, and what Federico and Martha said in response, he didn't understand. It didn't matter, he still wanted to hear everything. Zita had to remind him twice that his tamales were getting cold.

"A really good matadero is an artist. A great artist takes his art to the limits of what is possible. In order to do that, he has to risk everything, his sanity, his reputation, even his life. It is that way in all the arts, but nowhere is the danger so bloody, so mortal, as in bullfighting. And Manolete had the reputation of being not just a good or great artist but a genius. So that interested me, even though I had never seen a bullfight before. Also Franco was using Manolete to make himself look like a hero."

Pira knew who Franco was. He was the ruler of Spain, like a king. He had been a friend of Hitler when Hitler was still alive. He was a bad man. Bruno had fought against him in Spain.

"That would have been a reason not to go to see Manolete, wouldn't it?" Martha said.

That made sense.

"It would," Bruno said. "But here's the strange thing. A lot of Franco's enemies were crazy about Manolete. I mean the exiled Spaniards living in Mexico. Do you remember Octavio Sombra, the poet?"

Martha and Federico said yes.

"Well, Octavio was almost sick with longing to see Manolete. This torero, he said, is the soul of Spain, and that soul does not belong to Franco. Octavio told me things Manolete had said that Franco would not have liked to hear. 'Bullfighting is not about flags, it's about toros and toreros.' Which was an elegant way of saying: 'Franco does not own Manolete.' All this appealed to me. So when Octavio, who didn't have a lot of money, offered to buy me a ticket, I accepted. Later I remembered that Federico liked bullfights. What am I saying, he's an aficionado. And here Manolete was going to compete with the best Mexican bullfighter. It could be the greatest corrida in the history of bullfights, and Federico would miss it. So I called Octavio and asked him to buy me two tickets and said I would pay for one."

"I didn't think I could accept such a gift," Federico said to Bruno. "That ticket was expensive. But when I heard that your friend had paid for your ticket, I accepted."

For a moment they were all silent.

Then Federico raised his bottle of beer and said, "To the memory of Manolete," and Bruno, who drank his beer from a glass, raised his glass and said, "To Manolete," and then Martha and Zita raised their glasses without saying anything.

"How about you, Pira?" Federico said. "Won't you drink to Manolete? You can do it with milk." So Pira raised his glass of milk, and they all drank to Manolete.

*

The next day Bruno and Martha were going to take the bus to Mexico City to attend a conference, leaving Pira with Zita and Federico. It was Sunday morning. Zita asked Martha and Bruno if it was all right if she and Federico took Pira to the Cathedral with them. There would be a special Mass for the Virgin of Guadalupe. Martha hesitated, but Bruno said "Why not?" So they agreed.

They all went to the bus station together. Federico insisted on carrying the Vogelsangs' small valise. He had polished his red shoes with the little holes in them until they were super-shiny. Zita was wearing a rebozo embroidered with flowers and birds. Pira too was wearing something special: long pants with creases and polished leather shoes instead of sneakers. The last time he had worn such clothes was when his parents took him to see Hansel and Gretel in Mexico City.

The five of them walked through the market, which was even

more crowded than the day before. Pira looked out for the pig's head, but someone had bought it already. They passed three live goats with ropes around their necks. A man was holding the ropes tight in his fist so that the goats' heads were pulled together. Their yellow eyes were all staring in the same direction. One of the goats dropped many little round pieces of poop like marbles or berries from its behind. The man was also holding two chickens upside down by a string that was tied around their feet.

The chickens' beaks were open. Their eyes were round and staring.

"I hate seeing this," Martha said as they passed the man and the animals.

"Me too," Pira said.

*

The bus was late.

"If you wait with us you'll be late for church," Bruno said. "You should go."

"It's not so important," Federico said. "There are many Masses, but I don't see you so often."

"It's important to Zita," Martha said. "Isn't it, Zita? It's important for you to get there on time."

They all looked at Zita.

"Yes, but Federico needs to talk with Señor Bruno. That's important too. We'll keep you company until the bus comes."

And so they stood waiting for the bus while Federico and Bruno talked about the huelga, using words that Pira did not understand, and about how President Alemán wasn't as friendly to Mexican workers as Cárdenas and Camacho had been, and Zita talked to Martha about her family in Oaxaca and how they were all muy religiosos and Federico's family too but Federico himself was more political than religious and in fact was against the Church and the priests even though he did go to Church sometimes, and this, Pira thought, was a little more interesting.

"Es muy complicado," Zita said, and Martha agreed and said that she herself was Judía but not religious, so it was complicado for her too.

"Usted es Judía?" Zita said. Her hand went up to her cheek as she asked it.

"Yes," Martha said, "my father is Judío and my mother was Judía, so I'm Judía too. That's how it is."

"Yes," Zita said, smiling now and nodding, still with her hand on her cheek, "I understand."

Then the bus came and Bruno and Martha kissed Pira goodbye and shook hands with Zita and Federico and got on the bus. After the bus took off, Zita and Federico offered to hold Pira's hands, but he said no. He didn't want to look little when they went to the Cathedral.

*

On the way to the Cathedral, Zita explained that she and Federico would be receiving the hostia along with everyone else, and Pira could watch, and that it was very special and he would like it.

"What's the hostia?" Pira asked.

"It's a piece of bread. It looks like a tiny tortilla but it's really the body of Christ."

"Really?"

"Yes, but it doesn't look like a body."

"You eat it?"

"Yes."

"You swallow it?"

"Yes."

"And it's the body of Christ?"

"Yes. The priest calls it Corpus Christi."

"What's Corpus Christi?"

"El cuerpo de Cristo. It's Latin."

"What's Latin?"

"It's another language. It comes from Rome."

"Can I eat the hostia too?" Pira asked.

"I'm sorry. It's only for people who have been bautizado."

"What's bautizado?"

"It's when the priest sprinkles holy water on a baby's head and blesses the baby in the name of the Father, the Son, and the Holy Spirit."

"I wasn't bautizado?"

"No, mi amor, you weren't, because your parents aren't Catholic. Some people are and some people aren't. Both are good."

He could tell she knew he was disappointed, but she didn't know why. He felt sad because once again it was clear that being a gringo made him different from Mexicans. He wished he had brought his sombrero. If he pushed it into his forehead, which was how the campesinos wore their hats when they came to market, grown-ups looking down from above wouldn't know he was a gringo.

"Oye, Pirito," Federico said. "The body of Christ does not taste very good." He flashed a smile at Zita, who gave him a disapproving look.

"Psst," Zita said with a finger across her lips. They had arrived at the Cathedral. The broad, high door stood open. Above it hung a stone crucifix with two huge crossed bones underneath. They could have been dinosaur bones, but they weren't real, they were made of stone. Still, the whole Cathedral looked scary because of them, which was why Pira had never wanted to find out what it looked like inside. But now he was going in with Zita and Federico, and he felt safe. Zita drew her rebozo over her head and they walked in and it was like the moment when the whale swallowed Pinocchio. Silence swallowed him, silence and darkness.

"We're too late," Zita whispered in the darkness.

"Just in time," Federico said.

Then Pira's eyes got used to the darkness and it wasn't really dark, he could see white shirts and then black rebozos draped over the women's heads, lots of people shuffling together on a long path in the middle of the enormous room. And it wasn't really quiet either, there was a whispering and murmuring and once in a while the distant sound of a man's voice saying something a little louder. That was probably the priest. He couldn't make out the words. There was light coming in through several windows, some low and some very high up. He had never seen such high walls. There were paintings on them and sculptures and lots of gold. The whispering and murmuring came from the people in the aisle. They were praying. Some of the people were standing, but others were kneeling, and not just kneeling but shuffling forward on their knees, like the crippled beggar who wasn't supposed to beg in front of the Palacio de la Constitución but always did. But here there were many, and it didn't look as if they had leather pads on their knees like the beggar.

Federico offered him his hand, and this time Pira took it. They joined the procession. They weren't going to kneel, he was glad about that. Once he had seen Arón's mother make Arón kneel and pray on the stone floor after she had punished him. He didn't want to think about that. Zita was praying silently with her hands folded in front of her. She looked happy. Her lips were moving. Pira couldn't see the priest because the bodies in front of him were too big, but the priest's voice was not far away, and now he could hear him more clearly. His words sounded like a magic spell, and it was long. None of the words were Spanish, but he recognized three: Corpus, Christi, and Amén.

Each time, after the magic spell, the people moved forward, and Pira and Zita and Federico moved with them. Now Pira wondered: Was he supposed to eat Christ's body after all? He didn't really want to. According to Federico, it didn't even taste good.

"Corpus domini nostri Jesu Christi . . ."

But maybe that wasn't true. Maybe Federico had lied to make Pira feel better for not being allowed to eat the hostia. Maybe it tasted delicious. Why else would people line up for it?

" . . . animam tuam in vitam aeternam Amen . . ."

Pira turned his head and saw that they were the last in line. Everyone was murmuring, whispering. Pira thought of his poem. It was like a prayer, in a way. It wasn't about God, but it was about the mother of God. He could say it silently, the way Zita prayed. Maybe God wouldn't want him to say it here. He tried it out anyway, silently in his mind: "Cuando canta la verde rana . . ." It felt forbidden, so he stopped.

"Corpus Domini nostri Jesu Christi . . ."

He could see the priest now, a short man with dark glasses dressed in a long blue robe standing behind a low iron fence. He was holding a golden basket. A boy in a white robe stood next to him holding a plate, also golden. The boy was almost as tall as the priest was. In the background behind the boy and the priest, brightly lit, was a large crucifix made of shiny marble. Jesus was so pale he was almost blue, with a white cloth wrapped around his middle. Three black nails on his hands and crossed feet stood out against the red blood coming from the wounds. There were drops of blood coming from his eyes too, and from the thorns pricking the top of his head, and a long trickle of blood flowed from the cut in his side where a soldier had stabbed him with a spear. Pira knew about that from Zita.

The people in front of Pira were next in line to eat the body of Christ. It wasn't the body on the cross. It was a cookie. It didn't look anything like a tortilla. There must have been lots of them inside the golden basket, little white cookies. One by one, each person kneeled down on a cushioned bench in front of the fence with their hands placed together in front of their chest. Then the priest would take a cookie from the bowl, hold it up, make the sign of the cross with the cookie, and start saying the magic spell. The person would open his or her mouth, and the priest, still speaking, would put the cookie inside their mouth while the boy held his golden plate underneath the person's chin, and then, after the priest said "Amén," the person would get up and make room for the next person to kneel and get his or her cookie.

Now it was Zita's turn. She knelt down and put her hands together. The priest raised a cookie and started saying the magic words, "Corpus domini nostri Jesu Christi custodiat," and making the sign of the cross with the cookie while Zita opened her mouth with her eyes closed and stuck out her tongue a little and the boy held the golden plate underneath her chin, maybe to make sure she didn't drop crumbs on the floor. Then carefully the priest, still speaking, put the cookie into her mouth and said "Amén." Then Zita stood up and took Pira's free hand. At the same time Federico let go of his other hand and stepped forward and bowed to the priest. The priest was short and Federico was tall. But when Federico knelt down he was small enough for the priest to make the sign of the cross with the cookie in front of his face while he began the magic spell. After the priest said "Amén," Federico stood up and took Pira's hand again. The priest took a new cookie from the basket, expecting to give it to Pira, but before he could say "Corpus," Zita and Federico were already leading Pira away, and Pira saw the priest shaking his head and putting the body of Christ back into the basket.

*

That evening Federico turned on the radio. A Spaniard (you could tell he was Spanish by the way he pronounced his s's) and a Mexican woman were talking about Manolete, how he had lived and how he died. It was like a story. The man told the story and the woman asked questions. Then the man would tell another part of the story. A lot of it Pira didn't understand, but there were things he did understand that made him want to hear more, like how Manolete never stepped aside from a charging bull but instead stood still with his feet close together and drew the bull close and wrapped him around himself with his muleta, so close that the bull's horns grazed his body, tearing the golden threads on his traje de luces. Or how once, after he was gored by a bull and was taken to a hospital, someone asked him why he didn't step aside and he said, "If I did that I would not be Manolete." So Pira listened with Federico.

Every once in a while, the man and the woman stopped talking and there was Spanish music with trumpets. Pira liked Spanish music. So did Bruno and Martha. Sometimes Bruno put on Spanish records called flamenco where a man half sang, half shouted a long quavering "Ayyyyy. . .", followed by words that sounded both sad and furious. A guitar ran along with them, also angry, also sad, but listening didn't make you feel sad or angry. Martha said flamenco was like fire. The Spanish music on the radio wasn't flamenco but it was bright and exciting and Pira liked it a lot. Then the man's and the woman's voices came back. She wanted to know whose fault it was that Manolete died. Was it Manolete's fault? Did he make a mistake?

Now the man sounded angry. "There was no mistake. Blasco Ibáñez said, 'There is only one beast in a bullfight: it is the public.' Manolete's death was a sacrifice. The public needed him to die. We are that beast, we who loved him. He gave us everything he had to give. It wasn't enough. We wanted more. So he gave us his life. Had he not done that, we would have stripped him of his honor. Let us be honest. Like the monstrous gods of Mexico's old religions, we thirst for our heroes' blood, we drink it with satisfaction. Are we not relishing it even now, at this moment?"

The woman laughed nervously: "Diós mío! Strong words! But let us not forget, ladies and gentlemen, these are the words of a poet and a personal friend of the great Manolete, whose recent death is being mourned by aficionados of tauromaquia around the world. There remains only one question—briefly please, our time is running out: What can you tell us about the bull, the last bull that he killed and that killed him?"

"The bull's name was Islero. He wasn't born on an island, so I don't know why the people who bred him called him that. It could have been Manolete's name, because Manolete was certainly an islero, a solitarío. He was alone. No one who knew him could fail to have that impression, and it showed in the melancholy face we have seen in so many pictures. But you asked me about the bull. What do we know about bulls? Very little. He was strong, as all bulls are, and fierce, as all bulls from the Miura ranch are. He was brave. But he had something no other bull had or will ever have. He knew how to kill Manolete, el monstro. If bulls had knowledge, if they knew their own tragic history, Islero would be their greatest hero."

The trumpet music came on again and Federico turned off the radio.

*

Martha and Bruno came home long after Pira and Zita and Federico had gone to sleep. It was Tristan's barking that woke him.

"Shhh!"

That was Martha.

Tristan's claws scratched the tiles in the hallway and his tail knocked against Pira's door.

"Shhh!"

That was Bruno. The sound was sharper, shorter than Martha's. Pira didn't like it when Bruno got mad at Tristan. The door opened and both his parents came in. The room was dark, so he could barely see them. Bruno sat down heavily on the edge of his bed.

"Pira. My friend," he said. Pira was surprised to hear his father pronouncing his name in the Mexican way. He liked it. Then he felt Bruno's hand on his shoulder, shaking him gently as if to wake him.

"Yes," he said, to let Bruno know that he was awake, and in his "yes" there was also the meaning of "Yes, I am your friend." He had never thought of himself as Bruno's friend, and Bruno had never called him that, but he liked it.

Bruno removed his hand from Pira's shoulder, bent down to take off one of his shoes, and threw it against the wall. It hit the wall hard and dropped to the floor.

"For Christ's sake, Bruno!" Martha said. Her voice frightened Pira. It wasn't loud, but it was angry.

Bruno took off his other shoe. He threw it on the floor. Then he reached for Pira's hand and put it to his lips and kissed it. Pira smelled whisky on his breath.

"Your father is *drunk*," Martha said. The way she said the last word sounded very mean. Then they left the room and closed the door.

A few moments later Martha came back in and sat down on the edge of Pira's bed.

"I'm sorry we barged in like that," she said. "I'm sorry we disturbed you. Were you frightened?"

He shook his head.

"Bruno was drunk, that's why he acted that way. We had an argument on the way home. He was hurt and I was angry. But now everything's all right. Do you think you can sleep now?"

"Yes."

"Did you have a nice day with Zita and Federico?"

"Yes."

"You can tell me about it tomorrow."

"OK."

"Good night."

She kissed him. Pira smelled liquor on her breath too, and the sweet smell of her makeup. She closed the door. But it didn't close all the way—a draft made it open a little. Martha must not have noticed. If she had noticed, she would have gone back and closed the door. She wouldn't have wanted Pira to hear her and Bruno talking. Their conversation was private, he could tell. They were half quarreling, half discussing, keeping their voices close to a whisper so he couldn't hear. But he could.

"You shouldn't have called me that," Bruno said.

"Called you what?"

"A coward. You have no right."

"You were afraid. Why can't you admit it?"

"There was danger. That man had a gun. But you . . . You had no right to your courage. Think about it. The risk was too great."

She fell silent. Then she spoke again.

"You always argue so well. Your arguments stop me. But this time you didn't stop me, and I'm glad. I'm glad that girl is safe."

Bruno said nothing.

"You don't act," Martha said. "You talk about action, plan action, write about action, but when action is needed, you don't act. Remember that burro?" Her voice was sounding mean again.

"What burro?"

"Shortly after we met. We were out riding, and there was a man beating his burro, brutally. I just had to stop him, so I spurred my horse. Next thing I knew, you caught up with me and grabbed my arm and said something—I will never forget it: 'Spontaneous action is futile.' It sounded so knowing, so philosophical, it stopped me. But you were white as a sheet. You were scared."

"I remember."

"That's what I mean."

The draft knocked the latch against the lock. Martha got up and quietly shut the door. Pira listened, but they had stopped talking.

Pira hadn't understood all their words, but he understood enough to feel sorry for Bruno. Martha had called him a coward. That hurt. How could Bruno be a coward? It wasn't fair of Martha to call him that.

*

In the moment when Pira turned his head he saw a skull shining in the darkness. He wanted to scream but couldn't get a sound out. The skull's cheeks were narrow, the forehead wide, the top of the head and the chin hard clean curves like the edge of a plate. The face, without eyes, nose, or mouth, was a pale silvery white, like water lit from inside. It glowed. His body turned cold with fear.

Then he realized what he was looking at. It was his new mirror. Martha had recently hung it in his room. The frame with its carved trees and birds was invisible in the dark, and the glass was filled with moonlight. He looked away. There, in the window, hung the moon like a huge silver ball. The zapote tree stood black underneath it.

His heart stopped pounding. All was well. But now he was curious. Would the skull still be there if he looked? He looked: It was there. He knew it was nothing but moonlight filling the shape of a curved piece of glass, but at the same time it was evil, and he was scared again.

He got out of bed, turning his back on the skull, and opened the door to the patio and stepped outside. The roar of the crickets surrounded him. The tiles were cool beneath his feet. A breeze stirred the leaves of the zapote tree, each one of them black with a streak of silver, so that the whole tree appeared to be in motion. There was a deeper blackness behind the leaves, inside the tree. This wasn't the friendly zapote tree he knew by daylight. He lowered his eyes, and then closed them. The darkness was complete now, but this darkness was close to him. The feeling of the tiles under his feet was bright and clear, almost like seeing, as if he could see through his feet. There was nothing to see, but still, he could feel his way down through the softness of stone, down into the darkness of the stone world. It wasn't scary there. Didn't trees do that? Under the earth was a world where trees grew upside down. Just as birds made nests in the branches, other animals made their nests in the roots. Maybe there was an upside-down sky down there, black at night with a moon and stars, and blue with a bright sun by day. Maybe it was daytime there now. An opposite world.

Then he thought of the mirror and the skull in the mirror, and that brought up the memory of the mirror in *Snow White and the Seven Dwarfs*. That mirror was terrible. The way the Queen's face changed when she looked into it. The way she soared out into the night with her horrible eyes and teeth and laughing mouth. He remembered burying his face in Martha's lap. Later she said many children had screamed in the theater.

A soft sound nearby caught his attention. He opened his eyes and turned his head and saw a pair of bright yellow eyes in the shadow cast by the low patio wall. For a moment his whole body felt cold, but then he heard the soft sound of Tristan's tail thumping on the floor and knew that the eyes were Tristan's, so he wasn't afraid. He went to him and sat down next to him and patted his head.

"Tristan," he whispered. "My friend."

Still wagging his tail, Tristan whined.

Poor Tristan. He had been sad for weeks. Pira thought it was mean of the man who owned the little white dog not to let Tristan meet her at least once.

"Pobrecito," he whispered. He didn't want Martha and Bruno to hear him. "Te queremos todos." He always talked to Tristan in Spanish. "We all love you. Don't be sad."

Tristan understood. He rolled onto his side so that Pira could scratch his chest, and Pira lay down next to him and petted him for a while and eventually fell asleep.

When he woke it was still dark. He was shivering. He went back to his room and took off his pajamas, which were damp from the dew, and got back into bed. It took a while to feel warm again. The skull in the mirror was no longer shining. He asked God to let Tristan meet the little white dog. Then he thought of Bruno and how Martha had called him a coward. It wasn't fair. He didn't want to think about how Bruno felt. He thought of Federico. Federico was macho. When Pira grew up, he wanted to be like Federico.

10

He woke with a burning pain in his foot and screamed. But it wasn't a scream, he could barely hear his voice. He tried to sit. He couldn't. The pain widened and deepened. He tried to call Martha:

"Ma . . ."

His tongue couldn't form the rest of her name.

The pain ate into his foot—as if it had teeth, as if it hated him.

He tried to move his leg. It moved, but just a little. He couldn't get out of bed. The pain was getting worse. He called Martha again, almost voiceless:

"Maaa . . ."

Silence.

What if nobody heard him? That was a terrible What If. But the door opened and Martha came in.

"What's the matter, Peter?"

He moaned.

She lifted his body. His head fell back. His eyes, too, fell back. He saw the window doubled and blue morning light behind the bars.

Martha lifted his head. "Peter! Speak to me!" He saw a double Martha.

"Bruno!"

Bruno was already hurrying into the room, in his pajamas. He too appeared double. He touched Pira's forehead with his cool hand.

"He's in pain, Bruno!"

"Where?"

"Where does it hurt, Pira? Speak to us, please!"

With great effort, he said: "My foot."

Bruno yanked the blanket off his body and swiped something off the bed. There, on the floor, doubled like everything else, lay the black, shining, hook-like form of a scorpion.

"Oh my God!" Martha said.

Bruno rushed out of the room. Was he scared? But he came back with a sandal in his hand and banged the scorpion as hard as he could, three, four, five times—so hard.

Pira wanted to stop him, but the scorpion was already smashed and broken.

"I'll go call Amann," Bruno said, and he hurried out of the room.

Amann sometimes played chess with Bruno. Why was he calling him?

Martha put her hand where the scorpion had stung him.

"Does this hurt? Does this make it feel better?"

He shook his head.

"Amann is on his way," Martha said. "He knows how to help you."

That meant she and Bruno didn't know how to help him. That frightened him. He cried, and Martha cried with him and spoke to him, stroking his body:

"Oh, my Peter. My sweet, good boy. You'll feel better soon, I promise. I'm so sorry." As if it were her fault.

But Amann would help him. Usually when Bruno spoke about Amann, he smiled as if Amann was funny. Amann did this, Amann said that. Amann is a lousy driver. Amann almost drove us off the cliff. But now he had called him for help.

Bruno came in with Zita. Pira was still seeing double.

"Pobrecito," Zita said.

She was carrying a pail and several towels. There was water and ice in the pail.

"Duele," she said, "pero no es peligroso." It hurts but it's not dangerous. That was good. He felt less scared now.

She showed Martha how to wrap a piece of ice in a towel and dip the towel in the ice water and put it on top of the sore. Then she told her to do the same with the other foot and on his forehead.

"Don't be afraid, Pirito. Everything will be all right."

The cold made the pain worse, but then it was less again. He thought about Amann. Amann was on his way. In a car. Lousy driver, off a cliff. But no, Amann would help him, Martha had said so. Just thinking of Amann helped. The pain wasn't so bad now. How would Amann help? Maybe with magic. Bruno didn't believe in magic. If Amann helped Pira with magic it would prove that magic existed. Real magic, not like Sándor's magic tricks. A fly settled on the wall by the foot of his bed—one fly, not doubled. It was too big for a fly. It was looking at him. He cried out and turned his head away.

"Peter, what's the matter?"

Martha. Why was she so far away, when she was sitting next to him? Green eyes. Why did she have green eyes? They looked like marbles held to the light. And Zita was moving too fast for Zita. Out the door and in, out and in again. She was walking, but too fast. They were all moving so strangely. Like puppets. Something was stuck in his throat. He tried to cough it out. Martha helped him to sit up.

Bruno's hand came sailing through the air, getting bigger, took off the wet towel, and felt his forehead.

"I'll get a thermometer."

Bruno—that was Bruno. Why did he have antlers on his head? Like Bambi's father. He left the room. Too fast. So there *was* magic! But it wasn't good magic. He wished it weren't true, but it *was* true. Someone was making magic, and Bruno didn't know, *couldn't* know it. Under a spell! They all were.

"Bruno, look at his color!"

Someone was singing behind him:

"ooooooooo"

Someone was climbing upward slowly, step by step, with a deep bass voice:

"OOOOOOOOO"

Someone was scaring him, *wanted* to scare him. The voice was ringing in the middle of his back now, and was climbing.

Bruno came back with a thermometer, shook it, put it under Pira's tongue:

"Keep it there. Don't open your mouth."

A knocking began, like a fist pounding on a door. It was inside him, inside his chest. His head hurt. His face felt as if it was being held near a fire. The voice was still swelling and climbing. It was a man, a bad man, an enemy, climbing out of a well.

Didn't Martha hear it? Bruno? They didn't! They couldn't! Amann. Amann would help him. Everything became dark. In the darkness, Pira could see behind him. Dimly he saw the singing man, darker than the darkness, shrouded in a long black cloak, wearing a black top hat. He was climbing. He was the voice:

"OOOOOOOOO"

"Qué pasó?"

That was Federico. Where was he? The light was back but Pira couldn't move his eyes. They floated and slid to the side.

"Lo picó un alacrán," Zita said.

Alacrán	Scorpion

The two languages soared off in separate directions, but the singing voice in the middle was a third language, with only one word. It was climbing. It was going to his heart. It wanted his heart. The thing was still stuck in his throat. He was gasping. Martha slapped his chest, then his back. Now he could see the room again, Martha, Bruno, Zita, Federico.

"Where the hell is Amann!"

That was Bruno. Bruno was mad at Amann. Zita left the room and came back with more ice water. The bell rang. Tristan barked. Zita hurried outside to open the gate. A little man in a blue robe and wearing a tall pointed hat, blue with silver stars, rushed in. Amann! He was so little, he didn't look like Amann. But he was speaking German, so maybe he was Amann. He put a black bag on the bed. Bruno took the thermometer out of Pira's mouth to show it to Amann, but Amann was in a hurry. He waved Bruno's hand away. He opened the bag and pulled out—oh good, a magic wand!—and touched Pira's forehead with it. Bing!

Suddenly he was on a beach in the sunlight, digging, digging, with a small iron shovel by the edge of the sea. Groundwater rose in the hole he was making, and out of the water came a hand and an arm, a lady's arm like the arm of the Lady of the Lake in the book about King Arthur that his first father David had sent from New York. Wasn't she supposed to be holding a sword? Gently but firmly her hand pulled him into the water and under the earth.

The next moment he was in a small, dimly lit cave with a low ceiling. There, looking straight at him with little bright eyes, was a fox. His big ears stood up and were turned toward him.

"I'm your friend," the fox said, speaking only with his thoughts. "I'll protect you. I'm not strong, but I know many things. Come with me."

So Pira followed him through a tunnel, crawling on his hands and knees.

"Hurry," the fox said, looking over his shoulder, "otherwise they'll all die."

The tunnel led into Arón's house, and there was Arón kneeling on the stone floor in front of a big black crucifix, clasping his hands in prayer the way his mother told him to after she whipped him. The crucifix was taller than any crucifix he had seen in Arón's house. The ceiling was higher too. Where was he? The answer came like an explosion: under the ground!

"Hurry!" the fox said, but Pira didn't want to leave Arón behind. "Come with us, the fox is our friend!" But Arón didn't hear him. The fox was running out onto the street and looking over his shoulder, saying, "Hurry! Hurry! Or they'll all die!" and Pira followed.

There was a happy urgency in the fox's words, not fearful at all, so he knew that the fox wasn't afraid and that he knew how to keep ahead of the danger—just slightly ahead, which was why they had to hurry—and as long as Pira did what the fox said, all would be well, and if he didn't, or if he lost sight of the fox, something terrible would happen to him and to everyone else.

Where were they going? They weren't in the street any longer. He could see the outlines of hills. It was getting darker, and now there was nothing more to be seen, not the fox either, and something was moving nearby in the darkness. It was frightening, not knowing what it was. He called for his mother and this time he was able to say her whole name and it came out loud, but she wasn't there and neither were Bruno or Zita, only this dark thing moving near him on all

sides and underneath him, smooth and flowing, until he realized it
was a horse, and not just one horse but lots of them running together.
He was riding one of them, holding on to its strong neck with both
arms. He wasn't so scared now. He could see the horses dimly, rolling like waves and whispering wherever their bodies touched, and a
rumbling of hooves underneath. He liked that their bodies touched
as they ran, and he didn't mind being swept along as they ran like a
river with rolling waves, a river of horses galloping downhill, eagerly,
happily, toward something still farther down. Where were they
going? Where was the fox? Where were his parents and Zita? The
house, the garden, his room? What if they had all died? He screamed.
No one answered, no one came.

But someone did hear him. It was the fox.

"Listen and attend," he said.

Pira couldn't see him, but having heard him, he realized the
fox had been with him all along, running alongside the horses or
maybe flying in the dimly lit darkness.

He listened, he attended.

Something had changed. The horses weren't horses any longer
and he wasn't riding. Instead of rumbling hooves there were thousands of insect legs racing along in the dark with a rustling sound.
He saw them dimly as if by moonlight and they were ants. They
were scary, but strange too, so strange they were almost funny. They
were running upright like people. He recognized soldier ants by their
armor and by the pincer-like weapons on the sides of their heads, and
worker ants by their serapes and huaraches. Some of them had sombreros on their heads. He himself was running along with the ant
people, fast, fast, as if he were an ant, but he wasn't. He was himself.

"Hurry, hurry!" the fox said, and they were all hurrying, and
now he could see where they were going: to the Cathedral.

*

He woke in his parents' bed. Martha was practicing in the next room. Zita was sitting beside him. She touched the back of her hand to his forehead and smiled.

"Your fever is gone. You were very sick, but you're fine now."

She stroked his cheek.

"How good. Thank God." She made the sign of the cross over her chest.

They were silent together. That felt good. "What did you dream?"

He didn't know. Vaguely he remembered something.

"I was outside, I think. Under the ground. It wasn't a dream."

"I'll call your parents."

"Is Federico still here?"

"He had to go. He left yesterday morning."

That surprised him. Federico had been in the room just a little while ago.

"He made something for you."

She went to the dresser and came back with a sheet of paper and gave it to Pira. It was a picture of the two volcanoes, Iztaccihuatl and snow-capped Popocatepetl, with green hills and three red-roofed houses at the bottom, a horse next to one of them, and two flattened-out v's representing birds with wide wings, maybe eagles, in the blue sky. Beneath the picture were the words "QUE ESTÉS BIEN MI AMIGO." May you be well my friend. Federico could write now.

"I'll go get your parents."

Zita left the room. Martha's music stopped. Doors opened and closed. First Martha, then Bruno came into the room. They looked happy.

"Where's Amann?"

"He couldn't stay," Martha said. "He had to see other patients."

That reminded Pira of the way she used to explain Santa Claus's disappearance after he brought presents.

"He's a doctor?"

"Yes, didn't you know?"

"No. You just said he would help me. He's a funny doctor."

"What do you mean?"

"His pointy hat. His white stick. I thought it was a magic wand!"

"That didn't really happen, Peter," Bruno said.

"But it did," Pira said.

"Not really," Bruno said. "It's called a hallucination. It's like a dream. It feels real while it happens, but it isn't."

"But I saw him. He came with a black bag and pulled out a white stick and touched me on the head with it."

"You did see him," Bruno said. "He really was carrying a black bag, but he wasn't wearing a pointed hat and what he pulled out of the bag was a syringe in a white case. He took out the syringe and gave you two injections, one for the scorpion sting and one for something called anaphylactic shock."

"Anna?"

"Anaphylactic shock."

"That happened to me?"

"Yes."

"Like a shock, an electric shock?"

"Sort of, but stronger."

Pira thought of the current that ran through his body when he put his tongue to the bar in his window. If this shock was stronger, it must have hurt a lot. He was glad he couldn't remember it.

"Did I faint?"

"You did," Martha said. "For a moment we thought you had died. It was terrible. You could hardly breathe . . ."

"I remember that."

"You were delirious."

"What's that?"

"You saw things that weren't there."

"I saw antlers on Bruno's head."

Bruno and Martha looked at each other and burst out laughing. Bruno put his hand on top of his head.

"It's not true!" Martha said to Bruno, laughing but earnest at the same time, as if to convince him that he didn't have antlers. Maybe they were joking.

"Are you sure?" Bruno said, feeling the air over his head, as if looking for antlers.

"You'll just have to believe me," Martha said.

They laughed. Pira hadn't seen them laugh together like that, so happily, for a long time. Finally when they were just smiling again, Martha said: "Thanks for the laugh, Peter. That was funny."

"Why?"

"Bruno with antlers. It's funny."

"Like Bambi's father," Pira said.

"Oh," she said, her expression turning serious, "I didn't think of that."

"Were you afraid for me?" Bruno asked.

"What do you mean?"

"Did you think I might die?"

Pira nodded. He was embarrassed, and he was starting to remember some other things. The fox, the ants who looked like people. When Martha asked him if there was anything else he remembered, he said no, even though she was asking sincerely. She wouldn't laugh, and neither would Bruno. But they wouldn't believe the things Pira remembered. They would say they were dreams or hallucinations and didn't *really* happen. But they did happen. He was awake when they happened. He would keep those things secret. Maybe he would tell Zita.

*

Two days later Mr. Riley came by without calling first. He rang the bell and was there. Martha and Bruno didn't like it. They didn't like it because Bruno was working and Martha was practicing, and because they didn't like Mr. Riley anyway. They were nice to him only because he was Chris's father and Chris was Pira's friend.

The three of them sat down at the table on the patio. Pira lay down on the lawn to read in his *Golden Book Encyclopedia*, and that was how he heard their conversation.

Bruno asked Mr. Riley if he wanted a drink, and Mr. Riley said he would appreciate a whisky if he had it. Martha went inside and came out with a bottle of whisky and bottles of beer for herself and Bruno and glasses and an ashtray. She filled the glasses and then they raised their glasses and said "Cheers," and then they talked.

"I heard what happened to Peter," Mr. Riley said. "One of my maids told me. I don't think she knows your maid, but your maid must have told another maid, and so on. I call it the servant grapevine. News travels like wildfire that way."

He looked over to where Pira was reading.

"I see he's all right now. I'm glad. I heard he nearly died. Damn! That was no ordinary scorpion."

"It was an allergic reaction," Bruno said. "We were lucky we found a doctor in time."

"Thank God," Mr. Riley said.

"Yes, thank God," Martha said.

Bruno didn't thank God.

"That's one reason I came, just to see how he was and maybe help out. If you needed money for medical treatment, for instance. As you know, I have means. I hope you don't mind."

"We don't mind, Mr. Riley," Martha said, "but as you can see, the crisis is over. Thank you for the offer, though. It's very kind of you."

"That's OK. It's nothing."

He pulled a cigarette from a pack of Camels, and Bruno lit it with his lighter.

"There's something else. That charro you slapped the other night . . ." He was talking to Martha.

Pira looked up from his painting and saw his parents sitting unusually straight and still.

"I heard this through the servant grapevine as well. I own that nightclub, everyone there works for me, except for the prostitutes— they have their own boss, I'm not a pimp. Now that charro you slapped, he's one of my men. He was there on his off hours, and what he does on his off hours is his business. But I fired him anyway. That may have been a mistake—I'll explain why in a moment—but I did it. He shouldn't have slapped that girl around in front of all those people. It casts an unpleasant light on me. And that he did it in front of you offends me because it offended you." He was still talking to Martha, as if Bruno wasn't there. "Now, *your* slapping *him*, that was *your* business too. I'm not blaming you. You were protecting the girl, I understand. I just want you to know, you were very, very fortunate to come out of that incident alive. Mexican men are extremely touchy where their honor is concerned. And a charro . . . I don't think you understand this country as well as I do. A charro would sooner die, or kill, than allow himself to be dishonored by a woman, and a gringa at that. Which is what you did, in front of dozens of people. I guess he was too shocked to react. Your husband was wise to pull you out of the place, grab a taxi, and leave."

Martha looked at Bruno briefly. Then she glanced over at Pira, who pretended to be interested only in his book. Mr. Riley drained his glass, and Bruno refilled it.

"Thank you," Mr. Riley said. "Thank you very much."

He was talking to both of them now.

"I'm here, basically—mainly—because I'm concerned for your safety. A humiliated charro is more dangerous than a rabid dog.

I've ordered this man to leave town within twenty-four hours, threatened him, but he hasn't left yet, and he could take revenge. He's capable of it."

"What do you think we should do?" Bruno asked.

"I don't think there's much you *can* do, except maybe leave town for a few weeks . . ."

"That's not possible," Martha said.

"Of course not. I understand. No, my suggestion is . . . *I* can do something."

Pira too was now sitting upright and still. He was no longer pretending to read. He didn't want to miss anything.

"If you will allow me, I will post two charros in front of your house, day and night, for a while. They'll take turns, two at a time, like sentries. You can use one of them as a bodyguard when either one of you leaves the house. Peter too. Just to be sure. Give it two or three weeks. Meanwhile I'll see to it that this man leaves the state of Morelos. If he doesn't . . . But he will."

He leaned back and dragged on his cigarette. Martha and Bruno said nothing. Martha was frowning and looking away from Mr. Riley and Bruno. She looked angry.

"Think about it," Mr. Riley said. "But not for too long. Sleep on it, and call me tomorrow. I'm not asking for anything in return. I feel responsible, on account of this man having worked for me, and because you're the parents of my son's good friend."

After Mr. Riley left, Bruno said: "I think we should take him up on his offer."

"Really?" Martha said. "I was thinking the opposite. I was wondering, why does he want to scare us? So we'll accept his protection? I don't like it. I don't like *him*."

"I don't like him either. But I don't mind being under his protection. He means us no harm, I'm sure of that. My problem is with his charros. They represent everything I'm against. They're thugs, they're oppressors. They terrorize people who get in his way. He uses them to intimidate the workers on his hacienda. On the other hand— he's probably right about that man, he could be dangerous to us."

"You really think so?"

"I do. He's out of a job, dishonored by foreigners in front of his countrymen. Imagine how he feels."

She thought about it. Then she looked over at Pira and smiled.

"You've been listening to everything, haven't you?"

"Yes."

"Do you have any questions?"

He did have questions, but he wasn't sure they were the kind of questions she was thinking of. He decided to ask anyway.

"Wasn't Zapata a charro?"

"You're right!" Bruno exclaimed. "You're so right. They're not all the same. There are good charros, I'm sure."

Pira tried to imagine the slapped man's feelings. He must be ashamed. It must be terrible for a charro to feel ashamed. Charros had to be proud.

"Do you have any other questions?" Martha asked.

"Why did you slap him?"

"Because he was slapping a girl."

"But it was dangerous. Charros have guns."

"I wasn't thinking about that. I just wanted to help her."

"Maybe you shouldn't have slapped him."

"Maybe," she said.

"Maybe Bruno was right."

"About what?"

"That you shouldn't have slapped him."

"How do you know that?"

Pira felt himself blushing.

"I heard it through your door."

"I'm sorry you had to hear that."

"I wasn't eavesdropping."

"I know. The door must have been open."

They were silent together for a moment. Martha looked at Bruno again.

"Let's let them guard us for a short while," she said. "Or till Riley knows the man has left the state."

Pira's heart leapt. "You mean we'll have charros in front of the house?"

"Yes," she said, "starting tomorrow."

11

The next day began like a miracle.

The bell rang early in the morning and Zita let the person in and called Pira: "Pirito, come, look who's here!"

Pira came out of his room and there was Arón on the patio.

"Come with me to the canyon," Arón said with excitement. "I want to show you something. It's a surprise. You'll see."

As if nothing had happened! Pira could barely speak: "I have to ask my parents."

"Why? They always let you. Come quickly, you'll see. It's crazy. Es una cosa loca."

"I don't know if they'll let me."

"What happened?"

"A lot."

"Are they punishing you?"

"No. I'll tell you later. I'll be right back. Wait."

He ran into Martha's study. She was at her secretary writing a letter.

"Martha, Arón is here!"

"Really!"

"He's not mad at me anymore!"

"That's wonderful!"

She went out to welcome Arón: "Que bueno, Aroncito. I'm happy to see you!" She leaned over to hug him.

"He wants to show me something," Pira said in English. "He says it's a surprise. Can I go?"

"Where?"

"To the canyon. Please don't say no. We'll be careful. I promise!"

She thought about it. She wasn't sure. "I don't know. Let's ask Bruno."

She went to Bruno's office and knocked and went in and closed the door. Pira heard their voices murmuring inside. Then Martha came out again.

"Bruno says you should go. I agree with him. It's important Arón and you make up. But be very very careful, OK?"

"OK."

"Come right back after you see what Arón wants to show you."

"And the man? The charro?"

"Don't worry. I'm sure there's no danger. He doesn't know where you play, doesn't even know what you look like."

*

They walked to the canyon, their steps long, the way big boys and men walk when they're in a hurry. Arón said his uncle had told him about how Pira had been stung by an alacrán. His uncle had also told him about the thing they were going to see in the canyon. Then they ran. Both of them were laughing, for no reason. When they were out of breath, they stopped running and walked on, panting. Pira was grinning with pleasure. Arón had forgiven him. He was happy. So happy! Now he wanted to tell Arón about the scorpion. About how he had almost died. The terrible voice that said OOOOO. The other strange things, the hallucinations. And how Bruno spanked him. Especially that. He wanted Arón to know how it hurt. Then he realized he couldn't impress Arón with that. Chris maybe. But that was for later. Now he was happy.

"Look!" Arón said, pointing up at the sky, and Pira stopped to look. High above, vultures were circling. Then Arón started trotting again. "Come on!" He was leading. He didn't usually do that.

They reached the stream. Arón was barefoot and Pira had sandals on. He didn't want to get them wet, but Arón was already splashing through the stream, so Pira followed him. They crossed the big meadow, passed through a cloud of tiny mosquitoes. The meadow smelled of grass and cow dung. A group of cows lay chewing in the shade of a big tree, turning their heads to watch the boys as they passed.

They came to the canyon.

"Careful," Arón said, motioning with his hand for Pira to slow his steps. He didn't have to do that, Pira was already being careful. But there was something down there Arón wanted him to see, so he had to step nearer the dangerous edge.

"If you lie down it's safer," Arón said.

They lay down on their bellies and inched forward until they could look down to the bottom of the cliff. There a swarm of vultures were bunched together, their black bodies pushing and shoving, digging and pulling at something. Pira couldn't see what it was at first but then he saw that it was a bull. He was dead, that was good. His black head was on the ground, lying on its side with its mouth open and one long white curved horn jutting out.

Every few moments one of the birds hopped aside to gobble down something too big for its small beak, and instantly another one jumped in to take its place. Many vultures stood nearby, their small heads turned sideways, waiting for their turn. They looked a lot like German men with their hands behind their backs. Those who *were* eating, on the other hand, ate like pigs. Pira had to giggle, but then he realized Arón wanted to see everything all the way to the end, so he watched with him.

How polite they were! There weren't any fights like there would be with dogs. They were quiet. All you could hear was the wet smacking sound of their eating. A large vulture swooped down into the middle of the swarm, scaring the other birds so that they hopped aside, flapping their wings. Even then they made no noise except for some rustling.

Now Pira could see the bull's body. His hind legs and part of his back were just bones, the skin and meat were torn off. The newcomer grabbed a piece of skin on the bull's belly and yanked and tore the skin loose, peeling it back until you could see the ribs. The bird looked very strong. Immediately several other vultures dove in and drilled their heads into a mass of blue and pink organs beneath the ribs.

"How did he die?" Pira asked.

"He was sick, so the man who owned him came with some friends on horses and chased him off the edge of the cliff."

"Why?"

"Because he was sick. My uncle told me."

Pira was shocked. Why did the men kill the bull that way? Even if he couldn't be cured, someone could have shot him the way Bruno shot Tonta, the crazy dog. He hoped the bull had died right away. He wished this bull had been as brave and as strong as Islero. The men would be dead and he would be alive.

"Let's go down there," Arón said.

That seemed impossible, but Arón knew a path that went down the wall of the cliff where it wasn't so steep and you could hold on to the branches of bushes and small trees. Most of the vultures hopped away, spreading their giant wings for balance as the boys approached. When they came nearer, all the vultures got scared and flew away, stretching their necks and flapping their wings hard and fast. Some of them threw up before rising into the air. But they didn't fly far. They sailed above the boys and the corpse with their wings spread, and very high above them were others. The distant ones looked like Federico's drawings of birds in the sky.

The boys went to look more closely at the carcass. It smelled bad
near the backside because there was lots of poop there, inside and
outside the skeleton. Hundreds of flies were buzzing and crawling
all over the poop and the bloody meat and especially on a large
gray bag half filled with a wet mass of green and pale slime that the
boys agreed must be the stomach. Pira peered in through the ribs
and thought he could see the heart, a purple lump of bloody meat
with limp tubes hanging out of it. There were flies on the heart too.

"I have to go home," Pira said. "We can come back tomorrow."

Climbing up the path felt more dangerous than it had on the way
down, but they reached the top without falling. On the way home,
Pira told Arón how his mother had slapped a charro who worked for
Chris's father because that charro had slapped a girl and how Chris's
father had ordered the man to leave the state of Morelos so that he
wouldn't shoot Martha and that just to make sure she was safe he was
going to post charros in front of the house, and maybe they were there
already. That was so exciting for both of them that they ran most of
the way.

Two charros were standing in front of the house when they got
there, one on either side of the garden gate, so grand to look at in their
black suits with silver lace and bright silk bow ties and wide sombreros and boots with silver spurs and especially their cartridge belts and
their guns in holsters by their sides. It made the boys shy just to see
them from a distance. Their horses, one shiny black and the other gold
with a white mane and tail, had lassos attached to their saddles, and
their reins were slung over the spear-shaped spikes of the iron fence.
The boys slowed their steps as they came near. Pira was unsure what to
do. Should he say "Buenos días"? Should he tell them who he was, and
who his friend was? Could he just open the gate and walk in without
looking at them? But one of the charros said "Hola" as if he knew him
and opened the gate for him, and Pira said "Gracias." At that moment,
walking through the gate with Arón, he felt as if he were in a dream.

*

When Pira told Martha about the dead bull, the first thing she said was, "Did you touch it?" He said he hadn't. "And you?" she asked Arón, "did you touch it?" He shook his head. "Are you sure?" she asked both of them. They were sure. "Don't touch any part of it. You could get sick."

"Can we go back tomorrow," Pira asked, "just to look?"

"I don't like the idea," Martha said. "But I'll talk to Bruno about it."

At dinner that evening Bruno said it was all right to just look at the vultures and the dead bull, but that climbing down the side of the cliff was dangerous and they shouldn't do it again.

"But we found a way down, a path. We're not climbing, we're walking.

"Are you sure?"

"I'm sure."

*

That night as Pira dropped off to sleep he remembered a terrible thing he had seen the night he was bit by the scorpion. It was just a flash but he saw the whole horror. It was the Ant Queen, chewing. In the Cathedral. Her black bristling arms, her long black hands scooping worker ants, warrior ants, mother ants, baby ants, into her mouth, which was like a hole. He screamed and was wide awake. Martha came in.

"What happened, Pira?"

"I had a nightmare."

She put her hand on his forehead.

"Everything's all right, Peter. You're safe. Would you like me to sit with you?"

"Yes."

She sat down on the side of his bed.

"Would you like me to stay until you're asleep?"

"Yes."

He turned onto his side. Martha drew the blanket over his shoulders. Under the blanket he folded his hands the way Zita had taught him and closed his eyes. Somewhere the memory of the Ant Queen was waiting for him. He was scared again.

"What's the matter, Peter? What's frightening you?"

"Nothing."

"Is it the bull?"

"No. I like thinking of that."

It was true. He thought of the bull in the canyon and the flies. Those were real flies. The ants in the Cathedral weren't real. They were like the calaveras in the big green Posada book. Dressed like people. That couldn't be real. The Ant Queen wasn't real. She couldn't be. She was a hallucination.

All the while Martha was next to him and he felt safe. She would stay until he was asleep. If he had a nightmare he would call her and she would come back.

His thoughts returned to the bull in the canyon. That bull was Islero. Not really, of course, because Islero had died in Spain, but he could imagine it. When Bruno and Martha and Federico and Zita were talking about Manolete's death, they never mentioned Islero. Only the man on the radio talked about him. Pira wanted Islero to be famous.

Islero was dead and now the vultures were eating him and Pira and Arón had seen it and no one else. Tomorrow they would go again. He loved Islero.

*

The charros guarded the house for nearly a week. In the afternoon of the first day, two new charros came, one on a brown horse and the other on a white one, and the first two charros left. Then after dark two more came and replaced the second pair. The next morning the first two came back. So there were the morning charros and the afternoon and the nighttime charros.

Martha offered the men beer to drink and chairs to sit on, but they said that wouldn't look right because they were guards and guards stand and don't drink. Zita greeted them shyly in passing when she went in and out of the house, and the charros mumbled "Buenas," turning their faces away as if they too were shy. Bruno they greeted politely by touching the brims of their hats and saying "Buenos días, Señor." But they talked with the boys and even let them feed their horses apples.

People on the street stopped to look and wonder why the charros were there. Word got around and more people came to look, especially children. Pretty soon Pira was living in a famous house. Arón, too, felt proud walking in and out of the house. It was almost like being in a palace.

*

The day after the charros arrived, Mr. Riley came by to touch base, as he put it, with Bruno and Martha, and he brought Chris in his car. It was the first time the three boys had been together in a long time. Pira and Arón wanted to take Chris to the canyon, but Mr. Riley thought that Gutierrez, one of the charros, should go with them, just to be safe, and Bruno thought that was a good idea too. So they went, running most of the way, with the charro cantering behind them. He followed them through the stream and across the meadow to the edge of the cliff.

The vultures were gone. So was the bull, except for his skeleton. The top of the skull was still covered with black skin and shaggy hair, but the eyes were gone, their sockets rimmed with dried blood, and where the nose and mouth had been, there were just bones and white teeth.

At first Señor Gutierrez wouldn't allow the boys to go down the steep path. It was too dangerous, he said. But when Pira told him that he and Arón had already done it with Bruno's permission, and that this was what they had come for, to see the calavera from up close, the charro gave in. He told them to be very, very careful, or else he would get into trouble. He stayed on top, standing next to his horse, letting it nibble grass while he waited.

The first thing Chris wanted to do when they reached the bull was kick his head off so they could take it home.

"Why?" Pira asked.

"As a trophy," he said. Un trofeo.

"What's a trofeo?" Arón wanted to know.

"It's the head of a wild animal. You take it home to show that you killed it. We have the head of a zebra over our fireplace. My father shot it in Africa."

"But we didn't kill this bull," Arón said.

"We can pretend," Chris said.

"Someone else killed him," Arón said.

"So?"

"He's not ours," Pira said.

Chris tossed his straw hat like a lasso, meaning to make it land on the point of the horn, but it missed and dropped into the grass. The three of them felt uncomfortable now. To avoid looking at each other, they stared at the massive skull at their feet. Then Arón squatted down to look at it more closely.

"Look at all the ants," he said.

Hundreds of small red ants, different from the larger black ants in Pira's garden, were running in and out of the eye sockets and the holes where the nostrils had been. There were ants crawling in and out of a crack in the middle of the forehead too.

Those coming out of the eyes and nose were carrying tiny pieces of something that Chris figured must be the brain, but it was hard to tell what it was. You couldn't see anything through the eyeholes, and looking through the opening where the spine went into the head all you could see was light shining through the holes in the front.

They walked around the skeleton. The poop that had smelled so bad the day before had dried in the sun and hardly smelled at all anymore. But hundreds of flies were still crawling on it. There was dried blood on some of the bones, but mostly they were white. Chris noticed a row of thin bones standing up on the spine near the shoulders like the bones on the back of a swordfish. He wondered if they were ribs. Pira didn't think so, and Arón had no opinion.

Señor Gutierrez called down from the cliff. It was time to leave. Climbing the steep path, they held onto the branches of shrubs for support. "Cuidado!" Señor Gutierrez said several times. Of course they were careful, he didn't have to say that.

They walked home this time, instead of running. Señor Gutierrez talked with them on the way, riding slowly at their pace. He had heard them arguing about the bull's head. Properly cleaned and mounted it would be a pretty thing for the house, he said, una cosa bonita.

"My father says vultures have the best table manners," Chris said. "They finish their meal and don't leave anything on their plate."

Señor Gutierrez chuckled at Mr. Riley's joke.

"So there's nothing to clean," Chris explained. "The vultures already cleaned it."

"You could be right," Señor Gutierrez said.

Pira was always impressed by the bold way Chris spoke to his father's charros and by the respect they gave him.

"But there's blood on the eye sockets," Arón said, "and there's something inside."

Once again Pira noticed the change in Arón. He wasn't agreeing with Chris.

"The thing to do," Señor Gutierrez said mildly, "if the head isn't already completely clean, is to put it on an anthill. Black ants are best. After that you can wash it with soap and water."

"My mother wouldn't want it," Pira said.

"Maybe Señor Riley?" the charro asked.

"I'll ask him," Chris said.

"Tell him I can do it if he wants."

Señor Gutierrez didn't ask Arón to ask his mother. Maybe he wanted to get paid and knew she couldn't pay as much as Mr. Riley.

Many people saw the three boys walking into town next to a mounted charro. It was hard for Pira not to smile with pleasure and pride.

*

After Mr. Riley drove home with Chris and after Arón had left too, Martha noticed that Pira was trembling. She put a hand on his forehead.

"You don't have a fever. Are you feeling all right?"

"I'm happy."

"You're overexcited. Why don't you read a little? Or just lie in the grass, or on the patio?"

He lay down on the patio. But he was still trembling. He needed his marble. He got up and went to the toy box by the door to his room and took out the big marble and held it up to the light. Inside the marble was a blue swirl, and around the swirl there was just glass and no color. You couldn't see through it. It looked like water with a few tiny bubbles in it.

He went back to his listening spot and lay down, holding the marble, one side of his face on the cool stone. The pressure against his cheekbone was hard. As always when he lay like this, there were two sides, the air side and the stone side. Sounds on the air side were crisp and clear, and many. On the stone side there were few sounds, and they were muffled and dark. Some sounds he could hear in both ways, like Zita's singing "Por mi culpa" inside the house, or the faint clattering of Bruno's typewriter. Bruno wrote slowly, a few words at a time. When the words stopped, there was silence. Then there were more words. The stillness was longer than the words in between. Tristan's claws were scratching the patio as he came near.

Any moment now he would touch Pira with his nose. That moment wasn't yet, it was almost. As soon as it happened, it would be now. The moment came, a delightfully cool wet friendly nudge on his neck. Even though he had expected it, even though he remembered being touched by Tristan this way many times before, the feeling was new. Weren't new and now the same? The thought darted through him, fast, almost like an electric shock. Then there was another nudge, and now Tristan's wish couldn't be clearer. He wanted to play.

But Pira didn't want to move. If he moved, he wouldn't be able to move in the other way, into the stone world, and that was where he wanted to go.

Tristan was waiting. Pira could feel his breath on his neck. Then Tristan walked away. His steps sounded disappointed. I'll play with him later, Pira thought. Not now. Now was the new time. Now he was going underground. He wished Tristan could go with him, but that wasn't possible. No one could go with him.

No one. For a moment that thought scared him. But then he liked it. He liked being alone, as long as he wasn't afraid. And he wasn't afraid.

He turned all his attention to the stone side. Down, down. And already he was where he had been the last time he went down into the stone world. Standing among rocks and cactuses, a sword in his hand. It was the sword Excalibur. The sword and its name were one brilliant thing. He walked, not knowing where he was going. A black snake came out from behind a cactus and flicked its forked tongue, saw the sword in Pira's hand, ducked, and slithered away. He followed the snake. He noticed the ground beneath his feet was cool and no longer sandy. He was barefoot on a meadow with tall waving grass. The snake was gone. Maybe it was nearby. He stood still. Snakes were dangerous. He felt someone looking at him, or something. He remembered his marble. Far away, in the upper world, he could feel its weight and round shape in his hand. He could go back up anytime.

Then he saw who was looking at him. It was Islero. Standing in the distance near a clump of trees with his head turned toward Pira, just looking. They were both standing still and looking at each other.

Pira's eyes opened. There was Tristan, lying on his mat with his nose resting on his front paws, waiting.

"Good dog!" Pira said. His heart was thumping.

Tristan scrambled to his feet, and Pira leaped up to get the throwing stick.

*

Mr. Riley called to tell Martha that the charro she had slapped had left the state of Morelos. He knew this directly from the chief of police. So the danger had passed and he would withdraw his men, as he needed them for other work.

From one day to the next, Pira's house turned from a guarded castle back into an ordinary house. When he went with Arón to visit Islero's bones in the canyon, no one on the streets seemed to remember that these were the boys who had walked with a mounted charro.

Everything was back to normal. But normal now included Arón, and that was more fun than Pira remembered ever having. Arón had changed. He was the same but different. His climbing in the tree was bolder. He wasn't afraid of falling. He swung from a branch like a monkey and let himself drop to the ground. He wanted to play pirates, which he had never liked to do before. He decided to be a bad pirate, one that couldn't be trusted. He jumped on Pira's back from behind and tried wrestling him to the ground. He couldn't, because Pira was stronger, but he didn't go slack. He tried to win, and he didn't cry when he lost.

They went out on the street to play marbles with other boys, just like in the past, but now Arón introduced a new game where you tossed centavos as close to a wall as you could and whoever tossed his centavo closest won all the others. He had learned it from his

uncle, he said. Everyone had at least a few centavos. For fifteen centavos you could buy a good set of marbles. Winning this game was
better than winning at marbles. It was more exciting too.

They sat in the tree and told stories. Some stories were true and
others weren't. Some stories could be believed even if they weren't
true, others not. One story Arón told was about his uncle knowing
how to fly. Pira didn't believe it.

"Yes, he can," Arón said. "He told me. He learned it from a curand-
ero. He can see things other people can't see. He saw the farmer driving
the bull over the cliff and he wasn't even there, he was playing dominos
with a friend and he saw it in his mind. He sees a lot of things."

"And he can fly?"

"Yes, at night. He said he would teach me when I'm older."

Maybe it was true. "I want to learn that too."

"I'll teach you after he teaches me."

"I sometimes see things like that myself," Pira said. "Things
other people can't see."

He immediately regretted saying that.

"Like what?"

"I can see underground. Sometimes, not right now."

"That's a lie."

"It's not. I swear it."

"What do you see?"

He didn't want to tell Arón about Islero. He didn't want him to
think that Islero wasn't real.

"I see the roots of trees and plants, and different bugs, and snakes."

"Really? Snakes?"

"Just one snake."

Arón gave him a sly sideways look. Then he laughed and
punched Pira in the side.

"Liar!"

12

Two big things happened almost simultaneously, one after the other.

First a letter from Dorothy's uncle Harry came. It brought wonderful news according to Martha but it wasn't wonderful for Pira. Harry definitely wanted to turn Bruno's story into a movie. To prevent anyone else from making the movie he was sending Bruno money, and now Bruno was hopeful that he and Martha and Pira would be able to go to Germany not in two years but maybe much sooner.

"How soon?"

"It depends. We need twice the amount of money he's sending us, so that's a problem."

That sounded good.

"If the movie gets made we'll have plenty of money."

That didn't sound good.

"But that may not be for a while, and it may not happen."

That sounded good again.

Pira prayed that the movie wouldn't be made. He prayed to God, the Virgin, and Jesus as a group, which he had never done before. He thought of including Zita's ídolo too but he didn't know his name and couldn't believe in him anyway.

*

Two days later, Federico's strike began. It started in Mexico City
and by the next day railroad workers were striking all over the
country. Federico, who was going to visit Zita that weekend, called
to tell her he wouldn't be able to come, because of the strike. Bruno
asked Federico for the number he was calling from so he could pay
for the call because direct calls from Mexico City were expensive.
It was expensive for Bruno as well but he had more money than
Federico. He wanted to know how many men were marching, how
much money they had to feed people, whether people watching
them pass by were sympathetic. After Bruno hung up the phone,
Pira asked if the huelga was winning.

Bruno smiled and said it was too early to tell.

*

Every day at noon Bruno listened to the news on the radio. He
wanted to hear about the strike. Usually the news didn't interest Pira, but now that Federico's strike was in the news there was
the possibility that Federico would say something on the radio. It
wasn't likely, Bruno said, but it was possible. Many people spoke
on the radio. So now, when Bruno turned on the news, Pira listened
until it was clear Federico wouldn't speak.

Bruno was angry at the newsman for not saying anything
important about the strike and for talking a lot about other things
that Bruno thought weren't important. Pira didn't care about
most of those things either, but one of them was the fate of five
heroic Mexican mountaineers who had disappeared in the Swiss
Alps. That was what the newsman called them, heroic Mexican
mountaineers. Why was that not important? It was important to
the lost men, for sure. It was important to Mexicans. Bruno wasn't

Mexican, that was why he didn't care about the lost mountaineers. But he cared about the strike because Federico was in it. He cared about Federico.

*

Meanwhile letters went back and forth between Bruno and Harry. Pira learned about them from things Bruno and Martha said at breakfast or lunch or dinner. He didn't ask questions at first because he didn't want to know, but little by little the pieces came together and he understood.

Several times, they said it was complicated. That was hopeful. They were discussing how to find someone who could read Bruno's book in German and write English words for the actors to speak, how to find famous actors who would know how to play the characters in the story, and how to find someone really rich who would love the story and give Harry the money he needed to pay the actors and make the movie.

For a moment, Pira enjoyed imagining all these possibilities. He asked Bruno if they were looking for someone to play Hitler, because if they were, maybe Bruno could play him just like he had played the man who wanted to be Hitler.

"No," Bruno said. "There's no Hitler in this movie."

"Will it be for children?"

"No, I'm sorry. I don't think you would like it very much. Maybe when you're older, though."

Later, when he was alone, Pira remembered sharply why he didn't want the movie to be made. If Martha and Bruno and he went to Germany soon, he wouldn't be going to first grade with Chris. Federico would no longer visit. He wouldn't see Zita at all anymore. He would be separated from Arón again, maybe this time forever. No one asked him what he wanted. It wasn't fair. He cried at the thought that his parents were hoping so much for something to happen that, if it happened, would make him sad. Why would they do that? It really hurt.

When he complained to Martha about the unfairness (not to Bruno, because he knew Bruno wanted to go to Germany more than almost anything), his grief broke out with such force that he couldn't talk. Martha held him close, stroking his shoulders as he sobbed and clung to her.

"I know," she kept saying, "I'm so sorry."

It sounded as if she agreed that it wasn't fair, but it turned out she meant something else.

"It's sad, but it's nobody's fault. I hope you can understand that."

He shook his head.

"I know you're mad at Bruno, but he's not to blame. He needs to go back to his country. Just like a plant that needs water. It doesn't just *want* water, it would wilt without it. It's a need, not a want. Bruno didn't choose to have this need. It happened to him. It happened when he was forced to leave his country."

She stopped talking. Her breath cradled him silently for a while. Her hands stroked his shoulders. He listened.

She started speaking again. Her sentences followed one after the other as if she were reading from a book. As he listened, half focusing on her words and half on the sound of her voice, he was hearing her in the double way he heard sounds when he listened to the stone floor of the patio—one side of her voice coming from a little above him, out of her mouth and into his right ear, and at the same time her voice had an inside sound coming from inside her body into his other ear, which was pressed against her chest.

Her inner voice rumbled. It came from so nearby it felt almost as if she were speaking inside his body.

"When I was a girl about your age I had an older brother who went swimming in a pond near our house and drowned. He was a good swimmer, he shouldn't have drowned. But he did. I saw him at breakfast that morning, and a few hours later he was dead. That was the most terrible thing that had ever happened in my life. I couldn't understand it. Naturally I couldn't! No one understands death. But I also couldn't accept it. It felt so wrong. He was too young, I loved him too much, it shouldn't have happened. But whom could I blame? I tried blaming God, as if he had done it. But God didn't make my brother drown. It just happened. It was an accident. Life happens that way sometimes. Life happens sometimes in ways that make people sad. Or that make some people happy and others sad. It feels terribly unfair, but there's no one to blame. It's just life happening without any meanness."

He wasn't sure what she meant by life, but it didn't matter. He was no longer thinking. He felt a strange mixture of comfort and defeat.

*

Pira was in his room playing with his soldiers and Indians when he heard the newsman's voice. He was talking about the strike in a way that interested Bruno a lot, otherwise he wouldn't have turned up the sound. Pira went into the living room to hear better.

The newsman was saying that President Alemán was angry at the striking railroad workers because they were hurting the country. Then came the voice of the President. Pira recognized it, he had heard it before. The President said the ones responsible— "los responsables"—would be punished. "Criminales!" he said. "Traidores!"

"And now for pleasanter news," the newsman said. The heroic mountaineers had been found. One of them had a broken leg, but otherwise they were well and happy. Mexico was proud of them. Bruno turned off the radio.

Pira returned to his soldiers and Indians. He usually made the Indians win. Many of them died, but that made no difference. Sometimes there was a particularly heroic soldier who escaped capture by the Indians, but the Indians were always heroic.

Right now five soldiers in blue coats were ambushed by three Indians. They were probably going to die.

Pira's thoughts turned back to the President's voice. He sounded a lot worse than angry. He was furious.

A lot of people disliked the President, even children. Once, playing marbles with Arón and other children in the street, one boy taught them to say something bad: Alemán, Alemán, come caca y no le dan! The boys chanted those words in chorus, and to Pira's surprise the grown-ups who heard it laughed and weren't angry.

Was Federico one of the ones responsible? Would he be punished? How would they punish him if they did?

*

That evening at dinner Pira gathered from something Martha said to Bruno that she was going to sell her violin. When he asked her why, she said she was sorry she had mentioned it. Then Bruno said: "You have to explain, Martha." So she explained.

Selling the violin would bring in enough money to pay for the trip to Germany, even if the movie didn't get made. She already had a buyer—a friend of Sándor's who lived in Mexico City. They would be leaving as soon as tickets for a ship could be booked.

"How soon?" Pira asked.

"It could be in a few weeks."

"What about first grade?"

"We talked about that and decided it's best if you don't start school now. You would be making new friends, knowing you would have to leave them soon. It would be too hard."

"I don't think so."

"Think about it, Peter. It will be hard enough parting from the friends you already have. It's really better this way. I'm sorry, I know it's disappointing."

He wept quietly then, and his parents consoled him. He knew they wouldn't change their minds.

*

Amann came by to ask Bruno if he wanted to drive to the city with him. They were speaking German, so Bruno had to translate for Martha.

"He wants to give medical aid to the workers if they need it. There's probably going to be trouble with the police. He wants me to write a report for the émigré press. I think I should do it."

Martha didn't want Bruno to go, but he wanted to and it was clear that nothing she said would change his mind. He kissed her and Pira goodbye and promised to come back the next day. Something about the way he did that reminded Pira of a picture in Posada's green book where a man embraced his wife and children before being led away by armed soldiers.

At the gate Bruno turned around and came back inside to ask Zita if she had a message for Federico in case he met him at the demonstration, even though that was unlikely.

"Tell him to pray," Zita said. "Tell him he should be brave but careful. Tell him I love him."

Then Bruno and Amann left. Martha called Valéria.

"I'm worried," she said.

Why? Did she think Amann would drive the car off a cliff?

Suddenly everything felt dangerous.

*

Valéria came over. The two women lay down on the deck chairs beneath the banana tree, smoking and talking. Pira was going to his room to read or draw but on the way his mind changed and he went to the anthill instead. The General stood there as he always did with his sword raised overhead, and the ants scurried in and out of their home as always. They were no longer interested in the General.

Martha called Zita and Zita came out of the house and Martha asked her to please make some coffee and Zita went back inside.

Pira sat down in the shade with his back against the brick wall and watched the ants. Two of them were dragging a butterfly wing together. They hadn't reached the anthill yet. Their burden was slowing them down a lot. Dozens of other ants were running past them. How long would it take them to climb their steep house and pull the wing in through the door?

Zita came out with coffee and cups and saucers and sugar and some cake on a tray. Martha thanked her, and Zita went back into the house. She walked very straight, as always, her sandals slapping softly against the soles of her feet, and disappeared into the living room, where she turned on the radio, keeping it low so that Martha wouldn't mind, and turned the dial until she found a song that she liked. Then she started the vacuum cleaner.

Paco came fluttering down from the roof of the house, hoping for a treat, and Martha held out an arm until Paco hopped onto her wrist. She fed him a piece of cake with her other hand.

"Beautiful Paco," Valéria said.

Tristan came by with a lazy wag of his tail, and Martha fed him too. Maybe the danger had passed.

The two ants had pulled the butterfly wing halfway up the anthill, but now they were pulling in different directions. Pira thought of helping them. He imagined picking up the wing, carefully so they wouldn't fall off, and placing it, with them hanging on to it, next to the entrance. What if he did that? They would think he was a god.

The sound of the vacuum cleaner stopped and the radio got louder. Zita called from the living room:

"Señora Marta! Están dando las noticias!"

The clattering of the newsman's typewriter reached into the garden. Martha rose from her chair. Paco fluttered off her wrist onto the lawn. Valéria too stood up. They both walked nearer to the house and stopped in the grass with their heads turned sideways. Zita came out and stood next to the door. Pira, too, rose to his feet, he wasn't sure why. It felt a little like standing at attention.

The news was all about la huelga, so it was important, but the newsman used words Pira didn't understand, and after a few minutes he sat down again. Alemán's voice came on, saying the same words he had said the day before, calling the strikers criminals and traitors and threatening to punish the ones responsible. Then another man spoke, but this was a man who liked the strike. He said, "What we are demanding is justice. Justice in the form of sixteen centavos. That is all. Sixteen centavitos."

"This morning," the newsman said, "these same words were chanted by ten thousand railroad workers marching on the Paseo de la Reforma."

Then came the sound of their angry shouting:

"Dieciséis centavitos!"

"Dieciséis centavitos!"

"Dieciséis centavitos!"

"Dieciséis centavitos!"

Pira remembered Bruno and Federico talking about that sum, but only now did he realize how little it was. There were homeless boys with more money than that in their pockets. A bag holding ten of the cheapest clay marbles cost five centavos. When Martha and Bruno gave money to beggars, it was never less than fifty centavos. Why didn't the jefes, or the government, just give it? Why were they so mean?

*

The next day a fight broke out between the striking railroad workers and a band of men who wanted the strike to stop. Martha said
they were criminals. Two workers were knifed and taken to a hospital. The police arrested many people. The government ordered
the strikers to go back to work the next day, but they marched
again instead, and this time, instead of shouting "Dieciséis centavitos" they sang "La Cucaracha." Martha said they were making
fun of the government, calling the government a cucaracha who
could no longer walk. Then the government arrested the leaders of
the union and put them in jail. The workers marched again. Their
shouts on the radio sounded very angry. Then the jefes surprised
everyone by offering the workers a raise of ten centavos an hour,
provided they went back to work by Monday. It was Thursday
when the government said that.

Bruno came home the next day. He was very sad. The strike
was over, he said. "They broke its back."

That expression shocked Pira. It reminded him of Islero. Was
his back broken when he fell? Did he suffer? He hoped he had died
right away.

*

On Sunday the phone rang and Martha answered. It was Federico.
Martha called Zita, and Zita talked and listened and talked and
sounded happy. Then Federico had to hang up because the call was
expensive. Zita told Martha and Bruno that Federico hadn't been
hurt and the workers were going back to work, and that Federico
would write to say more and would visit as soon as he had earned
back some of the money he had lost during the strike.

"Thank God," she said, making the sign of the cross.

*

All the while, the first day of school was coming closer. Soon that day would be now, and his friends would be going to school and he wouldn't. He didn't want to think about it.

*

Martha and Bruno drove to Mexico City to meet with the friend of Sándor's who was interested in buying Martha's violin, and also to apply for visas to go to Germany. Applying for a visa meant asking for permission, Bruno said. They would come back the next day.

They left early in the morning. Pira was awake but still in bed. They came into his room to say goodbye. Martha kissed him. Then they left the room, closing the door behind them. Pira listened to the squeak of the garden gate opening and the click of its snapping back into the lock, the slamming of the car doors, the rumble of the motor as they drove off, and then they were gone. He folded his hands and prayed to Jesus: "Please make it so I don't have to go to Germany." He repeated the prayer many times in English and Spanish until he had that happy feeling that told him his prayer had been heard. Then he just lay there wondering what Jesus would do. Maybe the man who was supposed to give them permission wasn't at home when they rang his bell. Or maybe he invited them into his house and offered them drinks and was nice but then, when they asked him, he simply said "NO!" sternly, just like Bruno sometimes when he said no and meant no. Maybe not even knowing why he said it. Not knowing that Jesus was making him do that.

"NO!"

That made Pira giggle.

But what if they did get permission? It was possible!

He wished he could ask Jesus directly: "What are you going to do?" Why didn't Jesus answer prayers like a person: "Don't worry, I'll do this and that"?

Then Pira thought of another possibility. Even if Martha and Bruno got permission to go to Germany, Jesus could make the man who wanted the violin decide not to buy it. That way there wouldn't be enough money for the trip and they would have to wait another year and he could go to first grade after all. That would be just as good!

Zita opened the door and asked him to shower and get dressed so they could have breakfast together.

The water coming out of the shower was dirty and smelled bad. "Ay!" Zita said. "Come outside, I'll wash you with the hose." And she did that. He ran around the garden naked and screaming and she ran after him with the hose set to shoot strong like a fire hose so it almost hurt when it hit his body, but it didn't. It was just cold. Then she toweled him off. They both laughed at the way his teeth chattered.

For breakfast she served him two soft-boiled eggs and toast with strawberry jam and a bowl of Wheaties with milk, while she herself, sitting next to him at the card table on the patio, ate chicken, frijoles, and chiles wrapped in a tortilla.

Then they went shopping. He didn't really want to go, but she asked him to, so he went with her. As soon as they reached the market, he wished he hadn't come. He didn't like seeing the hobbled goats and the chickens hanging upside down. After buying what she needed to buy, Zita stood talking with another woman, their baskets at the height of Pira's face where he could smell the fish and meat they had bought. They talked and talked. It was so boring. He went to look at some canaries in a cage, But Zita called him back. She was stricter outside the house than she ever was at home.

Finally they got home and Pira sat under the zapote tree to

read the *Just So Stories*. "Hear and attend and listen; for this befell and behappened and became and was, O my Best Beloved, when the Tame animals were wild. The Dog was wild, and the Horse was wild, and the Cow was wild, and the Sheep was wild, and the Pig was wild—as wild as wild could be—and they walked in the Wet Wild Woods by their wild lones. But the wildest of all the animals was the Cat. He walked by himself, and all places were alike to him."

What if Germany and Mexico were alike to him? Was that possible? All he knew about Germany was that people spoke German there and not Spanish or English and that it was colder than Mexico. How could the two places be alike? They weren't.

For lunch, Zita made tamales and frijoles and gave Pira Coca-Cola to drink.

"Will you write to me when you're in Germany?" she asked.

"Yes," Pira said. That was a happy thought.

"I can read now," Zita said.

"I'll write you long letters," Pira said.

"You'll tell me about your friends . . . your school . . . your new house . . ."

He nodded.

"Your new maid, if you have one . . ."

That brought tears to his eyes.

"I want you to come with us."

She smiled. "That's not possible, Pirito. And besides, Federico and I want to marry and have children. We're Mexicans, so we should live in Mexico."

"I'm Mexican too."

She didn't deny it, but he knew it wasn't true.

"I'll write to you too," she said. "I'll learn how to write."

"Will you visit us?"

"I hope so."

"I'll come back to Mexico to visit you."

"When you're bigger."

"Yes."

"Then you can be an uncle to my children."

Pira laughed at the thought of being an uncle.

Then Zita peeled two mangos. After they ate them Pira helped
Zita clear the table. She wiped the sticky mango juice off his fingers
and face with a washcloth. Then she washed the dishes and went to
her room for a siesta while Pira lay in the shade beneath the zapote
tree, watching the leaves stir above him and wondering if Arón or
maybe Chris would come by in the afternoon, until he dozed off.

*

When Martha and Bruno returned the next day, they told Pira that
they had sold Martha's violin for a lot of money, and that this was a
good thing because it meant that in Germany they would be able to
live in a nice big house with a garden instead of a poor small house
without a garden.

Also, they had gotten their visas.

13

Something happened to time then. Pira didn't notice it right away, but he started feeling it as the days passed. The future, which earlier had stretched out from the present like a valley with a nearby red-roofed house called "school" and distant forests and mountains full of adventurous promise, was now more like the meadow where Islero had grazed before he was driven off the cliff. There was an end. There would be a new beginning in another country and another time, but between time here and time there was an ocean. He couldn't imagine his future life on the other side, and he didn't much want to.

Inside the Mexican time that remained, little changed. He went spazieren with Bruno and Tristan. Once Martha came along and they talked about the future.

"It's not good to just think about what you'll be leaving behind," Martha said. "We're all going together, you'll have your family. You'll go to school and learn German and make new friends. We'll get a dog, maybe a female. Then she can have puppies."

"And a parrot?"

"Probably not, Germany isn't warm enough for parrots."

"What else?"

"You'll learn how to ski, there's snow there. We'll get a piano,

and you'll learn how to play it. When you get good at it, I'll buy a
new violin and we'll play music together."

These thoughts were like strings stretched across the sea. They
weren't bridges, but they made a connection.

A couple of times Pira joined Zita on her walk to the stream to
wash clothes, and read there and watched the fish. Once he crossed
the stream and went to the edge of the cliff to look at Islero's
bleached bones. They looked the same.

At home, he played with his friends and by himself, as always.

Once Martha drove him and Arón to Chris's house. Mr. Riley
had bought Chris a BB gun and paper targets to shoot at. He taught
the boys how to shoot lying on their bellies and how to compete
in a grown-up way by keeping score. With each shot, the barrel of
the gun knocked against your shoulder. It hurt a little but not too
much. Bang! This was so much closer to real war than playing with
toy soldiers and índios. It was fun.

*

The first day of school happened without him, as he knew it would,
but he didn't feel lonely.

After breakfast he painted battleships and sharks with his
watercolors while Bruno retired to his office and Martha gave Zita
a reading lesson under the banana tree. Paco, sitting above them,
looked interested, which was funny.

At lunch Bruno and Martha asked him how he was feeling and
he said "fine," and it was true.

During siesta there was a downpour with thunder. Lying on his bed
with the door open, he watched the drops spring up on the patio like
little explosions. He had seen explosions like that in a newsreel about
the war. Children ran past his window holding their satchels above
their heads like umbrellas. He looked out for Arón, but he wasn't
among them. He had said he would come by to tell Pira about school.

In the afternoon, Martha and Bruno went spazieren with Tristan, and Pira stayed at home in case Arón came by. To pass the time, he told Zita the story of "How the Elephant Got His Trunk," and she liked it. Then he copied out a poem from Martha's *Treasury of Victorian Verse*, making the capital letters curl and twist to make them look ancient, and he showed it to Martha when she came back from her walk.

"I like it," she said, "but not as much as your poem about the white flower. Why don't you write another one? It could be about a blue flower."

She didn't understand. He hadn't set out to write a poem about a white flower. That just happened because of the rhyme.

"Don't you want to?"

He shook his head.

He climbed the zapote tree. Something must have died in the distant valley at the foot of the two volcanoes, because tiny vultures were circling there. It didn't look as if Arón would come. Probably his mother had punished him.

At dinner, Bruno looked more worried and distracted than usual.

"What's wrong?" Martha asked him.

"I'm trying to move a character in my book from one room to another. It's not working," he said.

"You do it like this," Pira said. He got up and walked out of the room. Martha and Bruno laughed, and Pira returned to the table.

The day darkened quickly after dinner. In bed, he reread "How The Leopard Got His Spots" until Martha said it was time to sleep and turned off the light.

Late that night Pira woke up. The house was quiet. Faintly through the door he heard his parents breathing in their sleep. He went out into the garden and took off his pajamas and lay down on his back in the wet grass. Maybe he would catch pneumonia. He would be taken to a hospital and the ship would leave for Germany and he would stay in Mexico with his parents.

The roar of crickets was all around him. The sky was black and blazing with stars. He had never seen them so brilliant. Some were white, some were silver, some were gold. Some were quivering. Many of them. As if *they* were making the sound. The moon was invisible.

He closed his eyes. The earth felt very large now. Bigger than the garden, bigger than the town. It was the world. He tried to imagine the earth, huge and round as it sailed through space, making a circle around the sun. On the other side of the earth, where Germany was, the sun was shining. But here it was night. What if he sank down into the earth here, in the dark? That could be dangerous. He didn't have his marble with him. But he was sinking already. He sank through empty space until his feet landed on a large meadow. The ground was cool and firm. There in the distance, near a thicket of dark leafy trees, stood Islero. He was grazing. He wasn't looking at Pira. That was good. Pira stood still. He was afraid to move closer, but he didn't want to turn away either. Where was his sword? It wasn't in his hand. But what good would a sword do against this huge bull? It wouldn't help, even if it were magic. He was just a boy, his arms were too weak. And besides, he didn't want to hurt Islero. Islero looked at him and returned to his grazing. At that moment Pira felt only love for him and no fear. He walked slowly toward Islero, and Islero made one step in the direction of the trees, grazing steadily. Little by little Pira approached Islero and Islero, still grazing, moved slowly, step by step, toward the trees. Now voices were coming from the grove. Or was it the gurgling, splashing sound of a stream? He was near to Islero now, almost close enough to touch him. They entered the grove together. Coolness and shadows enveloped them.

All at once everything was different. Five women surrounded the bull and the boy. They were happy to see them both, but they were most happy to see Islero. They loved him. They stroked his broad chest, hugged his neck, kissed his black nose, ran their fin-

gers through the curls on his forehead, caressed his beautiful glisten-
ing body. They kept saying and half singing his name as if they had
waited for him all their life and now he had come. Islero! Islero! They
looked like the women who came to wash clothes by the stream, but
they were more beautiful. They were barefoot. They wore long white
dresses. Their black hair fell loose around their shoulders. One of
them slung a bridge of white flowers between his horns. Another one
wrapped a rope of roses around his neck. Someone lifted Pira onto
the bull's back, standing. Two women held his hands on either side
so he wouldn't fall, "Mira! Mira!," pointing into the leaves above
him. There, held up by a forked branch, hung a toy he had lost long
ago, a wooden hoop with a blue half and a red half. The surprise of
that was so sudden that his eyes opened and he found himself lying
on his back in the garden looking up at the sky.

He remembered the blue and red hoop. He wished he still had
it. Even though Santa Claus had brought it when he was little and
still believed in Santa Claus. It came with a red stick for pushing
the hoop and making it roll. He had played with it on the street and
then left it leaning against a wall and when he went back to get it,
it was no longer there.

He was shivering. He put on his pajamas and went back to bed.
Tristan rose from his blanket and came into his room, tapping the
floor with his nails as he walked, and held out his head for Pira to pet.

Pira stroked Tristan's flat head and wept at the thought of the inev-
itable parting. Tristan went back to his blanket, and Pira fell asleep.

*

Arón and Chris told very different stories about school.

In Arón's school all the children were boys. In Chris's school there
were boys and girls. Arón's teacher, Señor Echevarría, was nice, but
he was also strict and sometimes shouted. The children had to fold

their hands when they weren't writing and reading. If you were bad
Señor Echevarría would make you hold out your hand and slap your
fingers with a ruler. In Chris's school no one was hit. The teacher
was a woman named Nancy, and she was only nice. She picked the
children up from their houses in the morning, bringing horses for
them to ride on, and rode home with them after school. Arón was
picked up and driven home in a bus. In Chris's school they made
sculptures out of clay and painted them and then fired them in a
kiln. In Arón's school the children sat behind benches in two straight
rows. In Chris's school they sat in chairs around several small tables.
In Arón's school the children ran around in a big dirt yard during
recess, playing marbles or kicking a soccer ball. In Chris's school
they played on the big meadow that came to an end at the cliff where
Islero had died. But they weren't allowed to go near there. Once in
Arón's school a girl was brought in and made to sit in a separate
chair for a day. All the boys made fun of her because she was a girl
and didn't belong there, and she covered her face with her hands and
cried. The teacher let them make fun of her.

*

A fair came to town, with a merry-go-round and a Ferris wheel on
the zócalo, and a giant slide and electric cars that you could steer
yourself. There was a shooting gallery where Bruno shot bandits
with sombreros that popped up from behind big cactuses. There
were stands where you could buy cotton candy, aguas frescas,
tamalitos, birds, flowers, and all sorts of toys. There were booths
where for a few centavos you could throw darts or toss a ring onto
a peg and win prizes. Bruno gave Arón and Pira a bunch of change
to spend on the games or on anything except the Ferris wheel. Martha said it wasn't safe. Together they went into a big booth with
mirrors that made them look enormously fat or wavy. For another
ten centavos you could go through a purple curtain with gold tas-

sels into a hall of mirrors where you could see yourself in hundreds of reflections all at once and from all directions, even from the back and from above. It made you glad to have a real live friend with you who wasn't a reflection.

*

Bruno's friends from the party came by to talk about something important. They kept interrupting each other. Their voices were loud. Some were shouting. The talk was all in German, but later Bruno told Martha what they had been saying, and Pira heard it. He used special grown-up words—anti-communist, enemy of the people, Trotzkyist, Marxist—but there was one word Pira knew well. It was Sándor's name.

"Sándor?" Martha said. "That's not possible!"

"What happened?" Pira asked.

"Sándor got arrested," Bruno said. "In Hungary."

"What did he do?"

"He didn't do anything."

"Why did they arrest him?" Martha asked.

"On a suspicion. They made a mistake."

"The party?"

"No, the police."

Valéria came over to talk about Sándor. Her face was puffy and red. She was wringing her hands.

"I don't believe it," Valéria said.

"I don't either," Bruno said. "It will all be cleared up."

"I'm so worried," Valéria said.

Then Bruno and Martha and Valéria said they were going to El Rincón del Sosiego, and left the house. Pira had the feeling they didn't want him to hear what they said.

*

Bruno and Martha didn't talk about Sándor much after that. Whenever they mentioned his name, it sounded as if they were talking about a secret.

"Is Sándor still in prison?" Pira asked once, and Martha and Bruno, speaking in unison, said, "Yes, he is."

"Will he get out?"

"Of course," Bruno said. "He's waiting for a trial. The judge will see that Sándor is innocent, and then he'll be let out."

Maybe the police suspected Sándor because he was a magician. They thought he could make things happen by magic, and that scared them. They didn't know his magic was just tricks. Why didn't he show the prison guards how he made things appear and disappear? Then they would understand.

*

Federico came to visit. Usually he came every two months but this time he came sooner because by the time of his next scheduled visit the Vogelsangs would no longer be in Mexico. Also, it was Saturday, not Friday morning as usual. The jefe wasn't letting him take Fridays off as he used to, just to be mean. It was punishment for the strike.

Martha made a special dinner that night and Bruno opened a bottle of wine.

"We should have worked harder to win over the other unions," Federico said. "That's why we lost."

"We learn from our mistakes," Bruno said.

"In the end we will win," Federico said.

"For our children," Bruno said, raising his glass.

"For all the children," Federico said. But because Federico was speaking Spanish, the words were "por todos los niños," which Pira remembered were words in his poem. No one else at the table thought of that, but he did, and it made him feel secretly proud. He

raised his glass of milk and drank from it while Federico, Zita, and
Martha drank from their wine glasses.

*

The next morning, Mr. Riley called to ask if Chris could come over.
"Of course!" Martha said. But before Señor Gutierrez brought
Chris in Mr. Riley's blue car, Arón came by. The Vogelsangs and
Federico and Zita were eating breakfast.

"Have you eaten yet?" Bruno asked.

Arón shook his head.

"Then join us," Martha said. "We have cornflakes . . . eggs . . . bread
and butter . . . marmalade . . . oatmeal . . . whatever you want."

"Butter," he said softly.

Federico cut open a white roll, spread butter on the two halves,
and held them up for him to see. "More butter?" Arón nodded.

Federico put on more butter.

"Marmalade?"

"No, just butter."

Federico gave him the plate with the thickly buttered bread.

"Would you like milk?" Martha asked.

He hesitated.

"Coca-Cola?" he asked, nearly whispering.

Zita stood up smiling and went to the kitchen and came back
with a bottle of Coke and a glass and a bottle opener, and took off
the metal top of the bottle, making it fizz.

"In a glass?" she asked.

"No, the bottle."

Then they all ate and drank together. Arón ate slowly, biting
small pieces off the edge of his bread and chewing thoughtfully.

Then the bell rang and Pira jumped up to let Chris in, and Chris
ran ahead of him through the garden and bounded into the house,
almost shouting: "Let's go to the Ferris wheel!"

Once again Martha put her foot down: "It's just not safe enough."

"But it *is* safe!" Pira said. "It's turned hundreds of times already."

"Maybe thousands!" Chris interjected.

"Doesn't that prove it's safe?"

"It doesn't prove anything," Martha said.

"But nothing bad ever happened!" Pira said.

"Yes, it has, with other Ferris wheels."

"But not this one!" He felt teary now. Why was she so mean?

"There's always a first time," she said.

"Not necessarily!" Pira said.

"Even if it happened on this wheel someday," Chris said, holding out his open hands to show the obviousness of it, "why should it happen to us?"

"OK, that's it," Martha said, "the answer is no."

"It's not fair!" Pira said, stomping the floor.

"I'm sorry," Martha said. She had made up her mind.

All the while they had been speaking English, and Arón, not understanding a word, watched their argument with wide open eyes. His mouth too was open. Zita noticed it.

"Aroncito," she said, leaning toward him, "they're having a disagreement."

Then Bruno explained to Zita, Federico, and Arón what the disagreement was about. Federico nodded, paused, and nodded a few more times, slowly, to show that he was thinking of something before he spoke, so everyone waited.

"Forgive me," Federico said to Martha. "I'm thinking two things. The first is that today may be the last time I see Pira. This is something he really wants to do. I would like to share it with him. It would be a special memory for both of us."

Martha sat up straight, listening.

"I have a suggestion," Federico continued. "Let me go with the boys and look at the Ferris wheel. I know how machines work. If I think it's not safe, we'll go home. If I think it is, I could take the ride with them. What do you think about that? If your fear is too great, I'm sure we can all understand that. I won't be insulted if you say no."

*

She didn't say no. The three boys and Federico went to the zócalo, walking fast. On the way, Chris said he had already taken the ride three times and it was chingón! How could he use such a word in front of a grown-up! But Federico just smiled and said, "We will see."

The Ferris wheel was taller than anything else on the zócalo, taller even than the Governor's palace, and the way it stood there slowly turning its painted cars in the bright sun, it looked proud and happy.

"Is it safe?" Pira asked.

Federico looked up and down at the wheel and from side to side. "It's well made," he said.

Pira thought so too. It looked like a giant cartwheel with eight thick spokes, each spoke connecting one of the cars to the hub of the wheel. There were grown-ups and children in each of the cars.

Now the wheel began to slow down. It slowed more and more until it came to a stop. Two older boys were in the lowest car, which was green with white stripes and hovering just above the ground. A man with suspenders wanted to let them out, but the boys swung themselves over the top of the door and ran off laughing. The man cursed them with bad words. Federico thought it was funny. The man stopped being angry and opened the door and held out his hand to help a woman with a long dress get into the car. She took his fingers with one hand and with her other hand lifted her dress and climbed up a step and sat down in the car. "No standing!" the man said sternly, and closed the door. The wheel started again, and the woman's car sailed off into the air.

Federico paid the man with the suspenders and the man gave him four tickets. They waited until the wheel stopped again.

"It's our turn!" Federico said.

The car at the bottom was red with a yellow door. The ticket man opened the door and a woman, a man, and a teenage boy climbed out smiling. Federico and the boys climbed in and sat down on yellow benches, Chris and Arón on one side and Federico and Pira facing them on the other. The ticket man shut the door and locked it. "No standing!" he said. A big sign on the inside of the door said the same thing: "DANGER! NO STANDING!" The Ferris wheel started with a jolt, lifting their car sideways up from the ground. Slowly they rose, higher, higher, until again the wheel stopped and Pira could see the top of the ticket man's sombrero as he opened the red door of a blue carriage below theirs. A young couple stepped out, and a woman and a little girl with pink bows in her hair took their places. They sat side by side. Again the wheel started. Now Pira could see not just one sombrero but a bunch of them and the shrunken bodies and feet of the men underneath the sombreros. It reminded him of the way things changed when you looked at them from above or below in a tilted mirror. It was sort of like magic.

The wheel stopped again and people stepped out of the lowest car and made room for others to climb in. Again the man with the suspenders locked the door and said "No standing!" and again the wheel started. Now you could see the wooden tops of the game booths and the canvas roofs of the fruit stands, the silvery dome of the merry-go-round, the Mexican flag on top of the bandstand, the flowers on the balconies surrounding the zócalo. Once again the wheel stopped and stood still.

"Look!" Chris said, pointing at a blue rectangle with little white circles in it. "The swimming pool in the Hotel Zapata!"

"Those are bathing caps!" Pira said.

The girl with the pink bows couldn't see the pool yet, but she would when her car was where their car was now. She wouldn't know it was the pool of the Hotel Zapata because the people who worked at the hotel didn't let índios inside, so she had never been there. Nor had Arón. Their car was rising again.

Chris wanted to stand so he could see better but Federico put a hand firmly on his shoulder, holding him down, and shook his head. So there *was* danger. It wasn't just the sign that said so.

Again the wheel stopped. They were at the very top, as high as the wheel would lift them. It was incredibly high, and scary. Pira clutched the edge of the car with one hand and the edge of his seat with the other. Federico put an arm around his shoulders. That made him feel safer. Arón, facing him on the opposite seat, stretched out an arm and pointed: "Mira, la catedral!"

There it was with its giant skull and crossbones and its huge open door, but it looked surprisingly small. It was Sunday. There would be a Mass. The wheel began to turn again, and as the rooftops, the trees, and the bandstand rose and the zócalo widened, the Cathedral descended and dipped out of sight, and suddenly Pira felt tears running down his cheeks and saw Arón's grave dark eyes looking at him, and didn't know what it was he was feeling, only that it was very big and not unhappy, despite the tears. He felt grateful too for Federico's arm still around his shoulder pressing him gently against his side.

The wheel stopped again. He looked up to see if the girl with the pink bows could see the Cathedral, but all he saw was the bottom of her carriage. He noticed Chris looking at him and felt ashamed of his tears and lifted a hand to wipe them away.

"Pirito," Federico's voice said near his ear, "I'm feeling sad too. Soon you'll be far away. But I'm happy we're here together."

The wheel started again. Pira leaned his head against Federico's shoulder. Federico squeezed him a little, then rubbed his back and removed his arm. Leaning his head over the edge of the car, Pira saw men and women and children rising toward him. The music from the merry-go-round was getting louder, and for a moment it looked as if he was slowly falling into a cluster of sombreros, but the men wearing the sombreros swung off to the side and two dogs appeared right next to the car, almost close enough for him to touch them, they were fighting furiously, white teeth gnashing, and already the car was sailing upward again. "From now on there's no stopping," Chris said. They were rising fast. Arón started giggling, holding on to the bottom of his seat. Pira craned his neck looking for his house, but it was hidden behind other houses. Now they were reaching the top of the circle. Chris let out a high-pitched "Whooooooh!" and for one tremendous moment Pira, stretching both hands with straight fingers above his head like a diver, felt himself sailing into the pure deep blue of the edgeless sky. Looking down he caught sight of the Cathedral with a cluster of tiny people in front of its doors, and already, again, the Cathedral dipped down and the zócalo rose and widened. So many people! He hadn't seen them before, men, women, and children. Somewhere above him the girl with the pink bows was seeing what he had just seen, as if his time had passed on to her and her time would pass on to the next person, on and on. Was time like that? There by the edge of the zócalo stood a row of toy tables and chairs and toy people standing and sitting. Wasn't that El Rincón del Sosiego? One of the toy people, sitting alone at a table, was dressed all in white. Could he be the man who thought he was Hitler? But already their car, still descending, was pulling away and other, bigger people rose up, the merry-go-round slid past with its organ music, and here was the bottom again. Instead of the dogs who had fought earlier, there were just scattered flowers and a mango pit at the feet

of the man with the suspenders, who was already slipping away as
the car soared outward and upward in a wide arc, the same as before,
except now branches and leaves he hadn't seen earlier were leaning
toward him. Over the treetops, beyond the roofs that hid the view
to the Calle Humboldt, he saw the tall house with the window from
which the little white dog used to look down at Tristan. Far away a
bell began to toll: the Cathedral. Chris and Arón were screaming
with laughter for some reason, the Cathedral sank behind the Governor's palace, and then there was only the hard, pure blue of the sky,
and suddenly there was stillness.

The stillness was made of many sounds, each one bright and
clear like a splash of color on empty space: the round gonging of the
Cathedral's bell, which sounded dark green for some reason, a burst
of laughter from some girls down below, mariachi trumpets, the
organ of the merry-go-round, a bright shout, "La Prensa!," cracks
of rifles in a shooting booth, and very far away, a braying donkey.

The bell stopped ringing. The wheel slowed and came to a halt,
and Pira's mind, too, became perfectly still. His head turned. His
friends had wrapped their arms around each other's shoulders. Their
heads were touching. Federico was watching them with a smile.

"We're getting out soon," Federico said, his voice sounding like
a gramophone record that was turning too slow. The wheel started
again, and suddenly Pira's thoughts were stirred into motion. He
remembered himself, and time was reborn.

"Federico," he said, "Zita told me there's a man with a bird on
the Calle De La Luz that tells you the future. Can we go there?"

"A bird?" Federico asked.

"Yes, he talks with the spirits through a little telephone."

Federico laughed.

"It's true," Chris said passionately. "I saw it with my own eyes.
That bird told me my future."

"What is your future?" Federico asked.

"I'm going to be a general."

Time had sped up without their noticing. Their car had arrived at its final stop. The man with the suspenders opened the door, and they got out.

"Can we go there?" Pira asked.

"All right," Federico said. "And then we'll go home."

*

There really was a bird that told the future. It was a canary in a pretty wooden house with a door and two windows. Both the door and the windows had bars like the ones on Pira's window. The bird sat inside on a little stand near a bowl filled with water. A man stood next to the birdhouse holding a tray with stacks of pink, yellow, green, blue, and white cards, each stack in its own compartment. The tray was held up by a leather strap that was slung around the man's neck. In front of the little house, on a table, stood something that looked like a tiny street lamp with a trumpet sticking out sideways on top. Federico said it was an ancient telephone. A woman who wanted to know her future gave the man money. The man opened the door of the house and put his hand inside, offering the bird a finger to sit on. The bird fluttered onto his finger and the man pulled out his hand with the bird perched on his finger and asked the woman to tell the bird her name.

"Adelita," she said.

The bird tilted its head. The little phone rang.

"Pajarito," the man said, "there's a call for you."

The bird hopped off his finger onto the table next to the telephone, chirped into the trumpet, cocked its head next to the trumpet as if listening, chirped into the trumpet again, and listened again. The man gave it something to eat. Then the bird hopped onto the tray, daintily pulled out the edge of a card so that it stuck out from the blue stack, and hopped onto the man's finger. The man put a small piece of food into the bird's beak and carefully moved his hand with the bird into the cage, where the bird hopped off his finger onto the little stand. Then the man drew his hand out of the birdhouse, shut the door, and with two fingers took hold of the blue card the bird had selected and lifted it out of the stack and gave it to Adelita.

"This is your fortune, Adelita. Guard it well."

Adelita's lips moved as she walked away reading the card.

It was the boys' turn now. Federico paid the man. Chris already knew his future and Federico wasn't interested in his, so the canary only had to tell Pira's and Arón's future. The bird did exactly the same things it had done for Adelita, but the cards it picked had different colors. Pira's was yellow and Arón's was green.

Arón asked Pira to read him his future as they were walking home. Pira read: "You are endowed with beauty of body and soul. You are loved and admired. Yet not a day passes when you don't feel the lack of that special person who would make you feel complete. Have faith. He is already dreaming of you, searching for you, though he does not know your name yet. Your marriage will be a happy one. You will live in a rich house with many servants and a beautiful garden. You will be blessed with three precious children and live a long and healthy life."

"I don't understand it," Arón said.

Federico was laughing. "It says you'll marry a man."

"How can that happen?" Arón asked.

"It can't. The bird made a mistake."

"I like the part about the house and the garden."

"Maybe you'll have that, Arón."

"I want that."

They walked on without talking.

"That card was for a girl," Chris said. "We should go back so the bird can pick the right card for him."

"There are no right cards," Federico said. "It's a superstition. No one knows the future."

"No one?" Pira asked.

"Nobody. No person and no bird."

"Maybe God knows," Pira said.

"Maybe," Federico said. "But he's not telling us."

Again they walked to the sound of their footsteps.

"You mean it's a lie?" Pira said.

"It's a game. A believing game."

Pira thought, a What If game.

"What kind of future would you like, Arón?" Federico asked.

"I want to be a policeman."

"You can probably do that. What does your card say, Pira?"

Pira had already read his future. "It says I can do different things," he said.

"Why don't you read it to us?"

Pira read the first sentence: "You will soon come to a fork in the road."

He looked ahead in case they were coming to a real fork in the road, but of course there was none. It was just a word picture. So, walking with his friends and looking up every few words to avoid stumbling, he read on: "One path leads to a great library where you can learn all there is to know. If you choose this path, you will become enormously wise."

"Enormemente!" Chris repeated.

"If you choose the second path you will explore unknown continents, suffer and struggle, and will stare death in the face many times. But in the end you will find great love and supreme happiness."

"Felicidad suprema!" Chris said.

Federico laughed: "Excellent! Which path will you choose, Pira?"

"The second one," Pira said. It sounded more exciting.

14

Suddenly Zita was leaving. A couple in Mexico City, friends of Martha and Bruno, needed a maid to help them take care of their newborn child. Martha told them about Zita, and also told Zita they wanted to hire her, and that they would be happy to have Paco live with them too. Zita didn't want to leave before Martha and Bruno and Pira left for Germany, but Martha said her friends needed her help right away.

"It's too sudden," Zita said. "I'm not ready."

But Martha said Zita would have to find a job soon in any case. Also, living with the Ortiz family she would be near Federico. And they were kind people and the pay would be good. Also they would be seeing each other again very soon. Once their belongings were packed and shipped off to Vera Cruz, they would drive to Mexico City to sell their car and say goodbye to various friends, and of course that included Zita and Federico. And even then it wasn't goodbye forever. They would stay in touch by mail.

In the end Zita was persuaded. There wasn't much for her to do before leaving. She went to the letter writer at the zócalo and dictated a letter to Federico. She went to the stream to tell her friends she was leaving. She packed most of her clothes, her framed picture

of Federico, the picture of the Virgen de Guadalupe in her jagged
halo, her metal crucifix, her green ídolo.

During siesta she practiced reading with Martha. Pira sat in on
one of those lessons. It wasn't really a lesson because Martha wasn't
teaching. Zita read from a novel about a young man in Spain long
ago while Martha listened. Zita could read well by now. She only
halted or stumbled when she came upon a word she didn't know or
when the sentence had several commas in it. Then Martha would
look at the word or the sentence with her and together they would
figure it out. A couple of times Pira was able to help.

The story went on for too long about things he didn't understand,
so he lost interest. But there was one part he liked. The young man,
whose name was Felipe, was in church during High Mass where
everything was very solemn. Suddenly he felt an itch, but he wasn't
supposed to scratch himself. If he scratched the itch it would look as
if he didn't love God, even though he loved God with all his heart. He
thought God would forgive him if he scratched himself, but nobody
else would. They would call it a sin. So he didn't scratch himself. But
not scratching himself was torture.

That word impressed Pira. How could just feeling an itch be that
painful? He had never not scratched himself when he felt like it. But
Martha and Zita found that part really funny. Pira asked them why
they were laughing. They said it was hard to explain.

At breakfast on the day she was leaving, Zita wept and smiled at
the same time, sitting very straight with her eyes lowered. Martha
too was weeping. She dried her eyes with a napkin. Bruno reached
out for the two women's hands. Then they held out their free hands
to Pira. He, too, was weeping. They sat holding hands around the
table for a few moments.

Part of Pira's sadness was about Paco. Zita was taking him with
her. He had been part of the family almost since before Pira was born,
and now he was leaving. Bruno said birds have a short memory, so

Paco wouldn't miss his family for long, but even if he missed them for just a week, that was a long time. But he would be with Zita, whom he loved as much as he loved Martha, maybe more because it was she who fed him. And once he got used to his new home, he would be allowed to fly in the garden, which tame parrots weren't usually allowed to do. So there were good feelings mixed into the sadness.

Paco of course didn't know what was happening. He was just surprised at being put in his cage. He didn't like it. The only time Pira remembered Paco being put in his cage was when he was sick and had to be taken to a veterinarian.

So off they went to the bus station. Zita was wearing a flower in her pinned-up hair. Bruno insisted on carrying her suitcase. Zita carried a smaller bag in one hand and held Paco's cage by its ring in the other. Paco tilted his head to see all the passing things. "Birds see from the side," Bruno had told Pira once. Now he could really see that this was true.

They didn't have to wait long for the bus. The driver pulled open the luggage compartment in the side of the bus and put Zita's suitcase inside. Other people put large bags and suitcases in there too. Zita put her small bag and Paco's cage on the ground. Then she and Martha hugged and Martha kissed Zita's cheeks. Then Zita and Bruno hugged and Bruno patted her back as they hugged. When Zita turned to Pira her face was wet with tears. He wrapped his arms around her and pressed his head against her body. She took his face between her hands and bent down to kiss his forehead, his cheeks, and his mouth. "Mi querido Pira," she said, looking at him with her beautiful brown shining eyes. Then she picked up her bag and Paco's cage and stepped into the bus.

*

That night Pira had a dream about a magician. He was dressed in black and wore a top hat. At first Pira thought he was the evil one with the O voice but it was Sándor. He was holding Pira's hoop. Smiling, he tossed it into the air, where it unfolded into a scarf, red and blue. The scarf floated back into his hand and turned into a hoop again. Sándor held out the hoop for Pira to step through. That was scary: No thank you! Then Tristan appeared. Jump, Tristan! Would he do it? Tristan leaped, and as he sailed through the hoop he turned into Paco and flew off on green wings. Pira woke up laughing.

*

In the kitchen hung a calendar where Martha marked special dates and appointments. For Pira, only three dates mattered: the day when Tristan would go to his new home, the day when Pira and his parents would drive to Mexico City and meet with Zita and Federico again, and the day when they would board the ship that would take them to Germany.

*

Martha and Bruno hired three men to help them pack their belongings. Their clothes would be put in suitcases, but they were also taking furniture, books, pictures, lamps, rugs, Martha's guitar, Bruno's collection of ídolos and two papier-mâché calaveras and a dragon Martha liked a lot. These had to be packed in crates, and that was what the three men were there for. They came in a truck filled with boards and boxes that were folded flat and spools of wire and rope and blankets and many bundles of old newspapers and a big toolkit and two saws, and brought all those things onto the patio. Then they measured the things they would pack and selected boxes of different sizes to put the things into, and stuffed newspaper between the things and the cardboard walls and sealed the boxes with tape. They also measured boards and marked them with a pencil and sawed the boards and hammered them together to make a crate and put the cardboard boxes inside it, and stuffed more newspaper into the spaces between the boxes and the crate, and built a top for the crate and hammered it shut. Then they started on a new set of boxes.

Gradually, as the crates filled up, the house started looking empty.

Arón came by. It was Saturday and he had no school. For a while the boys watched the men working. Martha watched too. The men seemed surprised by that, so she explained that she liked watching anyone do something well. They smiled and kept working. Once Bruno came out of his office to see their progress, but he was too busy to watch for long. He was writing an article with a deadline.

Later Pira brought out his magic mirror and showed Arón how to hold it sideways to make things look different, but Arón didn't see much of a difference, so they threw sticks for Tristan and then played with marbles and toy soldiers and made a palace out of blocks. Pira wanted to put the General in the central courtyard but Arón said the General belonged where he was. He was the King of the Ants.

Pira said, "He's yours now, I give him to you."

Arón said, "It's better if he stays here," and Pira knew it was because Arón's mother would think he had stolen the General if she found him in her house.

"I don't want him to stay here."

"Why not?"

"Because I want you to have him. . ."

Arón shrugged.

". . . And if he stays here after we leave . . ."

He imagined the empty house, the empty garden, the locked gate, the silence, and the General standing on top of the ant heap day and night. There would still be the ants scurrying in and out of their home. It was almost too sad.

"Let's put him inside the bull's head in the canyon!"

Arón smiled broadly: "Yes!"

Pira ran to his toy box and fished out the big, clear marble with the blue swirl and put it in his pocket. Then he ran across the lawn and took the General off the anthill.

"Let's go!" he said.

They hurried off through the gate. Pira turned back to shout into the house: "We're playing outside!"

"Where?" Martha said.

"On the street!"

He didn't want her to stop him from going to the canyon.

"Don't go too far!"

"We won't!"

Tristan wanted to come with them but Pira closed the gate so he couldn't follow, and then they ran, Pira holding the General in his fist and feeling the marble's weight in his pocket. They were barefoot. Every few steps a small stone would hurt Pira's feet, and Arón's too. The thing to do was to keep running, knowing the pain would go away, and it did. Only girls and small children would cry about something like that. At one point Arón was running faster than Pira, so Pira caught up and ran faster than Arón, and then Arón caught up and they ran fast together, laughing.

When they reached the stream, Pira had to stop and bend over and take deep breaths for a while. Arón too was out of breath. For a while they just stood there listening to the tinkling, chattering sound of the stream. It was siesta time; no one was there to wash clothes. Slowly the boys splashed their way through the stream, feeling with pleasure the soft squishy mud between their toes and the coolness of the current against their legs. Once they reached the other side they trotted, not as fast as before, through a copse of trees and onto the big sunlit meadow, and slowed their pace to a walk. Some cows were lying in the shade beneath tall trees in the distance. The boys reached the edge of the cliff and stopped.

Islero's bones looked very white in the sun. Nothing had changed about him. Not his position, not his shape. For the first time, Pira thought how surprising it was that none of his bones were broken. All the soft parts of him had been removed, leaving only the skeleton. In a way he was perfect.

Pira put the General in his empty pocket and started climbing down the narrow path alongside the wall of the cliff, holding on to branches of bushes and small trees. Arón followed him. When they reached the bottom, Pira took out the General, thinking to put him inside one of the bull's eye sockets. But he slowly walked around the skeleton instead. He didn't know why. Again Arón followed him. When they came back to the head, Pira said: "His name is Islero."

"Really? Who told you?"

"I called him that."

"Islero?"

"It's the name of a different bull. Federico told me about him. He was the bravest, strongest bull who ever lived. He killed Manolete."

"Who was Manolete?"

"Manolete was the greatest bullfighter who ever lived. He killed millions of bulls. People called him el monstro. No bull could kill him. But this one did. His name was Islero. He was from the Miura farm in Spain. I heard a man talk about him on the radio. He said if all the bulls in the world knew about Islero, he would be their greatest hero."

"Islero."

Pira felt happy at having told Arón his secret. It didn't matter if Arón told someone else.

He leaned over to put the General inside the bull's right eye socket. He was taller than the rim of the socket, so Pira had to put him in headfirst. Inside the socket there was more room above and below the rim, like a vaulted ceiling and a sunken floor. The bull's head was slightly tilted, so the General kept tipping over. But after several tries, Pira found a way to make him stand straight with his raised sword, looking out from Islero's right eye as if through a round window.

"I have something else," Pira said, "for the other eye."

He took the marble out of his pocket and carefully held it over the other socket. It looked like a big round staring eye.

"Don't," Arón said, "it's too precious," and drew a smaller, clay marble from his own pocket. Pira held on to the big marble while Arón put his marble into the bull's eye. It dropped onto the inner floor and rolled down into the jaw with a clinking sound.

"Let's go back," Pira said. "My mother will worry."

Before they went back up the path, Pira offered Arón the big marble: "I want to give this to you. Your mother won't know. She'll think you won it in a game."

Arón raised the marble above his eye and looked through it. A smile lit up his whole face. He stepped closer to Pira and kissed him on the lips. Boys didn't do that, but he did.

"It's the best marble," he said.

He put it in his pocket, and they started climbing. They ran home and played for the rest of the day.

*

The next day was Sunday. The workers would not be coming. It was the day Martha and Bruno had chosen to take Tristan to his new home. He would be living with Agnes, the nice woman who had given the farewell party for Sándor, and with her twin sons, Huitzil and Cuauhtémoc. Pira looked forward to going there again. He felt sorry for Tristan, but Martha was sure Tristan would be happy there, and Pira believed her. Martha said Agnes had said her sons were excited to meet him.

Tristan was excited too, but he always was when he got a ride in a car. He sat in the back next to Pira, panting and occasionally whining softly. Bruno suggested to Pira that he roll down the window so Tristan could stick his head out. That calmed him down a little. After a while he lay down with his head on Pira's lap and Pira petted him.

The bells of the Cathedral were ringing as they drove past it.

Pira was daydreaming when he heard Bruno say "István," the name of the man who had accompanied Sándor on that box-like instrument at the farewell party.

"This is crazy," Martha said.

"You and I know they're innocent, but the party doesn't," Bruno said.

"What happened?" Pira asked.

Martha and Bruno didn't say anything for a few seconds, and then Bruno spoke: "István was arrested in Hungary. Agnes told us last night."

"Just like Sándor," Pira said.

"It's because he was a friend of Sándor's. They think Sándor did something bad and now they think István was part of it."

"What do they think Sándor did?"

"They think he's a spy. But they're wrong. It's a mistake. They'll let Sándor go once they find out the truth, and István too."

"Who's going to defend them?" Martha said.

"It's a court of law," Bruno said. "They'll have a defense."

"How awful," Martha said.

They drove on without talking. Then Martha turned on the radio and found music played by a string quartet.

"Well, isn't that appropriate," she said, and then they just listened.

*

The Vogelsangs weren't the only guests at Agnes's house. Valéria was there too. They were sitting together around a table, Valéria, Agnes, the twins, Pira, Martha, and Bruno. The table was decked with porcelain plates and painted clay soup bowls, gleaming crystal glasses and silver utensils, bottles and glasses of beer for the grown-ups and Coca-Cola for the children. The twins, sitting side by side directly across from Pira, looked exactly the same with their long black hair, oval faces, and embroidered white shirts. Everyone spoke Spanish because the twins didn't speak much English. Tristan sat by the table too, waiting for tidbits. At home he wasn't allowed to beg at the table, but here he was allowed, so that he would feel welcome.

The last time Pira had seen Valéria she was crying about Sándor, and now her eyes were puffy and red, as if she were still crying. But she was smiling and being friendly.

Agnes's maid, Rosalita, cooked and served the meal but didn't sit at the table like Zita. First she brought fish soup in a tureen, which she rolled around the table on a cart, ladling the soup into each person's bowl—two ladles for each one. The twins looked suspiciously at each other's bowls before eating but seemed satisfied.

"Which one of you is Huitzil?" Valéria asked. They both raised their hands.

Agnes scolded one of them: "You shouldn't lie, Cuauhtémoc. You know who you are. If you keep doing this, I will give you different haircuts and different clothes. Then this nonsense will stop."

"We'll wear each other's clothes then," Cuauhtémoc said.

"We'll cut our own hair to make it look the same," Huitzil said.

"Do you like looking the same?" Bruno asked.

They gleefully nodded: "It's fun tricking people," Huitzil said.

After everyone had finished their soup, Rosalita rolled in the cart again, bringing chicken with mole and rice, peas, mushrooms, and fried plantains. The moment she filled the twins' plates, they started quarreling about who had more. Agnes said, "Huitzil! Cuauhtémoc! Don't start this again!" But they kept up their quarrel.

"Give me some of your plátanos. You have more!"

"You have less because you ate some!"

"I didn't!"

"You did!"

"Huitzil, there's more in the kitchen. You're not starving."

"I'm not Huitzil!"

Agnes threw up her hands, and the boys laughed.

"Every day they do this. I can't go shopping with them anymore. They're jealous of each other."

The boys looked at each other and grinned.

"I think they like teasing you, Agnes," Martha said.

Cuauhtémoc, or Huitzil, tried taking a piece of chicken from his brother's plate.

"All right, that's enough," Agnes said. "You sit here, and you . . ." but when she took Cuauhtémoc, or Huitzil, by the arm to lead him to another chair, he started to cry.

"It's not fair! You're always nicer to him! You give him more!"

"I have a suggestion," Bruno said.

At first no one listened to him because the boy kept crying, but then Bruno clinked his glass with a knife several times as if to raise a toast and everyone looked at him.

"I have a suggestion. Each of you is saying that the other has more on his plate. To me it looks as if you both have the same amount."

"No, he has more!" both boys said simultaneously, and burst out laughing. Pira thought it was funny too.

"Do you seriously want to solve this problem?" Bruno asked.

The boys looked at each other and agreed with nods that they did want to solve it.

"I propose that you allow a judge to make a decision. This judge must be fair, obviously."

The boys nodded.

"He must not favor one of you over the other."

They agreed.

"He must truly consider you equal."

They giggled together: "Yes."

"I think we have such a fair judge among us," Bruno continued. "It's not your mother."

The boys laughed.

"It's not me."

They agreed politely.

"I know who it is," one of them said, looking at Pira, who suddenly felt embarrassed.

"Well, I don't know," Bruno said. "Peter, do you think one of these boys deserves to have more food than the other?"

He shook his head.

"Do you think they have the same amount of food on their plates?"

He looked at the two plates. It seemed to him that if there was a difference, it hardly mattered. But it mattered to them.

"I'm not sure. I would have to look more closely."

"Huitzil and Cuauhtémoc, do you believe that Peter would be a fair judge?"

They both nodded.

"Peter, would you be willing to make a decision in Huitzil and Cuauhtémoc's quarrel? You could move food from one plate to the other until you feel sure they're both equal."

He nodded.

"Huitzil and Cuauhtémoc, will you accept Pira's judgment as fair?"

"Yes," they both said.

"You're in charge now, Peter."

In charge. As a judge? He was already in his new role.

It felt like wearing someone else's clothes.

"Move your plates near to me so I can see them."

Were those words really his? It sounded like an order.

The twins did as he said.

They were right, one dish had slightly more peas, the other slightly more mushrooms, and one dish had one piece of plantain more than the other. The drumsticks and mole sauce were equal. He gave the extra piece of plantain to Tristan. Then with a spoon, he moved peas and mushrooms from one plate to another, double-checked, made a correction, and pushed the plates back toward the twins.

"They're the same now," he said.

All the grown-ups clapped.

"Let's eat," Agnes said, "The food's getting cold."

"Good judge!" Valéria said, and the twins, already eating, agreed.

*

The twins gave much of their food to Tristan, and soon after Rosalita brought second helpings they left the table with their plates half full.

Pira joined them to play with Tristan and to show them the tricks he knew, and how to speak to him, and the kind of petting he liked. But first Tristan had to meet the peacock. The bird stood facing him with his tail feathers spread like a green and gold shield. The two hens stood by, watching. Pira called Tristan, afraid he would hurt the bird. But Tristan didn't listen. He lunged at the peacock. Instead of retreating, the peacock took three quick steps toward him. Tristan jumped back, surprised. He barked loudly a few times. The bird looked unimpressed. Now Tristan trotted around the peacock. The peacock turned with him, still with his tail spread. Again Tristan lunged at him, and again the peacock ran toward him, and Tristan retreated. Once more he circled the bird, watching him sideways, wagging his tail, and the bird turned with him again. Then Tristan gave up and went to Pira, smiling, and licked his hand.

"Paco knows how to fight," one of the boys said.

"Paco? That was my parrot's name."

*

Tristan played with the boys until Rosalita brought him a bone. He took it aside to chew in the shade of a tree.

"Let's play war! Come, we'll show you."

Pira thought he already knew how to play war, but what these boys did was different. They led him to a sandpit in the back of the house. One of them ran inside and came out with a sharp-pointed kitchen knife. "I'll start!" he said. "I got the knife!" and laid the knife on the ground next to the sandpit.

"All right," his brother said cheerfully. "It really doesn't matter who starts," he explained to Pira. Together the twins patted and smoothed the sand with their hands until it was all even. One of them drew a line dividing the sandpit into two equal halves and said, pointing at one half, "This is my land," and pointing at the other half, "this is Cuauhtémoc's. This line is the border." Then Cuauhtémoc picked up the knife, held it by the blade, and with a flick of the wrist made the knife flip through the air and stab the sand on his brother's land. With the knife then he cut a line in the sand that followed the blade's position to the edge of the sandpit in one direction and to the borderline in the other. Then he wiped out the border from one edge of the sandpit to the edge of the line he had just drawn.

"This is the new border," he said, "from here to here to here. That small part is his. The rest is mine."

He gave the knife to Huitzil. Huitzil took the knife by the blade, aimed it, and made it flip through the air and cut into his brother's land. A new line was drawn, again following the position of the blade, and most of the border Cuauhtémoc had drawn was erased. Now Huitzil had a lot more land than Cuauhtémoc.

But Cuauhtémoc regained everything he had lost and more. And when Huitzil at his next turn failed to make the knife cut into the sand, Cuauhtémoc threw up his arms with a shout. He took careful aim and reduced Huitzil's land to a narrow triangle pressed into a corner of the sandpit. But Huitzil's next throw reclaimed a large swath of Cuauhtémoc's land.

As the battle went on, Pira wondered how anyone could win or

lose at this game. He also wondered if the twins would include him
at some point, maybe as a judge. But they had no need for him. It
was a game for two. He felt like leaving but was hesitant because
they seemed to want him to watch their game and admire their
skill. He was their audience.

Finally he mumbled, "I'm going inside," and left them. They
didn't seem to mind.

*

The moment Pira stepped into the dining room, the grown-ups
stopped talking. He joined them at the table. Martha, Valéria, and
Agnes were drinking wine. Bruno was drinking cognac. They were
all smoking. There was so much smoke in the air that Pira had to
cough. Martha asked him to move his chair closer to hers and put
her arm around him and squeezed him a little. The others were
smiling. Valéria too was smiling, but her eyes were sad.

Then Bruno started talking to Valéria, and Valéria answered.
They were saying things Pira didn't understand, but he could tell
they were talking about the party because of the way Bruno spoke.
Whenever Bruno spoke about the party, especially when someone
disagreed, he would hold up one finger instead of gesturing vaguely
with both hands the way he did when talking about other things.
Instead of speaking in a tone of "maybe," or "hmmm, let's look at
this together," which was his usual way, his sentences now came out
hard and straight, like lines drawn with a ruler. Even while listening to Valéria, he seemed to be sending out hard straight thoughts
through his forehead.

All the while Martha's breathing, as she held him, was so quiet,
so steady. It had nothing to do with what Bruno and Valéria were
saying. What they said sounded boring.

"I object to your use of that word," Bruno said.

"What word?"

"Witch hunt. It's an investigation, certainly. But you can be sure it's a rational investigation."

"That's what the Inquisitors thought they were doing."

"You have no right to make that comparison," Bruno said. "Sándor and István will receive a fair trial."

Hearing those names, Pira listened more closely.

"I wish I could believe that," Valéria said. "I'm so afraid."

They fell silent. Pira was surprised. What was she afraid of?

Very gently, Martha started stroking his hair.

"Valéria is afraid for Sándor and István," she said, "because they're in prison. She's not afraid for herself. She feels safe here."

"So did Sándor," Valéria said.

Her speech was slurred. Pira didn't like it when people got drunk.

Agnes said, "Peter, do you like comics?"

"Yes, I do."

"Do you have a favorite comic?"

He could think of several. He wasn't sure.

"There's a pile of comics on the couch. Would you like to read them?"

He understood. He was in the way. He didn't mind. Their talk wasn't fun. And besides, he liked comics. He went to the couch and turned his attention to El Tío McPato, who was diving into a pool filled with gold coins while El Pato Donald asked his advice on playing the national lottery. El Tío McPato said the way to get rich was to buy cheap and sell high, not play the lottery. But no sooner did Donald leave McPato's house than he saw a vendor selling lottery tickets and bought one.

All the while, Pira listened with half an ear to the grown-ups in case someone said something about István and Sándor, but no one did. They were no longer quarreling.

Martha and Agnes had joined the conversation. They were just talking. It still sounded boring.

He turned the page. Donald was going fishing with Jorgito, Juanito, and Jaimito. The lottery ticket was hanging out of his pocket. Pira liked El Pato Donald. He always made mistakes, but he was always happy.

Suddenly Pira heard the name "Harry Taub" and listened.

"He's a Hollywood film producer," Martha said. "He's the one who bought an option on Bruno's book. He says the government suspects him of being a spy for the Russians or something like that. There could be a trial, or trials. It's not just him, it's a whole group of people in Hollywood."

"That sounds like the same thing under opposite auspices," Valéria said.

What was auspices?

"It's not the same thing," Bruno said. "Communism and anti-communism are not the same. The moral foundation is a different one."

They fell silent. In back of the house, the twins were taking turns winning new land with bright shouts, first one, then the other.

"You're being unfair," Martha said. "Valéria is talking about the victims. For them it's the same."

"And the rampant suspicion," Valéria said. "That too is the same. If Sándor and István can be suspected of treason, anyone can."

"It's Anyface!" Pira said.

They all looked at him.

"What do you mean?" Bruno asked.

Pira felt himself blushing. He had said something silly. Now he had to explain.

"It's a comic. Not the one I'm reading now. It's Li'l Abner's favorite comic. I read it at home. There's a detective named Fearless Fosdick. He's looking for a criminal named Anyface. The criminal can make himself look like anyone. So Fearless Fosdick is suspicious of everyone, because anyone could be Anyface. That's the story."

The grown-ups smiled, not in a way that made Pira feel silly. They were smiling at the story.

"Li'l Abner reads comics?" Martha asked.

"Yes."

"A comic in a comic, that's clever," Bruno said. "So does Fearless Fosdick find Anyface?"

"No. He kills a lot of innocent people. His bullets make holes in their heads and bodies. One man—Fearless Fosdick sort of breaks open his face, thinking it's not a real face, but it is. And Anyface, the real Anyface, just laughs and says, 'Fosdick is doing my killing for me.' His face is like plasticene, he can squeeze and pull it into any shape he wants. At one point he looks like a woman, then a man with wavy hair, then the chief of police. In the end Fearless Fosdick figures out that Anyface's face will melt in a very hot room. But the heat has to be five hundred degrees, no less. So Fearless Fosdick locks sixty-nine people who he thinks could be Anyface inside a big room and turns up the heat. He's in there with them, watching them. It gets hotter and hotter. Any one of them could be Anyface, but only one face will melt, and that will be the face of Anyface. The people are sweating and crying, 'It's too hot! I can't stand it!' But Fearless Fosdick says, 'We're just starting to get warm, it's only 250 degrees.' Somebody says, 'My false teeth are melting! Does that count?' But no one's face is melting. One man begs Fosdick to kill them all because the heat is so unbearable. But Fearless Fosdick says, 'No, Gentlemen. When the heat reaches five hundred degrees, one of your faces will melt like butter!" That's what he says. Then one man says, 'Look! Fosdick exposed Anyface all right! It's Fosdick himself!' Because Fosdick's face is melting. No one else's is. That's the end of the story. Li'l Abner is really upset, because Fearless Fosdick was his hero. He hates the story. He wants someone to explain it to him. The last words in the story are, 'Can you?'"

It felt like the longest story he had ever told. The end sounded funny to him, but the grown-ups weren't laughing. They looked shocked.

"That's a terrible story, Peter," Martha said. "I didn't know you were reading such things. It must have impressed you a lot. You memorized it."

"It's Li'l Abner," he said. "It's just a comic."

*

There was a slight drizzle during the drive home. The sun was setting over Popocatepetl. Martha drove slowly. The roads were not safe in this weather, she said. She turned on the radio, and together they listened to songs sung by Augustín Lara. All his songs were about his love for cities and women. They were more for grown-ups than children but Pira liked them well enough.

Pira remembered the way Valéria had said "Farewell." It was the same word Sándor had used. It felt almost too sad. It was like saying "Goodbye forever." But she had said it in a happy way, not sadly. The song on the radio was like that.

He wished he had said farewell to Tristan that way. Not only he but his parents too. They petted him, each in turn, and called him a good, good dog, but then the twins distracted Tristan by throwing a stick while Pira, Martha, and Bruno got into the car. It was like tricking him so he wouldn't notice. But he did notice. He looked up, pricking his ears as the car drove away and Valéria called after them: "Farewell!" He saw them leaving.

He didn't understand. But he would understand at some point that his family had left him.

But as Martha said, they had given him another family. There was even another Paco. The boys said they were going to teach Tristan new tricks. He would like that. Agnes would love him.

Sometimes Agnes was funny, but not on purpose. Like when she suddenly cried, "Good grief! Not that stupid game again!" and everyone thought she meant all the talk about enemies in the party, but she meant the twins' war game behind the house. They were shouting loudly at each other.

Now the sun was a huge golden ball above Popocatepetl. Most of the sky was still blue, but there were violet clouds near the volcano. Iztaccihuatl looked fast asleep.

Augustín Lara was singing about Vera Cruz. That was where they would board the ship, so Pira listened with interest.

Yo nací con la luna de plata
Y nací con alma de pirata.

Born with the silver moon, and born with a pirate's soul, Augustín Lara had left Vera Cruz long ago, but he missed her. Little corner where the waves make their nests . . . Little piece of my homeland that knows how to suffer and sing . . .

Suddenly, looking through the window, Pira saw his blue and red hoop hovering in space, framing the volcano. At first it was just a thought, but then, when he looked closer, it was real. It wasn't the real hoop, of course, but he knew it was real in a magical way, and that its reality depended on him to hold it in his attention.

The two halves were so perfectly half! They met at the top and the bottom. He imagined an ant crawling up the red side from the bottom. The ant wouldn't know it was going up a circle. It would wonder, Where am I going? Where is the ant heap? Where are my friends? So up it went, little by little, along the red half of the wheel. Walking around the wood, circling it as it climbed up and up. Off to the right side at first, because that was how the wheel went, until the ant reached the middle of the red half. Then the direction would change, gradually at first, and then more and more to the left, but still upward, on and on. What a climb for an ant! Eventually it would reach the top, the exact middle where the blue and the red half met. The moment it stepped onto the blue part of the wheel, it would start walking downward. It would think it was just going forward, but actually, more and more, it was heading back down. Eventually it would pass the middle of the blue, exactly opposite the middle of the red, the same but not the same, because one was up and the other was down, and would come to where the blue and the red halves met at the bottom, which was where it had started. Would it go up again? That would be sad. It would be better if it just got off the wheel and went home to the ant heap.

Martha's voice startled him out of his reverie. "I was thinking about Valéria," she said.

"What about her?" Bruno asked.

"Don't you think you were a bit hard on her?"

"She listens to the wrong people."

"Who are the wrong people, Bruno? There can't only be one right way."

Martha sped up the car as she said that and immediately put her foot on the brake. They were going around a hairpin curve. The car slipped and swerved. Martha said, "No!" and then let out a longer, very frightened wail. The side of the car struck a milestone by the side of the road and came to a stop. They sat as if frozen. Martha rolled down her window. An enormous stillness entered the car.

"Oh God," Martha said, very softly, and then: "I'm sorry."

They listened together.

"Is it safe to get out?" Bruno asked.

"I think so," she said. "Safer than driving."

"Let's get out."

There was a steep drop by the edge of the road. Pira imagined the car tumbling down there, down and down and down. They would have been dead. Or his parents would have been dead and he would have been alive. How would he have gotten home? Who would he live with if they were dead? Zita and Federico? Or maybe his first father David in New York? But he hardly knew him.

The stillness contained many sounds, some near and some very far away: the crunch of Bruno's shoe on gravel . . . tiny voices shouting somewhere . . . birds, lots of birds . . . the chug-chug-chug of a distant train . . . Someone was laughing . . .

Bruno's hand came to rest on his shoulder.

"Shall we get back in the car?" Martha finally said.

Once or twice on the rest of the drive home, Martha and Bruno talked about things they still needed to do before leaving. Mostly they were quiet. When they got out of the car and before going into the house, they looked at each other and hugged. Bruno held open the gate for Pira and Martha to step through. The house was so quiet. The emptiness of the rooms made their steps sound louder.

*

Bruno came into his room to sit with him before he fell asleep.

"In three days we'll leave for Mexico City."

Three days. That left two more days to play with Arón. He looked forward to that.

"And in ten days we'll be on the open sea. Are you excited?"

He imagined wind, sun, big waves, sharks, and pirates. He was excited.

"Yes."

The open sea. He loved those words.